INTERCONNECTED

JAMIE URQUHART

Dedication

This book is dedicated to my wife, Ellen. Without her continued prompting, it might still be only in my mind. She is my rock.

INTERCONNECTED

MIRRORS REFLECT WHAT THEY SEE. THEY DO NOT reflect feelings of anger, sadness, happiness—the very soul of whoever is standing before them. They are mere embodiments of the exact view in front of them. Move to the left or right, and the mirrors lose their subjects. Duck below the dressers, and the mirrors cannot follow. Jake stood in front of one of those mirrors. This one also did not emulate his feelings. Jake turned away and stood in front of his bed.

He was in a hotel off Interstate 77 in Oklahoma. This was a lonely stretch in a lonely place in the country apparently no one wanted to be from. The perfect place for Jake. The perfect place for evil to hide. Except Jake was not evil. In fact, he was the antithesis of evil. He had fought evil for what seemed like his whole life. He did not smoke; he rarely took a drink, only in groups where it was expected, but never alone. He never used drugs, except when prescribed by a provider. What he did do was walk into places he should never go to, at a time when he shouldn't be there. It was always by accident that he walked into situations. At least that's the way it seemed.

Jake turned to say something but stopped.

Last Saturday evening, about 11:45, Jake had been driving down the highway when he decided to get something to eat. He picked out a small diner in Shelbyville, Kentucky, off Interstate 64. He sat by himself, taking a table in the corner, looked at a menu, and ordered some food.

He told the waitress he wanted to eat, rest for a bit, then get back on the road, headed to California to spend time with his younger brother. The eggs were greasy, the bacon tough, and the bread soggy, but the coffee was hot...one of the best meals he had eaten in a long while.

Jake sat facing the window, looking out at the parking lot. Further out lay Interstate 64. He watched as cars and trucks moved from left to right and right to left, between Lexington and Louisville, Kentucky. It was the first time he had been to Shelbyville, and after last Saturday, it would be his last time.

Four men were seated at the counter, talking amongst themselves. They had ordered and were waiting for their food. As they waited, they talked about hunting, fishing, church going, the lottery, horse racing, and bourbon. Nothing Jake had not heard before, nothing that would draw him in, basically nothing that interested him whatsoever. They turned from time to time to look at Jake, but never entered into conversation with him. One of the four men stood up, stretched, and walked to the restroom.

The waitress brought Jake his check, which totaled $6.98 plus tax. Jake shoved a $10.00 bill under his plate, stirred his coffee with a spoon, and thought about heading out to drive west. But first, he had one task to do in Frankfort, the capital city of Kentucky.

As he watched the parking lot, he noticed a big car pull up, hosting six young men. They ranged in age from what appeared to be 20 to about 26, at least that's what he thought, but Jake was never a good judge of someone's age. He was 38, taller than most around him, and weighed a good 225-235 weight that had him in the same size pants for the past five years.

The young men came into the diner, talking a little louder than most, shoving and pushing each other in a more or less friendly manner, and crowded around the counter to get some food. None of the tables or booths technically seated more than four, but chairs could be added at the end to make room. The waitress asked the young men if they wanted a table or a booth. The boys indicated they would rather sit at a table, and they turned and sat one table away from Jake.

The boys ignored Jake and sat down and talked about football, girls, movies, the latest game device—which one Jake had no clue—and fast cars. They became louder, then softer; mostly they just visited with each other.

The waitress came out and took their order, and in a short time, had their ticket on the window for the cook to see. Jake stood up to leave, waved to the waitress to show her he had left money under his plate, and headed for the door. The man who had gone to the restroom returned to the counter and sat down.

The diner now held the waitress, the cook, the manager in a back room, four men at the counter, and six seated at a table for four. And Jake. That was 14 people in a diner that held up to 55, according to the sign on the wall. Jake walked towards the door when another vehicle pulled into the lot. An official, grey car with emblems on the sides and a light bar on top. A Kentucky State Trooper vehicle.

The driver climbed out of his vehicle and walked into the diner. Jake held the door for him. He smiled at Jake, nodded his head, and said 'thank you'. This made 15 in the eatery, before Jake left. It was the middle of shift, as far as Jake knew, mostly shifts changed at either six or seven AM, two or three PM, and ten or eleven PM, and it was none of those times. So, Jake figured it was time for the trooper to catch a meal.

Jake walked outside and sat in his car. He started it up, noting he needed some gas as it was below a quarter of a tank. He tuned the radio and started to put the vehicle in reverse when he looked back into the diner one last time.

He saw the trooper, gun drawn, pointing at the counter where the four men sat. All of the men had their hands in the air, and the trooper seemed to be shouting instructions to the men. The table full of young men sat frozen, looking at the scene unfolding before them.

The trooper grabbed his radio, shouting something into it, probably calling for backup. Jake surmised the lot would be full shortly and decided to go ahead and leave.

As he backed up, he heard a shout and saw the trooper at the door, pointing his weapon at him. Jake stopped the car in the middle of backing, put it into park, and placed both hands on the steering wheel. The trooper kept yelling at Jake, then looking back inside, then outside at Jake again.

Unsure of what was wanted, Jake slowly opened the door, placing his hands above the window, and slid his frame out till he was standing beside his vehicle. The trooper again yelled at Jake, but he could hear him now, telling him to come back inside the diner. Jake started walking towards where the trooper stood, half in and half out of the door, edged past him and into the diner once again.

The trooper, gun still in hand, motioned Jake to go back to his seat. The plate, coffee cup, and the ten-dollar bill were still on the table. Jake slid into the booth, looked at the young men at the table next to his, then at the four at the counter, then at the trooper.

"My name is Officer Larson, and I am a Kentucky State Trooper. This is a crime scene investigation. Everyone here is a suspect." The four men at the counter, hands still in the air, looked at each other and then back at the trooper. The six young men looked at each other, the four men at the counter, then at the trooper. Jake looked at each of the young men, the four at the counter, the cook, the manager, and the waitress, then at the trooper. No one moved more than their heads.

Finally, Jake spoke. "What are you investigating?"

The trooper looked at Jake. "There's been a shooting at the gas station across the street. It just came over the radio and the caller said whoever it was headed out the door and towards this diner." With that,

4

he looked first at Jake, then the young men, then the four at the counter, and back at Jake. "I take my job as a trooper seriously, and I need to get a grasp on what is happening here, so for now, everyone here is a suspect." He called out on the radio again, using a 10-code Jake was unfamiliar with, and then dropped the microphone back down to his lapel.

No one said a word, not the four at the counter, the six at the table, the manager, the waitress, or the cook. The trooper kept looking back and forth at everyone in the diner, holding his gun outstretched, but not pointing at anyone in particular.

The hat on the trooper's head flew across the room, and all eyes followed it as it flew, hitting the back wall and dropping to the floor. All eyes turned back to where the trooper stood, only now the trooper was on the floor, bleeding from a gunshot wound to the head. Fourteen people hit the floor, but no more shots came into the diner. The glass door was crazed and had a bullet hole through it, the same one that had hit trooper Larson.

Jake crawled towards the trooper, looking at the six young men and the four on the ground by the counter. "Did any of you hear a shot?" he asked. They all shook their heads as if they were on one cord being pulled by a marionette operator.

"Stay still." He looked at the manager, or at least where the manager had stood. "Call 911. Tell them a cop's been shot." He continued crawling towards the trooper, but as he neared, he realized there was little he could do.

"Have them send an ambulance and tell them there is probably a shooter out there still. Tell them they need a supervisor here as fast as possible." He looked back at the 13 others still on the floor. "Everyone remember what you saw, you're all witnesses to this." He reached the trooper and pulled him back from in front of the window, then behind the counter. Jake grabbed the trooper's radio and called out on it. "We are at the diner in Shelbyville by the Interstate," he looked at the manager, still on the ground, "What is the address here?" The manager told him and he relayed that information over the radio. "This trooper has been shot in the head, he's hurt bad." Jake tossed the radio microphone away from the trooper and grabbed some napkins and dishrags to put on the trooper's wound.

"I can't stop the bleeding. Someone needs to look out and see if you can see anyone out there who wasn't there a couple of minutes ago." No one moved. Jake stopped his care of the trooper long enough to lift his head over the counter and out to the parking lot. Nothing moved outside. Jake stood and walked around the counter. He walked over to the table of young men, all scattered across the floor.

"Any of you know first aid?"

"I do," said one of the young men.

"Come over and start with the trooper. He needs all the help he can get."

Jake reached down and took the pistol from the outstretched hand of the trooper, then slid out the door. It was dark, about midnight-thirty, and Jake was wearing dark clothing. He blended in with the surroundings, good for him now, not so good when other police and troopers and EMS workers arrived on scene.

First, Jake made sure he did not track up the area where the shot might have come from. Judging from the angle of the bullet, the broken glass in the door, the hat on the back wall, and what looked like a bullet hole in the wall, the shot would have come from a line of bushes about 20 yards from the diner.

Jake sat down against the outside wall of the diner, letting his eyes adjust to the darkness. Nothing moved. He figured if anyone was still out there, they would have shot him by now as well, but there was nothing. No movement, no grating of shoes on the gravel in the lot, no cars or trucks moving, nothing. He heard a long, piercing, whining noise coming from somewhere, and he knew reinforcements were on the way, but, just as with General Custer, they would probably be too late.

Jake got up and walked back inside the diner. He placed the gun back down by the trooper's hand. Everyone stood back up when he came in, but no one left.

"Remember what this guy said, you are all suspects in a shooting now a double shooting," he said. "Think of what you were doing when he came into the diner. Remember what he said, how he looked, remember the time."

Twelve of the people in the diner looked at Jake, each other, the clock on the wall, and then sat down. The 13th was still taking care of the downed trooper. Jake walked over to his seat, where his coffee was now cold, the $10 bill still under the plate of what was left of the runny eggs and hard bacon. Tones were low, all wondering what had just happened, who would shoot an officer, why, and what happened at the gas station across the street.

Three cars turned into the lot of the diner, light bars racing, sirens blaring. Three men in uniform rushed into the diner, guns drawn. Twenty-six hands went up in the air as the police entered the door; the one exception, the young man working on the trooper. The police went to where he was working on Larson. All three looked around at the crowd, then one spotted Jake, seated by himself.

"Sir, can I speak with you?" the officer asked Jake. Jake stood and walked over to where the officers stood. The other two officers took over care from the young man, and one of them radioed for the ambulance to hurry to the scene.

"What did you see, from where you were seated, Sir?" asked the trooper.

"I saw your officer come in here, and I was walking out the door. He smiled at me, I got into my car, looked up, and he had his gun drawn, pointed at everyone in the diner. He then opened the door and told me to come back into the diner. So, I did."

"What happened next?"

"We all saw his hat fly off and hit the wall, then we looked back at him and saw him lying on the ground, bleeding."

"Everyone agree?" said the officer.

One of the men at the counter said, "No, officer, that man exited the building, went to his car, got out a rifle, and shot Officer Larson."

Jake looked at all the men, four at the counter, six at the table, three behind the counter, and knew this would not end well.

"I do not have a rifle in my vehicle. When your officer was shot, I was sitting here at the table, as he had asked me to do."

The officer turned and looked at the manager. "Joe, what happened here?"

Joe said, "Just like Luke says, Bill. This guy went out to his car, got a rifle out, and shot Larson. Just like that. No warning, nothing."

Jake looked at the waitress. She would not look back at him. Jake looked at the officer asking the questions.

"Let me ask you something. If I shot this officer here, why would I come back in and sit down? Why would I not just leave? These people have put up a story, one that they made up to incriminate me, for reasons I do not know."

The supervisor said, "I need you to walk slowly towards me, hands outstretched, and then turn around. I don't want anyone else to get shot tonight."

Jake complied and walked slowly towards the officer, then turned and stretched out his hands behind his back. The officer took Jake's left hand and snapped on a set of cuffs, then reached for his right hand and pulled it back as well.

"You are not under arrest, you are just being investigated for possible criminal activity," said the supervisor. "I do not want you to move unless I tell you to move, understand?"

Jake nodded his head that he understood. The supervisor frisked Jake, first up one side, then down the other, and then asked Jake to turn around.

"Why do you think these people would put up a story on you?" he asked Jake.

Jake shrugged his shoulders. "No idea. This is my plate over there, my coffee, and that's my car, halfway in and out of the parking lot. I was pulling out when this officer told me to come back in."

"He's lying," said the one at the counter. "Larson tried to get him to come back in, but he just reached down in his car and came up with a rifle, shooting."

The supervisor, named Kowalski, looked at the other 13 in the diner. They all nodded in agreement with their counterpart.

One of the troopers walked up to Kowalski and said something to him. Kowalski looked at Jake. "They found a rifle in the bushes."

Kowalski walked Jake out to his squad car and placed him in the back seat. Jake was so tall he had to sit completely across the seat, legs on one side of the car, his head on the rear headrest on the other side. Kowalski moved to the driver's door, opened it, and got in.

"Are you willing to talk to me?" asked Kowalski, as they drove east towards headquarters in Frankfort, Kentucky. "I mean, can you tell me something about yourself?"

Jake looked at the image in the rearview mirror, which was hard to do because of how he was sitting. "What do you want to know?"

"Where are you from, why are you here, what caused you to eat in that diner tonight?" All good questions, but Jake was cautious.

"I'm no one, going nowhere, from nowhere. I stopped because I was hungry. Any law against that?"

"Only when you shoot one of my troopers," came the answer from Kowalski.

"Go back in and ask that one guy, Luke? Ask him why, if your trooper was calling to me to come back inside, why was he shot in the side of his head."

Kowalski didn't say anything. They drove in silence for the rest of the 30 miles to headquarters.

Kowalski parked the squad car and opened the backdoor for Jake to get out. It took quite a bit of effort for Jake to move from the cramped quarters to standing upright at his full six feet-three-inch frame. They walked in to barracks 12 on the west side of Frankfort.

Kowalski opened two doors with the push of a button, then had Jake stand facing away from him while he patted him down again. Jake figured there were cameras associated with the push buttons so that not just anyone could access the police barracks. They walked into the barracks and Kowalski told Jake to stop.

"Turn around, facing away from me," said Kowalski. Jake did as he was told, and Kowalski removed the handcuffs. Jake rubbed his wrists the get blood flow to his hands again, as the cuffs had been very tight.

"Now, before I ask you any questions, I need to read you your rights." Jake listened as Kowalski pulled out a card from his left top pocket and read to him about lawyers and silence, and giving up rights, and appointments. "Do you understand your rights?" asked Kowalski. Jake nodded. "Gotta hear you say it, OK?" Jake said he understood.

"Okay, I'm not sure why you were in that diner, but I sure haven't been doing this job for the past 28 years not to feel a vibe and go with my gut feeling. I felt I had to remove you from that diner because not everyone ever has the same story. Why do you think that is?"

"Probably my fault," said Jake. "When I picked up Larson's gun to go outside to see if the shooter was still there, I told everyone in the diner to make sure they had their stories straight. I moved out and to the right, then sat down against the wall behind my vehicle to let my eyes adjust to the dark. I surmised where the shooter would have been aiming from, but I didn't walk over there for fear of destroying any evidence. I walked back inside, put Larson's gun down by his hand, and asked if anyone knew first aid. The young man who was helping your trooper was the only one who responded."

"Why blame you?" said Kowalski.

"Not sure. Because I'm not from here?" mused Jake. "Maybe I shouldn't have told them to get their stories straight, huh?"

"Well, I have to write this up. We'll have teams going in to question each of the guests and workers at the diner, and if anything could change, it would be during that one-on-one with my detectives. They can get water out of rocks." With that, he pulled out some paper and stuck it in a printer, turned on a computer, and let it warm up.

"Tell me about yourself, Jake. A little background goes a long way here."

"I'm unemployed. I travel around. That's about it."

"Yeah, where do you get your cash from, Jake? Do you rob diners and gas stations?"

Jake looked tired. "I receive a pension from Golden Bear Investments. They pay me every month."

"What did you do for them?" said Kowalski, as he started typing.

"Security. I worked for them on the 80th floor of the south tower at the World Trade Center in New York… till 9/11. I worked with Don Ramirez, head of Morgan Stanley security. Don called me after the first plane hit the north tower and told me to get everyone out. I did. He didn't. I survived because I made sure all my employees got down and left the building. Then I exited. I never went back to work for them. So, every month, I get a check. Plus, I got 2 million as a settlement. I don't need to rob or shoot anyone." Jake sat back and crossed his arms.

Kowalski looked at him. "Why would someone shoot my trooper?"

"Your trooper closed off his peripheral vision while looking at the 14 of us in the diner. He lost his ability to assess threats around him. He never moved, making it easy for a shooter to take aim and hit a stationary target. He had us in a V line of sight but he was in a V himself, with the V inverted, so he was the point of the letter. Easy shot and easy kill."

"Are you blaming my officer for being shot?" Kowalski raised his voice. "I'll be darned if you or anyone else tells us how to hold prospective criminals until help arrives." Kowalski turned and began typing again.

"No one blames your officer, and no one, especially me, thinks your man, what's his name, Larson brought this on himself. You need to ask yourself why the store was robbed across the street and the clerk shot. It seems to me this was a set-up, an ambush, something planned for days if not weeks, and I dropped into the middle of it."

"What, you think terrorists? This is Kentucky, not New York or LA. No one is going to come to Kentucky and start a war, not here. Heck, Washington, D. C. thinks Louisville is the capital of the Commonwealth. Idiots." He hesitated for a second. "It's Frankfort. The capital, I mean." He looked at Jake. "Okay, so I need some information from you to start processing. I don't think you're part of this, but I still have to have some information since I did put you in handcuffs and transport you here."

"Jake Thompson. Aged 38. I stand six feet three, weigh about 230. I come from the northeast, outside New York, but I was born down south, in Texas. Mom and dad moved there when I was three. I like the Yankees and the Giants; I hate the Jets and the Mets; I like classical music, but rock and roll, oldies stuff, is still good to hear too. I like to eat good food; I hate sushi; I like pasta; and I've never been married. I have a brother and a sister, both still living, and mom and dad live up north. You can call them if you like. I don't do things like shoot cops or rob gas stations, and I don't carry weapons. I trained to be a mixed martial artist; I am a seventh-degree black belt in Korean style Tae

Kwon Do. I served three years in the military, Special Forces, but they never needed me, and I never went to college. I like a beer on very rare occasions; I don't smoke or do drugs, or get into trouble, except when it comes to find me."

Kowalski looked at Jake for a minute. "How would you have done this, and what would you have done if you were my officer?"

"First, I would never have gone into the diner. I would have waited until backup arrived, and I would have spread out from the gas station, looking for clues. Of course, he didn't know the gas station had been robbed, so there is that. I notice a lot of cops standing around, usually inside yellow tape, as if that tape would ward off bullets. Too much standing around by those guys. But your guy, Larson? Like I said, he apparently didn't know about the shooting when he walked into the diner.

"Anyway, I would have set up a perimeter, working from the gas station out, up to and including shutting down the interstate, so a random shooter would not be able to get off more shots. I would have ordered a bus to take away all the patrons in the diner to be able to interview them separately. I never would stand in one place and let myself be a target when a shooter might still be outside.

"As for doing it, I guess I would have done it the same way. Wait for a cop to arrive and shoot him. But why? Why wait around to shoot a cop after you shot a clerk at the gas station? What made Larson come into the diner as I was leaving?" asked Jake.

"He was going to sit down and have some dinner. He and the rest of the troopers in this area like that diner. The staff treats them well, sometimes gives them a donut or a piece of pie for no charge, you know, cop stuff." Jake nodded as if he understood, but he didn't really, not ever having been a police officer himself.

"Larson's married with two kids. My boss is on his way to tell his wife. They transported him to Louisville by helicopter. Not sure if he's gonna make it or not. What made you get that one kid to provide care for Larson?"

"Just a guess on my part, is all. I figured he was shot in the head, and someone with better knowledge than me oughta take a look at him." With that, Jake sat back and re-crossed his arms. "I'd like to head on to California, if possible. My brother is out there working, and I wanted to spend some time with him."

"You are hip-deep in a shooting investigation, Jake. I'm not sure if the cashier at the gas station next to the diner is alive or not. You're not going to California or anywhere till I find out what happened." Kowalski went back to typing again.

Jake was led back to a holding room, not quite a cell; there was a coffee pot, a TV, a candy machine, and a soda machine. He was allowed his wallet after it had been examined for contraband. Jake looked over the selections and decided on coffee. He got a cup from a holder by the sink, filled it with coffee and sat down at a table. Jake tried to think about what had happened at the diner, but he was tired, so he decided he would move to the sofa and try to get some sleep.

About an hour into his nap, Jake was awakened by someone coming into the room. It wasn't Kowalski but another trooper, higher in rank, maybe a lieutenant or captain. The officer looked at him for a moment, walked over to the coffee machine and poured himself a cup, then stood in front of Jake.

"How did this go down out there tonight, Sir?"

Jake looked at him and shrugged his shoulders. "I'm not really sure. I was looking at your officer and his hat flew off his head. None of us turned and looked out the window, but we all watched his hat fly off and hit the wall. Then when we turned back around, that's when we saw he was down on the floor. All of us hit the floor as well."

"Where were you when the shot was fired?"

"I was sitting at the table where I had had my food. I had a perfect view of all the others in the diner, and none of them had left, in fact, all but the waitress, the cook, and the manager had just gotten there before the shooting started. I was the only one finished."

"So, do you know where the shot came from?"

"Like I told your man Kowalski, I think it came from the bushes at the edge of the parking lot. One of your troopers apparently found a rifle there. You should be able to find out who it belongs to by tracing the serial number on the rifle."

"It's been ground off," the officer said. "Nothing there to see. All of the others in the diner say you did it. Why would I not believe them and believe you?"

"Because if I had shot the trooper, I would have kept on moving. I would not go back in, sit down, watch the trooper's hat come off, go to his aid, lift his service weapon from his hand, go outside to see if I could survey a threat, then come back in and sit down as if nothing happened. Not the way I work."

"How is it you work, then?" asked the officer.

"First, let's get one thing straight," said Jake. "I don't even know your name and I am not going to try to solve this case for you. I was driving from the east coast to California to see family, and I want to get back on the road as soon as possible."

The officer said, "My name's Captain Tanner. And like Kowalski told you, you're not going anywhere for a while. We need to get some answers about what happened tonight, and buddy, you are one of the lead suspects in this case."

The phone rang, and Tanner reached out and took the handset off the wall. "Tanner here." He listened, said okay, and hung up. "Larson's still hanging in there, he's 50-50 on surviving. Whoever shot him is going to do life in prison, and if he dies, they're going to get a needle in western Kentucky." With that he turned and started to walk out of the room. "Do you need some time to think of a better story, Mr. Thompson?" he asked.

Jake just looked at the captain. "I did not do this, I have no knowledge of who did this, and I was in the diner when your trooper was shot. I don't care what those others are saying; I am the one telling the truth."

"Is it true you shot from the car and not the bushes?"

"As an officer, you need to let the forensics team work to show you where the shot came from, which, in my humble opinion, was from the bushes. The trajectory from my car is not accurate for where Larson was hit or for where his hat ended up."

"There is that," said Tanner. "Kowalski has some more questions for you. Get up and follow me to the ready room."

Jake stood and followed Tanner through the break room door, into the hallway, and then into Kowalski's office.

"He's all yours," said Tanner. The captain then walked away.

Kowalski was seated at his desk, and he motioned for Jake to sit down. "Anyone you want to call?" he asked.

Jake shook his head. Kowalski arranged some papers on his desk, moved his mouse to activate his computer, then looked at Jake.

"You know, this could be really bad for you, if we don't find out who else might have been out there, right?" Jake shrugged his shoulders.

"Why should I talk now, if no matter what I say, you keep telling me it's going to be bad for me? Why don't you have the rest of the diners down here, each in a different room, asking them questions? You've allowed them to stay together to firm up their story, to make sure each knows what the others might say, and you say it's going to be bad for me? I think, if you want my opinion, you've decided to stop the investigation now because everyone in that diner has, for some reason or other, turned on me. I guess because I'm not one of the locals. That's all I can come up with for an answer. I think the one you should be talking to is the waitress. She's the one who took my order, the one I tipped, the one who knew for a fact I didn't leave that store until and only until your trooper showed up. I came back in as soon as he told me to, I sat at the table where I had been served, and I have nothing to hide. The others, the four at the counter and the six at the table—what is happening with them? Ask yourself, why are they all saying the same thing? You and I know if two or three people witness a traffic accident, you get two or three different answers as to what happened. How can 14 people out of 15 in that diner say I did it, especially after something so traumatic?"

Kowalski said, "Because 14 of the 15 aren't you."

"I was talking about your trooper. If he could talk, he would be the odd one out, and it's my presumption the other 13 in that diner don't want him to talk." Jake sat back.

Now it was Kowalski's turn to look at Jake. "You think there is some great conspiracy at that diner? You think they planned to have this happen when you showed up? Really?" Kowalski shook his head. "I think you need to write books or make movies or something like that. You'd be pretty good, if you get my drift."

Jake said, "Kowalski, what if either the four who sat at the bar or the six young men who came in after are the ones who robbed the gas station and shot the clerk? Could you, even for a moment, give that some consideration?"

Kowalski eyed Jake for a long minute. "If you think they are all in cahoots with each other, we've got bigger problems than even I can handle. Those are local boys, all from that town. They know each other, heck, one or two of them have worked at the gas station before, for goodness sakes. I'm not going to go to their mothers or their wives and ask if they are having troubles or if the boys decided to shoot a Kentucky State Trooper. Where would that get me?"

"Maybe it would lead you to the truth. Maybe one of them knew that Larson was on duty and maybe they planned it out because he frequented the diner. It was late at night and that gas station was not hopping like some I've seen. I was getting ready to head there because I needed gas when Larson called me back inside." Jake continued. "If I was a betting man, I would say one or more of those boys or those four men have run afoul of Larson and it was their time to get even. I would check and see if there is possibly a fifth, who would have been seated at the counter or a seventh who would have been at the table. Or maybe another cook or waitress or a co-manager. Who would have been so mad they were ready to kill a cop? That's who I would be talking to right now."

A large man pulled his vehicle into a hotel in the western part of Louisville, Kentucky. It was about 3 AM and only ambulances and prostitutes were on the streets.

He rented a small room, paid cash, and walked to the door that had the number 6 on the front. He opened the door, set down his bag on the bed, and picked up the phone on the table.

Jake was led back to the break room. He asked if he could now make a call, but was told he would have to clear that with Tanner, the captain. Jake sat back down and poured another coffee for himself. It was stale and old but still hot, so it felt good going down. He knew he was in a really bad situation with some really pissed off people as well as cops—for what reason he knew not.

It was over an hour before Kowalski came back, opened the door, and told Jake to follow him. Jake stood, taking a while, poured himself another cup, draining the carafe, and walked after the supervisor.

Jake went back to Kowalski's office and sat down. Kowalski looked at him, shuffled more papers, then set them down on his desk. "You know, I tend to believe the ones who are not believable and I tend to doubt those who I think I can trust. This is something I have learned over the years. Trust but verify, I always say. So, I called this company you said you worked for in New York. All I got was security, but they said you up and quit after 9/11, just walked away. Said you couldn't take it anymore. Like you were a quitter all around. You said you did three years in the military, but they didn't want you. Why would they not want you to stay in? Why not make a career out of it like I have being a trooper? These, of course, are questions I asked myself, meaning to ask you, but I figured I would never get a straight answer if I had you in here, so I did some more searching. I looked up 9/11 and found the guy you said was your friend, this Ramirez fellow, then I went and found images, but I don't find any of you with him. I saw all kinds of pictures of him walking around the towers, talking on the phone, doing things like that, but nothing about you. The person I talked to acted like you weren't even that important to the company. So, are you hiding some-thing and your company is in on it, or were you really just a piss poor employee who did only what was needed and nothing more?

"So, I called a friend with the New York Port Authority and I am waiting for him to give me a call back. Should be anytime now. Before he calls, is there anything you want to tell me? To get something off your chest? Come clean? Drop the act?" He waited. Jake just looked at him, a serious stare that made Kowalski a little uncomfortable.

"We'll just sit here until my friend calls back with the information I've requested. I hope, for your sake, he knows you and he tells me you are the salt of the earth, the savior of all saviors, the one in a million who saved a whole group of people from sure death. Want to wager with me on whether that's what he'll say?"

Jake again just looked at Kowalski.

"Okay, but it's going to go bad on you here, my friend, because if you are not who you say you are, this attack on my trooper is going on your neck, and none of my other troopers like anyone messing with the family." He said it like he considered the family of officers more like a family of La Cosa Nostra from Sicily than state troopers from Kentucky.

Jake sighed, and said, "It looks like you've made up your mind. I did not, nor ever would, jeopardize the life of a police officer. But I can't convince you of my innocence, so is it okay now if I make a call?"

Kowalski pointed to the next office over. "There's a phone in there. I think Tanner will be okay with it. Dial 9 to get an outside line. If you're making a long-distance call, dial 4, 3, 2, 1, then the number, that is, after you dial 9."

Jake got up and walked to the next office. He sat down in the roller chair by the desk and picked up the handset. He dialed as he had been instructed, and a voice answered on the other end. Jake talked for about 5 minutes, then hung up. He walked back into Kowalski's office and sat down.

"Still waiting for my contact to call from New York," said Kowalski. I would offer you some food and something more than coffee, but with budget cuts and all, and since you are not headed to the local jail yet, my hands are tied." He held out his hands as if they were magically cuffed, then dropped them to the desk. "Why don't you either confess to what you've done or help me find out who did this?"

Jake said, "I'm not helping you catch whoever did this, because I'm not a cop here in Kentucky or anywhere else, for that matter. It's not my responsibility to find out who did this, but I can only tell you it wasn't me. That is the end of the story I have for you." Jake sat back in the wooden chair, which scrapped across the floor as his big frame moved it.

The phone rang then, and Kowalski reached out to pick it up. "Kowalski here. Yep? Don't know him? Never even heard of him? Can you check with Golden Bear Investments for me? Yeah, I'm having trouble getting through to someone high up. How's the family? Good, good to hear. We gotta go fishing next time I'm up there, which, if I play my cards right, will be in about 4 months, when I retire. Okay, you, too. Tell Amy hi for me. Yep, bye." He looked at Jake. "He's never heard of you and no one with the Port Authority has heard of you either. So, I think you're some kind of storyteller or I'm not getting through to the right people. Can you explain that?"

Jake just looked at him and shook his head.

"Well, I think the only thing I can do with you now is to take you over to the jail so you can get some rest and I can go home. I'm not a babysitter but the jailers sure are." He stood up and told Jake to do the same. "Turn around and put your hands behind your back." He cuffed Jake again and led him out to the squad car in the parking lot.

The sun was just coming up as he put Jake into the back seat of his car, moved to open the front door, when Tanner came out of the building and headed for Kowalski. The two talked for a minute, then Tanner turned and got into his SUV, and left the lot. Kowalski pulled the door open and sat down behind the steering wheel.

"Larson's gonna make it, they think. But he's in a coma, so there's no talking with him now."

"Can we go to the hospital to see him?" asked Jake.

"Not all the way to Louisville, no way. He's in ICU there, under guard in case someone else decided he needed to finish the job—the one either you did or someone else did, I don't know. You're going to jail now, where you can get some food, clean clothes, and some rest. I'm headed home to do the same. I've got more questions, but apparently you don't have the answers. Why don't you think about it while you're in jail, for a little while?"

Kowalski started the car and they pulled out of the lot, headed across town to the jail. While driving, Kowalski got a call on the radio. "Go ahead," he answered. The radio squawked and beeped, and Jake had trouble hearing what was being said, as he was not used to the speaker or the way they talked.

Kowalski looked in the mirror at Jake, again, across the entire back seat. "Do you own a pair of sunglasses, prescription lenses, dark gray?"

Jake nodded. "I do. Why?"

"The detectives found a pair just like that by where they found the rifle, in the bushes. This just keeps getting worse and worse for you. Unless you're gonna tell me they're O. J.'s glasses, I think we have our boy."

With that, he turned the car into the lot of the jail and radioed for the sally port to be opened.

Jake was put in an isolation cell for the intake, but he was assured he would be placed in general population as soon as the jail finished his documentation. Jake had to empty his pockets, take off his clothing and his watch. The jail staff intimated Jake about retribution, revenge, repayment, all said with spittle at the corners of their mouths. Jake stood there in front of the guards, listening until the door clanged shut.

Twelve hours went by with no contact by the jail staff. Then, the door clanged open and the captain of the jail stood at the opening of the cell. "Time to move to general holding," he said. "This jail has some pretty bad people here; I sure hope you can take care of yourself. The guards won't help you at all." With that he turned on his heel, Jake followed with two guards behind him.

The door to the general containment area stood ajar, allowing for passage for Jake from a sterile hallway to where about 200 men stood or sat in a central holding area. Individual cells ringed the central gathering area for almost 360 degrees. Jake saw there were four beds to each cell, but he also noted there were mats thrown on the floor of each room, so five or six men were housed in each individual cell.

Jake surveyed the area as he followed the two guards towards one cell at the far end of the day room for prisoners. He walked into the cell, the guards gave him a pillow without a pillowcase, mat, and two threadbare blankets, then turned and left. He sat down on one of the lower bunks, looked out at the prisoners, closed his eyes and smiled to himself. He was in.

The big man in the hotel room slept well after completing his phone call. He woke, showered, dressed, and made coffee out of the small coffee maker on the table. The coffee maker leaned to one side because one leg of the table was shorter than the other. The big man had to hold the coffee cup at an angle so the coffee would pour into it.

Jake woke when someone started nudging him. Three men stood before him in a row.

"What's your name?" the biggest one asked. The three blocked Jake from seeing what was happening in the central meeting area of the jail.

"What's your name, I said," the big one asked again.

"What's it to you?"

"Just like to know who killed a cop's all," he said. The three stood still in front of Jake.

Jake tried to stand, but one of the men pushed him back down onto the bunk. "You move when we tell you, in this jail," said the smallest one. He had a loud, ugly kind of voice, like he hid behind it because of his size.

Jake sat up to make himself bigger, but not to be a threat. The three moved forward as one, pressing in on Jake, more to make a point than anything else, at least for the moment.

Jake lifted his head and looked at all three. Their stomachs were about his nose level. Not advantageous if you have become soft while in jail, as these three had been.

Jake said, "I'm going to stand up now, so you might want to move back."

None of the men moved, so Jake looked up at the three of them. "Sorry, I wanted to be friends." As he said 'friends', he swept his right leg from right to left, dropping the smallest one onto his left side. Wind escaped from the small one and he did not move. The other two took a second to look down at their friend, and that was one second too long. Jake kicked out with his left leg straight into the knee of the biggest one, bending it backward, out of shape, tearing cartilage and sinew, sliding the kneecap off to the side of the big one's leg, dislocating it. The middle one didn't fare much better. Jake scissored that man's legs with his, then turned to his right, dropping him on the little one who was still down, again knocking the wind out of the one already down. It took no more than about 5 seconds, and all three were down. Jake stood and moved past them. Turning and bending down, he told the biggest one, "Let's just forget this conversation ever happened. How about it?"

The big one's eyes bugged out of his head and he held his leg in pain. The other two were throwing up, gasping for air, and throwing up again.

Jake walked out of the cell and into the general population. There was someone out there he needed to see. Someone who deserved all the anger and fire he had been holding in for the past 15 years. It was 9:30 at night. Lights were out at 10:00, so he had to hurry.

Kowalski awoke to the ringing of his phone. "Yeah?" He listened for a few moments, then turned off his cell phone. "Crap," was all he said.

He got up, showered and dressed, put on his official black shoes, gun belt and hat, and walked outside to his car. He turned on the key, picked up the microphone to his car radio, and called dispatch.

"This is 821; I'm in route to the jail. Call Franklin County P.D. and let them know someone's been killed out here. I just got a cell phone call on it." The voice on the other end of the radio copied and asked if Captain Tanner needed to be notified as well. "Yeah, might as well get him in on this, even though this is their jurisdiction. 821 out."

Kowalski drove the 10 minutes it took to get to the jail, and there found four county deputy cars, two ambulances, as well as the county sheriff's car in the gravel lot. Kowalski stepped out of his vehicle, but left it running.

"What's going on in there, Pat?" he asked the sheriff. The sheriff looked at him.

"Like a scene from a movie," he answered. "If you're going in, I suggest gloves and shoe covers. I won't even let EMS in. No use."

Kowalski went to his trunk, opened it, and put on gloves, shoe covers, and took out his camera. The state always wanted pictures of crime scenes—was it for posterity or just because someone got off on the gore, he wondered sardonically.

Kowalski entered in through the sally port, through two sets of locking doors, down the sterile hallway, and into the gathering room, however, no one was gathered in there. All prisoners were locked in their cells, all doors closed, no one was allowed to come out until the scene was secured, investigations complete, and the body or bodies removed. Standard procedure. Although, when Kowalski got to the middle of the room, he realized this was anything but standard.

In the middle of the room lay not one but four bodies. All four had their necks broken as well as all four extremities; they were naked, and all had been disemboweled.

"Geez!" said Kowalski. "What the hell happened here?"

The captain of the jail walked over to where Kowalski stood.

"All the prisoners were accounted for last night, lights out at 10 PM, no one moving. We have video of the room and no one left their cells at any time. The guards made three rounds last night, 11 PM, 2 AM, and 5 AM. All the guards, two different shifts, said there was nothing to report. Nothing to see on the video either.

"Lights on at 6 AM and we found these four out here, just like this."

"Who are they?" asked Kowalski.

"All four are from the same family from back east, somewhere around New England, from what I can gather. Not brothers but cousins maybe. One's an uncle to another."

"And no one knows what happened? Have you started interviewing the prisoners?"

"We were waiting for the sheriff and his deputies to get here. They and you lead the investigation. We just hold them." He turned and walked over to where two of the sheriff's deputies were setting up tables.

"Let's get these bodies out of here, pronto. I don't want these prisoners seeing them up close. Were any of the other prisoners friends of these four? Maybe start interviewing them?"

The captain of the jail turned around. "No, these four kept to themselves. Kinda looked out for each other, if you know what I mean. There was one or two who wanted to get in their good graces, but, no, not really." The captain called to one of his jailers to phone the coroner to get him out to pick up the bodies for autopsy.

Kowalski started taking pictures. First, he took an overall picture of the meeting area. Then, he took a picture from 90-degree angles until he had completed a circle. Next, he took pictures of the four bodies, then a picture of each body, each broken arm and leg, and each stomach area where their guts extruded from their bodies. He laid a ruler next to the stomach of each man for clarification during autopsy and for crime scene information, then he got out four yellow markers from his bag, numbered one through four, and placed a marker by the head of each body.

After he finished taking the pictures, he called the sheriff back over. "Pat, who here would do something like this? One of the jailers, maybe? I mean, they're the only ones who have access to the cells and to this area at night, right?"

The Sheriff said, "Not sure where to start this investigation. We have 200 prisoners who probably saw nothing, and I have to interview all of them. If one talks and someone doesn't like it, then we'll have another dead body before tomorrow morning." He turned and said something to one of his deputies.

Kowalski put his camera away, picked up the markers, and sat down at one of the tables. "I think there's someone here who might be able to give me a clue as to what happened here last night. Where's that new intake? Jake Thompson?"

One of the jailers told him which cell Jake was in, and Kowalski asked for the cell door to be opened. The door slid open slowly on an automated track, and Kowalski stepped to the entrance.

Jake was still asleep on the lower bunk, but the other beds in the room were empty. Kowalski shook Jake and he sat up, rubbing his eyes.

"Jake, I need you to come with me. We need to talk."

Jake sat down behind a table in the jail captain's office. Kowalski leaned over, took off his shoe covers, and sat on the edge of the table.

"I'm gonna start this investigation with you. Did you see or hear anything last night?"

"What was I supposed to see and hear?"

"Four dead people are being taken to the state morgue for autopsies, and you and 200 of your closest friends were in here last night. I thought you might have seen or heard something."

"Why not start with the guards? They have unfettered access to the central area. We were locked up all night."

Kowalski nodded. "We're going to start talking to the guards. But what gets me is in two days, you are near the deaths of four people, and the wounding of two, including the clerk at the gas station, and the attempted assassination of a state trooper. Those are pretty high odds, wouldn't you say?"

"Statistics are just that. If I'm at an airport and a plane crashes, I'm near about 150-200 casualties. Does that make me the main suspect of the plane crash?"

"No, but if you were on the plane and you were the only survivor, I'd be asking you these same questions. Again, see or hear anything?"

"No."

"Back you go, to your cell. I'd talk to your cellmates and see if they can give me a clearer picture, but I don't know where they are."

"They won't talk either."

"What, did you kill them, too?" Kowalski asked, almost half-believing that somehow, Jake just might have done that.

"No, they were hurting too badly last night to do much of anything."

"Hurting? How? What happened after you came in here yesterday morning?"

Jake described in detail his 12 hours in single cell confinement, his introduction to his new facilities, the three who tried to roughhouse him—to their detriment—and then lights out.

Kowalski asked the captain of the jail to call the hospital and check on Jake's roommates. He then turned his attention back to Jake.

"Got word on the way over here—Larson's still in a coma, but the bullet hit and then moved around the crown of his head, it didn't enter the brain. He has a subdural hematoma, but they've put in a drain and they are pretty sure he's gonna survive."

"Glad to hear it. Maybe if he wakes up, he can clear me, and I can get on the way to California."

"Not so fast, Jake. Now we have four dead inmates in the jail and 200 people to interview. Not sure, but I think you might be with us for a while longer." With that, Kowalski stood, motioned for one of the jailers to take Jake back, and walked out of the jail to his car.

Kowalski placed his kit in the trunk, closed the lid, and, turning, leaned on the back of the car. Something was just not right about what was happening in central Kentucky. Nothing right at all.

A guard came out to where Kowalski was leaning on his car.

"Hey… Ski. Those prisoners in with your new one? Man, they are all messed up. Three of them, leg problems, one I've sent to the hospital. I think his leg is broken. The nurse here wouldn't touch it. She says you need to get your camera and take more pictures. Says she wants someone to file charges against whoever did this to those three.

"Wait, wasn't there another inmate in my prisoner's cell? I thought there were five or six in each room. Am I right?"

"Yeah, you were right. But one of those six, he's one of the dead ones the coroner is picking up."

"Crap. Any of those three talking?"

"Not a word from any of them. And your boy, not a scratch on him. Like he just kicked all three of their rears yesterday without breaking a sweat. They are mum."

Kowalski walked around from the back of his squad car and sat down in the driver's seat. He picked up a bottle of water from the console and took a long drink.

He saw the sheriff and called out to him. "Hey, Pat, I'm heading over to Shelbyville to the diner. If anyone needs me, call my cell, okay?"

He put his car in drive and pulled out of the lot and on to the connector road, heading west. Five minutes later his cell buzzed and he picked it up.

"Kowalski here. Hey, Walt. Any news from Golden Bear?" He listened intently. Kowalski pulled his car over, got out his pocket notebook and began writing furiously. "Geez, are you for sure?" He listened some more, then hung up. He sat on the side of the road for a few minutes, trying to decide what course of action to take. He waited for traffic to thin, turned on his blinker and pulled out onto the road, still headed for the diner.

Jake sat back on his cot. All three of his still living roommates were either in the infirmary or at the local hospital. One, the kneecap guy, would never walk again without a cane. The other two had minor injuries to their abdomen, but the bruising on their chests and thighs would take weeks to go away. The nurse noted in her report all three men refused to say who did this and would not implicate their new cellmate. The other cellmate now lay in the state morgue with his three relatives—also with nothing to say, thought the nurse.

Kowalski pulled in to the diner and went inside. The place was closed for business still, but the manager, cook and waitress were all there, looking tired and sleepy. The waitress and the cook had cleaned the floor up of the blood where the trooper had gone down, but none of the tables had been bused, under the authority of one of the other state troopers, in case there was evidence to implicate one of the people who had been there Saturday night. One of the state troopers had a measuring tape out and was writing on a pad.

"Hey… Ski, wondering if you were going to come back today. I've line of sighted the shooter's position here, if you want to take a look." Kowalski nodded an affirmative response and walked outside with the trooper.

"From what I can tell, the shooter stood here, in the bushes. I've followed the footprints, and they come from the interstate, not the gas station." Kowalski looked at the interstate, 20 yards away, then turned 90 degrees to the west and looked at the gas station.

"No footprints from the gas station to over here at all? How about this? Did whoever shot the clerk move towards the interstate, then double back? Any chance of that?"

"Not from what I'm seeing," said the trooper. "And, it looks like the shooter had been here for a while. Tracks through the grass to and from the interstate can be seen. And, we got some tire marks on the side of the road. Looks like a car had been sitting here for a while as well. No cigarette butts or anything, no Coke cans or liquor bottles thrown down. But, peculiar that a car would stop right here, line of sight of the diner, and then there are the tracks up to and from the diner." He finished and looked at Kowalski.

"Jake had it right. He said it might be someone from the interstate," said Kowalski. "But none of what everyone else in the diner says makes any sense. If Jake was inside, would he have a confidant who took the shot? And how can someone shoot through glass, hit my trooper in the head, and make that shot so perfect it just skims the top of my trooper's head and doesn't kill him? That's just impossible."

"Yeah… Ski. Impossible. But, that's what the details say. One more thing. Those footprints? Made by a big guy. Heavy. At least 230 pounds maybe more. And, those tracks come from the car parked here at an angle in the parking lot to the bushes and back. Or, maybe from the car to the bushes and back. Looks like the tracks belong to that guy you have in custody." He turned and walked back into the diner. Kowalski followed.

The captain of the jail, a man named Fry, walked up to where Jake was sitting on his cot. "I need you to come into my office," he said. Jake looked at him, nodded, stood, and walked out behind the captain. They walked down the sterile hall, past the single cell, turned and walked into an office marked 'Captain'.

"Sit down," said the captain. "My name's Captain Fry, and that's what you'll call me, get it?" Jake nodded. "Those three in your cell were hurt last night. I need to know what happened."

"Ask them," said Jake.

"I did, but I got no answer."

"Why ask me, then? You need to concern yourself with finding out who killed those four, then find out what happened to my cellmates," said Jake.

Fry studied Jake. "You talk like someone who's been around police work, but my records show you told the State Police you were a security guard. Like at the mall or something?"

Jake shook his head. "New York City. I was working there on 9/11. Couldn't go back. Too much trauma for me."

"But you're trained military, right? Says here you were Special Forces. I was airborne. How long were you in?"

"Three years."

"Long enough to learn some things, I guess. Let me ask you… how do you think those four ended up dead in my jail this morning?"

"Took too long in the shower? Took too many donuts from the box? Forgot to tell everyone they played nice? I have no idea." Jake leaned back in his chair and looked at Fry. "You would do well to hand me back to Kowalski and have him send me on my way. I've had nothing to do with any of this stuff, from the diner to the gas station to my three bunkmates to those four dead guys on the floor."

"I started this by telling you to address me as Captain Fry, and so far, you have not done so. Why should I acquiesce and send you on your merry way, so you could inflict this kind of harm somewhere else? No way, buddy."

Fry stood up straight, and said, "Back to your cell. You're getting new bunkmates tonight, and a camera in your cell room, just so we can watch and see what you are doing. Think anything'll happen tonight after lights out?"

"Not unless someone brings it to me, it won't happen." Jake stood up, turned and headed back to the central holding area.

Kowalski had been on the phone for almost an hour. He looked at his battery percentage and realized he needed to plug in. "Walt, can you send me that information? I sure would like to have it when I go to talk to this young man," he said. "Again, thank you for your police work up there, and tell your family 'hi' for me." He hung up, plugged in his phone into the car charger, and went back into the diner.

"We got us a real top-notch, true-blue hit man in jail over to Frankfort," he told his troopers. "This guy has got a file a mile long on what he's done and where he's been. Afghanistan, Iraq, Libya, Suriname, the Maldives, Russia, Iran, the Crimea, Syria, on and on. And everywhere bunches of people die. All bad guys mind you. He's like the hit man of hit men. Expert marksman with a rifle, a pistol, expert at explosives, expert at circumventing electronic and static motion detectors. This guy's a ghost, as far as my contact in New York tells me. He told me he was in the military three years, and they never used him. My contact says he just got out, maybe four months ago. That's 20 years of service, if I'm counting right. All those hits, when jets dropped bombs on the bad guys in Iraq and Afghanistan? He was there, painting the targets with lasers.

"My contact told me he has three medals of valor, two bronze stars, a silver star, one Purple Heart, and maybe this guy's up for the Congressional Medal of Honor. For what, he doesn't know. I've gotta get back over to the jail and talk to this guy. As Ricky Ricardo says, 'He's got some 'splaining to dooo."

Captain Fry walked back to his office, sat down, and tried to think through what Jake had told him, but more importantly, what he hadn't told him, in their conversation. Fry remembered in his conversation with Kowalski that Jake had worked with some kind of securities company, and was there on 9/11, but couldn't go back. Too much trauma. Fry would have to see if Jake was in the World Trade Center or was he just in New York City or was he just making all this up. No telling. From what he could surmise, Jake had a long list of things he was not telling him and Kowalski and the Captain at the State Police Post. Why would someone leave a job, take two million dollars, get a retirement or severance check—whatever—each month for the rest of his life, and act this way? Fry needed to contact Kowalski and talk to him about it. After all, the jail staff was not an investigative team, though they did have police powers. Sometimes, Fry felt like the biggest and worst babysitter ever.

The big man walked out the door and got into his car. It was a dark green sedan. He turned over the motor and pulled out of the parking space and headed towards the Interstate.

Kowalski walked back inside the diner. "I'm running over to the jail to talk to our guy Jake," he said. "Annie, come over here for a minute; I need to talk to you." The waitress walked over to where Kowalski was standing. He said in a low voice. "I need a gut feeling, truth-telling moment with you, right freakin' now. I don't care what your boss says, what the cook says, or what those other diners say, I need to hear from you what exactly happened, and it needs to be right now!"

Annie looked down at the floor, then back at Kowalski. "Just like we said on Saturday. He got a gun out of his car and shot Larson in the head. Is Larson going to be all right? I worry so much about his wife and their kids. Really, I do." She ducked her head again.

"Look at me," Kowalski said. "Larson is going to be fine. The bullet just grazed his head. He's gonna have to get a different haircut, I think, after this, but he's gonna' make it, okay? You shouldn't be afraid to talk to me. I'm a friend here. No one's gonna know we talked. An innocent man may spend the rest of his life in jail if I don't get some answers. Now, I am all-good inside until I get upset, and I'm gettin' upset. Talk to me, Annie. Tell me what really happened."

Annie teared up. "It was like they all said, he was the shooter. He done it. Then he came back in and sat down like nothin' ever happened."

"I'd like to believe you, but I talked to him before I talked to anyone else, and he knew the story just the same as everyone else. From the same perspective. And, there was no evidence of gun residue on his hands. We checked at the jail. You never said he went and washed his hands. We did find his prints on Larson's pistol, but that had not been fired. He would have had something, some kind of powder on his hands if he had used that rifle to shoot Larson. See how I am putting holes in your story? Now, I need you to tell me the truth. Or, we can go to Frankfort and you can talk to the detectives there. Which do you want?"

Annie stood looking at Kowalski, then at her manager, then back at Kowalski. "I don't know any more than I've told you, I told you that already. Now, I've got to get on prepping for when we open back up, if you don't mind." She turned and walked away.

Kowalski headed out to his car, waved to his troopers, and pulled out of the lot. He wheeled his vehicle east down I-64, back the 30 miles to Frankfort. He stopped at Post #12 in order to pick up the information

Walt sent him from New York. He had to load two reams of paper into the copier and had to change the toner once.

He pulled into the lot of the jail, locked his car, and headed inside. He went through the sally port and turned down the sterile hallway, then turned back to Captain Fry's office.

He stuck his head in Fry's office. "Hey, you're not gonna believe what I found out about our guy Jake," he said to Fry. "This guy's a freakin' war machine."

Fry looked up at Kowalski and grinned. "Sit down."

Kowalski pulled up a chair. "He's up for the CMH for some kind of service. He's got three medals of valor, two bronze stars and a silver star as well as a Purple Heart. He told me he was only in for three years. I count about 20."

Fry nodded. "I brought him in here a couple of hours ago. He's a cool one. I'm putting some new guys in his cell tonight. These guys are teddy bears. No harm'll come to him or them tonight." Fry continued, "I tried to get him to tell me what happened in the cell, but he just scoffed it off like it was nothing. We're probably going to get sued over this."

Kowalski shook his head. "If I'm right about this guy, he's got the government or some big company affiliated with the government behind him the whole way. I'm starting to think, like him, that this is a big conspiracy, and you and I have been dropped into the middle of it." He pulled out a folder from the briefcase he was carrying. "Feast your eyes on this." He passed the file to the captain.

"This must weigh five pounds," said Fry. He opened the file and started turning the pages. "If this is true, why would the feds let this information out? I was in the military long enough to know the more you do, the more they deny. Plus, what if there's more than one Jake Thompson in the military. Stands to reason. Heck, there's two Thompsons in my jail right now, besides yours."

Kowalski said, "My gut tells me this guy is the real deal, he's some kind of killing machine, and he put himself in here to kill off those four family members this morning."

Fry turned around and picked up some folders of his own. "Take a look at these. You might want them for your investigation. I think it'll tie nicely in with what happened over in Shelbyville Saturday night." He passed four folders across the table to Kowalski. "These were bad dudes, but they were not a threat to anyone in here. I don't think they deserved to be killed the way they were."

Kowalski turned page after page in the folders. "These all read the same. They come from the same place; they did the same crimes; and they got the same time. What gives?"

"I don't know. These guys weren't even from the U.S. They were Russian wannabes. All four of them had more warrants out for their arrest. And, they had international warrants from Interpol. Who comes to Kentucky who is wanted by Interpol?" he asked Kowalski.

"Beats me. I'm gettin' too old for this mess. The deeper I look, the worse it gets. Back in the 80s, they had something called the Bluegrass Conspiracy in Lexington. Some cop from Lexington was running drugs and killing people. This could be even bigger. I'm thinking of calling the feds or the military to see if they want to take this guy off our hands. I've got to propose this to Tanner first and have him run it up the line to see if my superiors agree, but all the same, the more I see, the less I want anything to do with this." He closed all four folders. Fry looked at Kowalski.

"You know, I had this feeling I have seen this guy somewhere before. Maybe not him, but someone just like him. I was in the airborne, and I hung around with a couple of guys. I'll give them a call and ask if they've ever heard of Thompson. And, I'll ask if they know of any other Thompsons who were Special Forces, Recon, whatever. I'll let you know what I know, when I know it." Kowalski stood and waved his hand, then picked up his folder.

"Make copies of these, then put them in a safe place. If this guy is a real ghost, he'll come through the walls and take them with him." With that he turned and walked out of Fry's office. Fry picked up the files and dropped them into a desk drawer, then picked up the phone.

Jake got four new cellmates that night. Four guys, all older, all missing some teeth, all there for petty crimes. The four only nodded at Jake, they tried no bluster, no bravado, and especially, no talking. Jake laid back on his cot, stretched his hands behind his head, and closed his eyes. In a flash, he was asleep. The military taught you to nap early and often, because the time was coming when action would be the word and it would not stop when the clock struck 5.

Next, one of the jail guards woke Jake up, made him stand in the corner of the cell, brought in a camera, placed it on the wall above Jake's cell door, then covered it with a metal grid and Plexiglas. Finally, they took Jake out of the cell, into the shower, and gave him a full body and cavity search, in order to make sure he had no contraband on him. They also pulled his mat, sheets, pillow and pillowcase off and gave him new ones. They went over the bed from top to bottom, front to back, to make sure he had not hidden anything in a spot a casual check might not reveal.

They brought Jake back into his cell, pulled the other inmates out, and locked the door. "Dinner is through the hole tonight," said a guard. That meant Jake would be eating his meal on his cot, not out with the others. He would be served a tray through a three-inch opening in the door, the kind the guards used whenever there was a problem; unruly inmates, a jailbreak, or an outbreak of the flu or some other communicable disease.

Kowalski pulled in to Post #12 in Frankfort. He shut off his vehicle, stepped out and to the rear of his car, opened the trunk and took out both his briefcase and his camera bag. He walked up to the door, hit the buzzer and heard the door click open. He pulled the door and stepped through.

Captain Tanner was waiting for him inside. "Need you to come into my office."

Kowalski said, "I need to get these pictures over to the lab. I took photos of the four dead bodies in the jail. Be with you in just a minute."

"NOW," said Tanner. My office, at once."

Kowalski put down his briefcase and his camera bag outside the captain's office. "What's up, Cap?"

"I just had a visit with a guy from the Department of Defense. He sat me here and bent my ears back. He wanted to wait for you, but I told him you weren't coming back today. He left a card with his number. Why do you think a DOD guy, in uniform, wanted to visit me?"

"Search me," said Kowalski. "Something to do with the attempted murders of the service station clerk and Larson?"

"Yes and no," said Tanner. "The DOD guy asked me about the four guys at the diner. What are their names? The ones sitting at the counter."

Kowalski pulled a notebook out of his pocket. He named the four men sitting at the diner.

"What did you tell him?"

"I told him the Kentucky State Police had a criminal investigation that was unfolding, and we were neither at liberty to discuss the case nor at liberty to release any information about the four men at the diner or anyone else eating or working at the restaurant. I told him we had a possible suspect in jail. Plus, I told him about the four dead inmates at the jail."

"And?"

"He seemed unfazed, like this was expected. I've never been so mad in all my years here with the state. He told me he had assets we did not want brought down to Frankfort, and it was best to get along by going along."

"What'd he say after that?" asked Kowalski.

"Nothing. He picked up his things, headed out the door, and got into one of those dark sedans the feds use. Only this one didn't have a fed license plate on it. It was from Georgia. I took note of the number and ran it through NCIC. It came back to a rental company in Atlanta. Like this guy flew into Georgia, rented a car, drove up here and tried to bully me into giving up our man.

"One more thing. This guy was the biggest uniformed fella I've ever seen. Must have hit the scales at 300, 325 easy. And, he talked with an accent. Like an eastern European accent."

"Well, our man, the one we have in jail, it turns out, never did three years in the military. More like 20. He apparently just got out. I'm still waiting for information to come from that Golden Bear Investment and Securities Company in New York. Haven't heard anything else from my friend on the Port Authority, but he did send me a folder on Thompson. He's trying to get a handle on him and his 9/11 connections with Golden Bear. I think after 9/11, he got pissed and went back into the military, maybe to kick some butt or work out some repressed anger issues he had as a kid. Not sure which. He's been in more countries than I can count on two hands and two feet. Apparently he was or is some kind of an assassin. He hunted down people who were totally bad buys and offed them. Maybe he's still doing it, here in the good ole US of A."

Tanner shook his head. "Had to come here. Had to be on my watch. He's going to mess everything up." He looked at Kowalski. "Do you think Thompson was trying to kill Larson and missed?"

"I think he was trying to save Larson and purposely aimed high." With that, he stood. "I've gotta get these pics over to the state lab. They need to see the position of the bodies, how they were found, all that forensics stuff. And I've got that information on Jake Thompson you need to feast your eyes on, right now." He turned, walked to the door, picked up his briefcase, pulled out the folder and tossed it on Tanner's desk. It landed with a thunk.

"This'll fill your day." He walked out the door again, picked up the camera bag, and headed over to his desk.

Kowalski sat down, turned on his computer, and waited for it to warm up. He was getting more and more skittish about dealing with Jake Thompson as each hour moved by.

All the cell doors were locked, two guards were on video monitor watch, and guards were patrolling the inmate's central room every 30 minutes. They also walked past Thompson's cell and looked in the three by thirty-inch window, just to make sure he was still in there. And, Captain Fry called every hour, just to make sure nothing else was happening. What a night.

Kowalski headed home, arriving at about 4 AM. A little late, but earlier than he had been home in the past three days. He pulled into his driveway, pressed the door-opener to the garage, and stopped. He needed to get milk for in the morning. He could go now, or he could get up, get dressed, hit Kroger's doors… He was too tired to think about waking back up in the morning.

Kowalski put his car in reverse, backed down the drive, then hit the garage door opener to close the door. There was a tremendously bright light, followed immediately by a BOOM, and Kowalski's garage was simply not there anymore. Shrapnel from the blast hit his car and he reflexively covered his face with his arms. Flames shot more than 25 feet into the air, and the fire spread to the backside of his house. No one but Kowalski lived there, no family, no love interest, no pets, no housekeeper, no one else, so there was no imminent danger to life or health.

He stopped the car, put it in park, grabbed the car radio microphone from its holder, and called dispatch. "Alert the fire department to come to 128 Sunset Drive, east side of town," he shouted into the radio. "Also, send the local police. My garage just blew up." He threw the microphone down on the seat and watched what was left of his garage burn.

Jake sat up in his bed, finding the beam from the guard's flashlight too bright to keep sleeping. He rubbed the sleep out, stared through the light and into the eyes of the guard. The guard shined the light around the rest of the room and then moved on.

The guards on the video monitor sat watching nothing. No movement, except for the guards every 30 minutes, but nothing else. There were 14 guards working at night. The night supervisor, actually one of Captain Fry's right-hand men, was on duty from 11 PM to 7 AM. Donald looked at the clock on the wall, then at his watch. It was 4:15 AM. The police were mostly finished coming in and out, dropping off drunks that would be in jail for six or so hours; long enough to sober up, but not long enough to make them lose their jobs over a public intoxication charge. Fry had called in 15 minutes before. Donald told him, "Nothing to report, Cap." All was well.

The guards left the day room and went about their rounds of the outside halls, the outside grounds, the sally port, and then back to the break room for some coffee and a stale donut. Pete, a guard on his 12th week of service, told the others, "I'm creeped out by what Fry and Donald are doing to us. They must think this fellow is some kind of a Shazam or something."

"Alakazam, that's the guy's name. Alakazam. You know, the magician. He says Shazam. Like Gomer always said."

"Who's Gomer?" asked Pete.

"Young pups. You guys need to watch more TV Land. You'll lea…."

The lights in the break room flickered off, on, off, on and then off again. Emergency lighting lit up the hallway with a much dimmer but perceptible light. Pete reached for his radio.

"What's happening, control?" No one answered.

"Control, this is 728. Can you hear me?" asked Pete.

"Power's out," said one of the other guards. "The backup generator will start in a few seconds. Give it some time." Seconds turned into a minute. A minute into two. No lights.

"What do we do?" asked Pete. "Let's head to control and see why the generator isn't on."

The three guards headed down the hall, passing through two doors with keys instead of using their radios to call control to open doors. When they got to the control door, they knocked but got no answer.

Pete said, "I'll go into the prisoner day room and look through the glass to see if I can let them know we are trying to get in." He pulled out his set of keys, turned his flashlight on to high, and headed down the sterile hallway.

The key fit but didn't turn. Pete pulled out the key and put it back in. Still no action. Pete radioed his partners. "No luck with the door into the day room," he shouted into the mouthpiece. "I'm heading back!"

Pete came back down the sterile hallway to the door of the control room. The three took their flashlights and beat the ends on the metal door. 'Pound, pound, pound, pound'. No response.

"What do we do?" Pete asked the others.

"We're secure here, but we need to check for an outside breech, either into or out of the jail. All three headed to the sally port. The keys failed to function in the exit doors as well. Each tried their own key in succession. They felt and knew they looked like the Keystone Cops. They stopped and looked at each other. One of the guards took his radio and tuned it to the local police frequency. "This is 725 at the jail. Can anyone on this frequency hear me?" No response.

Kowalski was standing by his car at his house when Captain Tanner drove up. He walked over to the captain's car.

"Sorry, boss. Glad I wasn't in there."

Tanner looked past Kowalski. "What in the hell is happening here?"

"Don't know, but I sure as hell care. Someone or something is trying to put me out of business. Think this is related to our man Thompson now?"

Tanner looked from the embers of the fire of the burned-out garage to Kowalski's face. "This has gone from serious to critical. Anyone connected to this case needs protection. No questions. I'll call the governor's office at 8 AM."

"I'd go straight to the governor's office, if I were you. I've got to stay here and go through what's left of my garage."

"No way. It's too dark and the fire department won't release this scene till morning at least. You're coming with me. Follow my car to my house; we'll park it around back so no one sees it, then you come stay with me and the wife. You can have one of the kid's rooms, they're away at college. It's comfortable, the bed is big, and I got beer in the fridge." Kowalski started to protest but Tanner would have none of it. "At least for the rest of the night. Then we'll see."

Kowalski nodded and walked back to his car. He started it up and pulled in behind Tanner's. He flashed his lights and Tanner pulled away.

In 10 minutes, they arrived at Tanner's home. The house was dark; the sky was almost ready to start to lighten in the east. Tanner pulled in and motioned for Kowalski to pull past him to the left. Kowalski did as instructed and shut his car off. He stepped out and walked up to Tanner.

"You think this is a good idea? I mean, if someone is trying to harm me, wouldn't they try your house as well?"

"I guess we'll see in a few minutes." Tanner took his keys in his hand, took a flashlight from the door of his SUV and walked up to the backdoor of his house. The door looked intact, the screen closed tightly. Tanner felt around the outside of the screen and found no wires, no plastique, no C-4, no alterations of any kind.

"Geez, are we just really paranoid or what?" he asked Kowalski.

"My garage says we're not paranoid."

Tanner opened the screen door. He again felt around the backdoor and for anything out of the ordinary. "Should we call the explosives team to come out and look at all the doors before we go in?" Kowalski didn't answer.

The key opened the backdoor, and both Tanner and Kowalski entered without further problems.

"I think having the bomb squad look at your garage is probably very important, don't you?" asked Tanner. Kowalski seemed to be in a trance, whether from being over tired or from abject fear and doubt, Tanner could not tell.

"Let's call it a night. Get some good rest and we start anew in the morning, which is only two hours away."

Neither man slept a wink.

The lights in the jail came back on 35 minutes after they went off. The generator never started. One minute, Pete and the other two guards were in full darkness, no air, radios not working, the next minute, lights were on, the radios operated, and the doors buzzed open.

Pete and the other guards called for the control doors to be opened.

"Why didn't you open this door?" Pete demanded.

Donald, the control supervisor, looked at him. "Directive 518, Standard Operating Procedures. And I quote. 'In case of a power failure, do not use radios and do not operate control room doors'. The doors are kept closed, so the inmates can't jump the control guards and take over the jail. Don't you remember anything about jail safety?"

Pete and the other two guards looked a little sheepish. Then Pete remembered. "I tried to open the door to the day room and it would not operate. I also tried the keys on the sally port doors, and none of our keys worked at all."

The control supervisor said, "Hand me your keys." He took the keys, looked closely at them, and said, "When were you issued these keys?"

"When we all started. About 12 weeks or so ago."

"Did you try them then?"

Pete looked quizzically at their supervisor. "I don't recall."

"These locks were changed out more than five months ago. You were given a set of old keys. No wonder you couldn't get through most of the doors."

"What about the generator? It never started," said Pete.

"Probably out of fuel. I'll put a note in and have the day shift order more diesel. With that, the supervisor closed the door to the control room.

Pete and the two guards stood there for a minute, then called on the radio for the door to the day room to be opened. They needed to do their 5 AM check and it was already 5:25.

The guards walked into the dayroom, flashlights playing across the walls, floors, tables and chairs. Nothing moved. Nothing was out of place. The guards walked to Jake's cell and looked in. Jake was fast asleep.

"That really made me jumpy," said Pete. "I'll be glad when this night is done." The other guards agreed and went back to their regular patrols. Pete wrote the incident up as a power failure without backup protection, keys not functioning due to out of date status, put it in the day log, and filed it back on the shelf. The donuts and coffee tasted pretty good right then.

Tanner and Kowalski got up, dressed, and went out to Tanner's SUV. Tanner told Kowalski to back up, opened the door to his vehicle and pulled the hood release. The hood jumped up slightly. Tanner walked around to the front of the SUV and moved the hood latch. It slid easily, and the hood rose up on its own. Tanner looked over the engine, the battery, and the starter, but saw nothing. He told Kowalski to stand fast while he started it up. He left the door open, just in case. The engine rumbled to life and settled into a low growl. Tanner looked at Kowalski. "Get in," he said.

Kowalski stepped around the SUV and opened the passenger door. He saw no wires, no plastique, no C-4, nothing. He closed the door.

"Gee whiz, Cap. I think I am getting really paranoid in my old age."

"Your paranoia is validated by what's left of your garage." They headed over to Sunset Drive to see if the fire department had any clues as to the explosion and subsequent fire in Kowalski's garage.

Frankfort Fire Department's Station 4 was still on scene, as well as the fire marshal, the assistant chief of the fire department, and a member of the state police bomb squad team.

Jim, the bomb squad tech for the State Police, walked up to Kowalski. "Hey… Ski. We found out what happened. Do you have any animals?"

"No, I live alone."

"Well, you have some kind that's been getting into your garage. Maybe a squirrel, a possum, raccoon, something like that. We think it tipped over a gas can in your garage. I guess you have a tight airspace in there, so when the door opened, air flowed into the garage. The triangle of fire—you know, air, fuel, ignition—took hold. You closed the door with your remote, and a spark from the electronic opener apparently caused the fumes from the spilt gas to ignite, resulting in an explosion. We've found no other signs of explosives." He looked at Kowalski. "Did you keep anything else in the garage?"

Kowalski shook his head. "Nothing out of the ordinary. I keep guns in my house, I do have a reloading station in the garage… at least I did have one. There was a little powder out there. Not much, and it was in an explosion-proof box."

"Yeah, we found that,… Ski. I think this was just dumb luck on your part, not getting killed." Jim walked back over to where the state troopers were combing through some more remains, and the fire department hit a few more hot spots with water.

"Can this be real?" asked Kowalski. Tanner shrugged.

"I guess anything's possible. I'm just glad we're not combing the remains looking for you." The two walked back to Tanner's SUV.

"I gotta head over to the jail and talk with Thompson some more," said Kowalski.

"You gonna tell him what just happened?"

"I'm not sure yet. I want to see what happened at the jail last night. If any more inmates died." He looked at Tanner. "Boss, I just have that feeling. And it's never good when I get that feeling, you know."

Tanner fired up the SUV and they headed back to his house.

The lights popped on precisely at 6 AM in the jail. Some inmates were already standing at their cell doors, waiting for them to open. The guards walked around, completing a head count before central opened all the cell doors. When they came to Jake's cell, they counted one inmate, checked the roster, and counted five names on their sheet. The other four men had been moved to another cell for the night. Two always counted at sunup and lights out, just so one guard could not be compromised. The count in the jail was 204. The count on their sheet met the same number. 204.

The guards signaled control to open the cell doors. They exited the day room and central hit a master button, which opened all the doors at once. 204 prisoners stepped out from their cells and into the day room, in an attempt to get away from the nasty smell of five or six people in a 5x8 room.

Jake moved and sat at a table by himself. Never one for talking, Jake was wondering what Kowalski was working on, and how soon he would be released. He didn't have long to wait. The door that led to the sterile hallway opened up and a guard called out Jake's name. He stood up and walked over to the door.

"Yeah, I'm Jake."

"State cop here to see you. He says you know him. This way."

Jake followed the new guard, who was just coming into one of the interview rooms, down past the new holding room.

Kowalski was seated inside at a desk. Jake dropped down into a chair and sighed. "You going to be able to get me out of here today, Kowalski," he said, more as a statement than a question.

Kowalski shook his head. "It's way past my pay grade, Jake." He looked at Jake, and said, "Any idea why someone would want to blow up my garage, with me in it?"

Jake sat up. "No, I don't know, and I hope you're not trying to pin anything else on me. Crap, Kowalski, you and the State Police are trying to pin four murders and two attempted murders on me already. I've been in here for the past 48 almost 50 hours and I have had no contact with the outside world except through you."

"Things just started going haywire when you showed up, is all. I went home last night, opened my garage door with the remote, remembered I needed something, and closed the door again. The garage blew up, burned to the ground. The fire department and the police department are still there, searching for clues. Do you have any insight into this, Jake?"

Jake looked at Kowalski for a long, hard minute. "I've been in here, no contact. I don't even know where you live—don't even care where you live. I've been nothing but helpful the whole time I've known you, and you continue to hurl accusations at me for no reason other than I'm your patsy for the day." Jake stared back at Kowalski.

"I'm not blaming you. I just need to know if there's a cleanup crew following you around the country, trying to get you out of trouble." He didn't tell Jake about the so-called fed, who came to Tanner's office the day before.

Jake said, "You've got to be kidding. Are you some kind of fantasy writer that you think I am capable of hiring, paying, keeping on staff, to follow me all over the country, just in case I fall into some sort of crazy, off-the-wall, science fiction, voodoo thing like this, and they can rescue me? You need to see a shrink."

Jake sat back in his seat. "I told you I have a brother in California, mom, dad and sister in New York. I retired from Golden Bear Securities because I couldn't go back after 9/11. Why doesn't anyone here listen?"

Kowalski held up his hand. "I've listened to you each time you've talked. But weird things are happening here—things that have never happened to me before. This isn't some *X-Files* TV show I've fallen into, but strange things are happening with players I still don't know showing up. And how did four guys end up gut-cut on the floor of this jail? Can you answer that? Or do ghosts come in through the walls and get these men out of their cells and kill them? I've never had a case like this, not ever." He pulled out a notebook, opened to a blank piece of paper, and placed a pen on it. "Write down what you did on the night of the four murders," he said. He added, "And write down what you did on the night of the gas station attendant's attempted murder as well as my deputy's attempted murder."

Jake looked at the paper, picked up the pen and started writing. In about 5 minutes he was done. He turned the paper around for Kowalski to see.

"What's this?" demanded Kowalski.

"This is a timeline to show I could not have killed anyone, not at the gas station, not at the diner, and not here in jail. It's given me some clout here; no one wants to talk to me because of the three hurt in my cell and the four dead in the day room being attributed to me. The guards here are really poor. They should have found those guys before morning check. I was in the military for three years, and that was beat into our heads during basic. Know your numbers before the drill instructors come asking. I did a lot of pushups to learn that lesson."

"About those three years," said Kowalski. "I've got good information you might have extended your stay in the military by about, oh, say, 17 years. Any response?"

"Why would I tell you three if I had made the military a career? No one at my rank makes a career out of the military." He looked at Kowalski. "I'm more concerned with what those people accused me of at the diner. I again tell you I had nothing to do with either shooting. But apparently you aren't going to question those men or the waitress to see where the truth lies." He stood up.

"I'm going back to the day room. Do you have anything else you want to accuse me of doing before I leave?"

"Sit down, Thompson. I'm not done here," sighed Kowalski.

Jake sat back down, crossed his arms and looked at the sergeant.

"What would you have me say, Kowalski? I don't have any place to take this from here. I am innocent of all charges, but I can't prove it beyond a shadow of a doubt. You have me in here, and I can't help you find out what is really happening. I've not been before a judge, no formal charges have been filed, and by my count, you've got about 22 hours before the Supreme Court says you're out of time. You can't hold me longer than 72 hours without charges being preferred."

Kowalski sighed and sat back. "I told you before, I believe what I can't prove, and I disbelieve what I can. Too many years of going back and changing reports, going over crime scenes again and again. It's tough being me."

"Well, try being me for once. Geez-o-Pete, Kowalski. Why would I drive though Kentucky, stop in some random spot-on-the-map diner, after supposedly shooting a clerk, wait for a cop to show up or not show up, leave, shoot the cop, then come back inside? That goes beyond all reason, and you know it."

Kowalski nodded. "There is that. By the way, ballistics came back last night. The rifle we found in the bushes matches the bullet that grazed Larson's head."

"Did you match my prints on the rifle?" asked Jake.

"No, and that's another piece of the puzzle. But, we did find plastic gloves, the kind EMS uses, by the sunglasses you said were yours. I guess they might have fallen out of your pocket after you shot Larson?"

"Come on, Kowalski. I was seated in the diner when Larson was shot. And I bet if you look in my car, my sunglasses are still in the glove box. That's where I keep them. In a case. I'm not in the habit of carrying sunglasses around with me in the middle of the night. You need to start talking to those others at the diner. Someone's going to change their story. They always do."

Kowalski stood and called for a guard to take Jake back to the day room. He walked outside to his vehicle. He did need to get back to Shelbyville to talk to the others in the restaurant. Something just didn't seem right. Jake was correct when he said two or three people who saw an accident would have two or three different stories. But now, he'd let almost three days go by, and the crew and patrons at the diner would have had time to put a story together that would be basically impossible to break.

He opened his car door and stopped. He saw a wire he had never seen before, drooping down below the nadir pin where the door hinged to the A-frame of his sedan. He stepped back, turned away, and went back inside the jail. He took out his phone and called Tanner.

"I want you to come out to the jail, and see if you can ring up Jim, the bomb guy, to come with you. Something's up with my car."

It took Tanner less than 15 minutes to get to the jail. Kowalski had gone back out and placed DO NOT CROSS yellow tape around his vehicle. The bomb guy was about 10 minutes behind.

Tanner asked, "How long were you in the jail?"

"About 20 minutes or so. But I locked my car like I always do." They went back into the jail and asked for the footage from above the sally port where prisoners were brought in and out. The video showed no one near his vehicle.

Jim walked out and looked at the open door. "I think this might be a wire from the stereo system in your car. Did you have one added after you got it?"

"No, I don't listen to the radio in my car, and it was issued new to me three years ago. I don't use it for car chases or PIT maneuvers, so it has to last me a long while."

Jim walked over to the car, bent down and looked at the wire. He reached out and touched it, pulled on it slightly, then pushed on it, and then pulled on it again. He walked around to the passenger side, opened that door, and crawled across the seat. Jim bent down and looked under the driver's seat. He stood up and looked at Kowalski.

"Good thing you didn't sit down in this seat," he said. He reached under the seat. "You might have turned this over." He held up an open, half-eaten bowl of clam chowder, with the lid firmly closed. "How long has this been here... Ski?"

"Probably since the last time I ate clam chowder," Kowalski said, laughing nervously. "Geez, Tanner, I feel like I'm seeing shadows around every rock. I've never felt like this before." He sat down on a bench outside the sally port.

"Maybe I just need to go ahead and retire. I think my edginess is going to be a detriment to the department. I think I'll turn in my paperwork next Monday."

Tanner replied. "Well, I think we're all seeing ghosts after Larson's getting hit the other day. Why not take the rest of the week off? Maybe go fishing, up to see your buddy in New York, or just sit at home. I don't want you thinking about this case for the next four days, okay?"

Kowalski nodded. "That's like telling me not to think about the elephant in the room." He turned, walked to his car, started it and drove away.

Jake sat in his cell, not because he didn't want to be outside with the other inmates—it was because he wasn't an inmate and he had nothing in common with any of them. Of course, he supposed most of the inmates felt the same way. They weren't guilty, and they weren't supposed to be in there either. But all of them had been dealt a sentence by a judge or a jury of their peers, or they were being held over after being accused of a major crime. Jake still had not been formally accused. And time was running out.

Kowalski drove home, intent on resting. When he got there, he knew he had plenty to do regarding the garage. Call the insurance agent, sift through the remnants and see if anything was salvageable, order a dumpster to throw what was ruined away, see if his house was damaged, call for someone to give him a bid on building a new garage. He had plenty of work to do for the next four days.

Tanner and Jim were still at the jail. Jim told Tanner he would stop by his house and give it a good once over, to check to see if anyone had planted anything. Tanner told Jim that was not necessary, that what was happening was more in his mind than in reality. Jim nodded and got into his suburban and drove away.

In the jail, the three inmates who had tried to strong-arm Jake were back. The biggest one, named Dave, walking with both a limp and a cane, sat down at one of the tables. "Boys," he said. "I've got to make that guy pay for what he's done to me and my friends. I've got to come up with a plan before he leaves here. Anyone wanna help?" He said it in low tones so no one past two tables could here. Several of the men said they would help, but only if he could guarantee their safety.

"I can guarantee but one thing—this guy's not gonna walk outta here tonight." With that, he stood, leaned heavily on the cane, and went to get a cup of coffee.

Jake saw the three inmates come back into the day room, but he made no move of reconciliation or acknowledgement of their presence. He did lie back down on his cot, closed his eyes, and rested. He knew things were going to heat up before lights out. He had to be ready.

In the end, six men decided it would be worth it to jump the guy who put their friend on a cane. They planned for about an hour, then talked four others into starting a staged fight on the other side of the day room, to draw attention away from Jake's cell. They set the time for one hour before lights out, after all had eaten, and before the guards came to do their nightly count.

Jake awoke at dinnertime and filed in with the rest of the men to the canteen, where breakfast, lunch and dinner were served. He got himself Salisbury steak, mashed potatoes, green beans and some coffee. Jake walked back to the day room and sat at a table by himself. He saw the six, plus the one he put on a cane, crowded around a table on the other side, talking and looking at him. He ate his dinner quickly, took the tray back to the canteen, and returned to the day room. He pocketed three dish towels and put two of them under his mattress, then walked back out. He went over to the dish cleaning area and dipped the third towel in the hot water. He wrung it out and pushed it into his pocket. The six had split up, three on one side of the room, three on the other.

They kept looking around, watching the clock, and looking at the guy with the cane. Jake stepped back into his cell and sat down on the cot. He now knew how many were going to come after him, he just didn't know from where their attack would take place.

Kowalski stood in the middle of his garage, picking up charred pieces of his loading station and shook his head. Conspiracy theorists never think something as small as a rodent could do something as big as this. These theorists never wanted to admit Lee Harvey Oswald was the lone shooter in Dallas. That Jack Ruby was not paid by the Mafia or the Cubans to kill Oswald, that John Hinckley acted alone in trying to assassinate President Reagan.

He continued sifting through the rubble that was his garage. He bent down to pick up something on the floor and stopped. He reached for his pen and inserted it into a cartridge he had been planning to reload. He held it up in front of his face for a long minute.

"That's it!" he exclaimed. He turned and went into his house, careful to take off his shoes before entering. He pulled his cell phone out of his pocket and called Tanner.

It was an hour before lights out. Eight hours before the end of Jake's 72-hour hold on a non-charge. Jake awoke from his nap, sat on the edge of his bed, and prepared himself. He pulled the dish towels out from under his mattress and wrapped them tightly around his knuckles. This was the time he would have done it, so he thought this might be the time the six had set to go after him. He felt the sturdiness of the bed. It and the one across from him were bolted to the floor. Nothing gave. In fact, the bunk beds didn't move an inch. No weapons were available for him to use in the room. No pens, no newspapers he could roll up and use as a small ram, no hard coffee cups he could put in a pillowcase. Heck, he didn't even have a pillowcase for his pillow. He looked at his clothes. An orange one-piece jump suit, t-shirt, slippers, and boxer shorts were all he wore. There was nothing to be had there for his immediate use. He would have to use each of the six against the others. One advantage he did have was the small size of his cell room. Not more than two at a time could come through the door to attack him. He stilled himself, breathed deeply, and closed his eyes. He would know when it was time, just by listening. He tightened the dish towels one more time.

Tanner answered the phone. "Tanner here."

"Thompson's telling the truth. He didn't shoot Larson. I've got the proof."

"What? Did someone confess?"

"No, can you come over to my house? I'll show you when you get here."

"Headed your way," said Tanner. He clicked off his phone, picked up his keys and walked out to his SUV.

At two minutes after 9:00, a fight broke out in front of the glass partition between the day room and control. The supervisor on duty hit the alarm button, and 12 guards headed towards the day room, stopping to get rifles that fired non-lethal bullets and tear gas, plus helmets, riot gear and bulletproof vests. The other two guards headed outside to make sure a breech was not about to occur. These guards were armed with M-16s, fully loaded and ready for an outside interdiction. They also radioed the sheriff's office and informed them of what was happening.

The sheriff's office automatically sent two cars as backup for the guards on the ground.

In the day room, the fight between four inmates caused a back swell of men towards the outer walls. The six who had decided to help the inmate with the cane turned as one and moved towards Jake's cell. At 9:04 they reached his cell door. The two biggest men, named Jeff and Trey, stepped into Jake's cell room. They looked at his bed, where he had been sitting five minutes before, but he was not there. They looked under the bed, at the other bunk, and into both corners of the room. He simply wasn't there. Jeff and Trey turned around and lifted their hands to show the man with the cane he was not in his room.

Tanner drove the short distance over to Kowalski's house and pulled into the drive. The stench of the doused garage rose to meet his nose and caused him to hold his breath. Maybe one of those rodents was killed in the fire. Karma was good but when it was bad, it was really good.

The six men fanned out across the day room to find Jake. Most of the other inmates were watching the fight. Some were yelling for the fight to stop, others were yelling for a particular man to beat another. Any trained observer could tell the men weren't landing full blows, and they kept each other from falling into any of the tables that were bolted to the floor.

Jeff and Trey walked over to the man with the cane. "Dave, we can't find him. He's disappeared."

"He's here and he's got to pay for what he did to me," said Dave. "Split up and find him!"

The men moved between those watching the fight. The guards would be coming from the sterile hallway into the day room at any moment. Their chance to take the big guy down was growing slimmer by the second. They split up, two went one way, four the other.

In the group of four, the last man, a little guy named Willie was half-looking for Jake and half-watching the fight. He really wanted to be in that fight, but he also wanted to get into the graces of one of the groups that provided protection. At 5' 1" and 124 pounds, Willie needed protection.

As he turned to watch the fight again, the whole room turned upside down. His feet hit the ceiling and he hit a concrete table with his left shoulder, which immediately separated, then his collarbone, which snapped in two, and then hit his head on the concrete floor. Pain seared through his body for a couple of seconds. Blackness and unconsciousness couldn't come too soon.

Tanner knocked on Kowalski's backdoor. He noticed some charring that had impinged on… Ski's back siding, but it looked like it could be cleaned up.

Kowalski opened the door. He was on the phone. "Come in, boss," he said. He continued talking on the phone. "Yeah, that's what I thought. This case has been driving me crazy. You've just added some sanity back into my life. Thank you so much. Hope to get together with you very soon. I may even turn in my paperwork next week, if I can get this case closed." He listened. "Yeah, my deputy's gonna make it. He's out of the coma, but he's got one heck of a headache. He's seeing double. Hopefully, that'll fade after a while. And he has a case of amnesia. Okay, say hi to the wife. Talk to ya later." He hung up and looked at Tanner. "I don't think Jake's got anything to do with shooting Larson, but he does have something to do with the deaths of the four in the jail."

Jeff and Trey kept moving around the room, looking at the faces of over 190 inmates. They couldn't figure out where the big guy had disappeared to. The day room was only 30 feet by 30 feet, with an offshoot to the canteen. They looked at each other and headed for the canteen. The other three kept circulating, looking for Jake and not finding him.

"What's the new evidence you have on Thompson?" asked Tanner, as Kowalski put his phone down on the table.

"I've had that peculiar feeling you and I have been played," said Kowalski. "When I was looking through what was left of my garage, I thought about not what we had, but what we didn't have. We've got a gun, his sunglasses, gloves, a hole in the glass, a wounded officer, and we're waiting on ballistics to see what kind of gun was used to wound the gas station attendant. What we don't have escaped me until I sifted through my garage floor and found this." He held up a cartridge.

"Is that the shell casing used to shoot Larson?" asked Tanner.

"No, I want you to see past the shell casing. I want you to think about what was and was not said at the diner the night of the shooting."

"I'm not following your drift," said Tanner.

"Think back to what Jake said. I had to come inside and find my pocket notebook to make sure. He said, 'Think about it. It seems this was a set-up, an ambush, something that was planned for days if not weeks, and I was dropped right into the middle of it.'"

"What's your point… Ski?"

"My point, boss, is, what if it was a set-up, an ambush; what if it was planned for days if not weeks, with Thompson dropped right into the middle of it?" Tanner still shook his head. "For Pete's sakes, Captain, we're being played for fools. Thompson set this whole thing up so he could get into the jail, to kill those four!"

Jeff and Trey continued walking towards the canteen. Jeff looked back at the other four, but now there were only three. One of them, Parker, was a meth-head from eastern Kentucky. He had lost almost every tooth in his mouth. He reached back to grab his friend Willie's shirt, to make sure they made it through the crowd together. But something wasn't right. The shirt was too big, too tall, too something. He turned and looked, and it wasn't Willie but the big guy whose shirt he had. And the big guy had his arm raised, with his elbow pointed at Parker's face. The point of the elbow came down, plastering Parker's nose across his face, knocking out the last remaining three teeth in his mouth, and rendering Parker even more unconscious than he was from day to day. Now there were four, plus the guy with the cane.

Tanner looked at Kowalski. "Do you really think Thompson made us take him into the jail, so he could call a hit on four guys none of us knew anything about?" There was almost a look of concern on Tanner's face. "I think you need that time off, and it needs to start now."

"I think we need to get over to the jail and see if Thompson has anyone else on his hit list."

Jeff and Trey looked in and around the canteen, but no big guy. They turned and only saw one of their own, standing on a table, looking for the others. The guards would be coming through the door after three announcements were made over the loudspeaker. Jeff and Trey knew the guards would be putting on riot gear, loading their non-lethal bullets, and be waiting in the sterile hallway for the door to be buzzed open. Jeff looked back just in time to see the third guy, Brett, suddenly turn head over heels and fall to the floor, as if by magic.

Jeff grabbed Trey. "Something's wrong. I don't see any of our other guys. C'mon!" He took Trey by the arm and pulled him towards the back of the day room.

The fight was still going on, though the actors were tiring, mostly just pushing and shoving. Jeff looked for Dave, but didn't see him either.

"Where'd everybody go?" asked Trey.

"Don't know. I got a bad feeling though. Maybe we just need to cool it until after lights out." The two walked back around, stood at the very rear of the day room and started to watch the fight.

Trey turned to his left, to talk to Jeff over the yelling and cursing. "They're pretty good players, huh, Jeff. I wish I was in there, swingin' away. Get rid of some of this boredom." He shadowboxed for a few seconds, then turned back to his left. Jeff was on the ground, bleeding from both ears and his nose. "Jeff, are you okay?" No reply. He stood back up just in time to see the big guy moving at what he considered light speed. Trey didn't have time to move, he could only stand there, dumbly, and watch the towel-wrapped fist fly forward and break his jaw. For Trey, the lights went out in the room. Jake unwrapped the towels from his hands and threw them into the trash. Lady Luck looked in on him tonight. He actually hadn't needed the protection for his hands. But, need not, want not, as the old saying goes, or something like that, Jake mused. He walked over to Dave, the man on the cane. Dave moved back slightly. But not enough. Big elbow to the face. A big twist to the injured leg. Lights out for old Dave.

Tanner and Kowalski called ahead and were told a fight was in progress in the day room. Four men were fighting by the main door, and the guards were starting to make entry. Kowalski looked at Tanner. "I told you this guy, Thompson, is a lot more than he told us he was."

"We don't know if this is Thompson or just a regular fight. I've seen plenty of them in the jail over the past years." But Tanner wasn't really feeling the confidence in his own voice. He mashed the pedal to the floor, pulled out of Kowalski's driveway and hit his lights and siren.

"The day room is about to be breeched. Everyone drop to the floor! The day room is about to be breeched. Everyone drop to the floor!" The order was repeated a third time, the door buzzed open, and 12 guards rushed through yelling, "Get down, get on the floor. We will shoot you with rubber bullets. We have tear gas!" All 12 yelling the same thing but at different times made the cacophony in the room seem like 100 guards were coming through the door. The fight stopped, the players probably glad as they were punched out. All 200 plus inmates were on the floor. No one trying to fight back against the guards, no one challenging them, no one claiming harassment. The guards told all the inmates to stand up as one unit, walk to the far wall, face it and wait for a head count. All but seven stood and faced the wall. The guards walked over to the seven on the floor, at first exhorting them to stand up, then realizing they were either unconscious or nearly so. One guard called for medical aid. They requested three ambulances from the city and had the on-duty nurse come to the day room.

The nurse, an older, retired ER nurse who had seen it all, walked from inmate to inmate. "This one's in a coma, this one's still breathing. Hey, this one, we sent him to get his knee fixed. He's not ever gonna walk again." She continued until she had checked them all.

I've got four in comas, and three that'll wish they were dead tomorrow," she said.

"Head count!" shouted one of the guards. The rest of the guards separated the men into groups of ten for ease of counting and for command and control.

"Hundred ninety-six, plus the seven down, that's 203," rang out one of the guards. "We're one short!"

"Check all the cell rooms," called out the supervisor. Four guards stayed and watched the group of men while seven fanned out and checked the individual rooms.

"I got one in here," said a guard. "It's that new guy."

The supervisor hurried over to the cell, thinking the new guy might be hurt or dead. He found Jake lying on his bed, eyes closed, sleeping. "Wake him up!" said the supervisor. Another guard shook Jake, who rolled over and sat up on his elbow.

"What's the problem, guys?" Jake said. "Can't a fellow get some sleep around here?"

Tanner and Kowalski pulled into the jail parking lot, which was filled with two squad cars, three ambulances, and two guards armed with M-16 rifles. "Move aside," ordered Tanner. The county sheriff's deputies and the EMS workers stepped aside, as did the guards.

"What's going on in there?" asked Tanner.

"Riot, Sir," came the reply. "We got seven in there who're gonna take a ride to the hospital—if they make it out of here alive, that is."

Tanner pushed his way through and into the sally port. He saw the evening supervisor coming on, receiving a report about the incident.

"What gives here?" he asked.

"We're not sure," said Donald. "The control people said it looked like they were watching a play instead of a fight. There were four inmates, pounding on each other, but not really hurting each other. The guards didn't look much past those four. But when we breeched the day room and cleared the inmates, we found seven on the floor. All seven hurt, real bad."

Kowalski looked at the captain of the jail. "One of those hurt that new guy, Thompson?"

"No, Sir," said the captain. "He was in his cell asleep, as far as we could tell. We're gonna take a look at the video from the cameras."

"Did you put a camera in his cell?"

"Sure did. Just getting ready to go to the computer and look at that one before we look at any other footage." He turned and walked to an IT room, filled with radios and antennae, computers, editing booths, time code source machines, and banks of old video tape machines not being used.

Tanner looked at the tape machines. "Old technology. Not used any more. We have all the cameras running into two computers. We have two computers, so in case one dies, we can catch whatever happened on the other computer. But sometimes that old Murphy and his law still steps into the room."

He reached over and stirred a mouse awake and moved a cursor up to a time bar at the top of the cathode ray tube. "We can see most places from here, but there are still a few dead spots, and when these guys are up on the tables, there's more blind spots as well."

He shuttled the video left and right, right and left. Tanner and Kowalski saw men up on tables, yelling and screaming while the fight went on, cheering and booing, almost as if they were on cue to get involved as well.

"Here's that guy's cell. You can see his legs here. Let's see, that was at 8:50." He shuttled the video forward. Suddenly, the screen went blank. No video until 9:15, after the fight was over. The video came back up. They could see Jake lying on his bunk, looking like he was asleep.

"That is the strangest thing. I'll have to get my tech guy to look at the camera. Usually, if it goes dead, it stays dead."

Donald moved his mouse again, to another camera view. He shuttled until he hit 9:04 PM.

Kowalski saw what looked like a fight starting. "Stop, look at these three here… and here. They're not involved in the cheering. Are these our guys?"

"Let me get one of the guards who knows the floor to come in here and tell me." He called out over the radio, and Pete, the late-night guard, keyed into the IT room.

"You know these guys here, Pete?" Pete looked at the screen.

"That's Willie, there's Jeff and Trey, they're buddies. Here's Parker and his friend William. That's Dave. He's the one who had his knee blown out. I don't know the other guy, but he hung around them as well." They watched the video.

The first thing they saw was Willie with his feet straight up in the air, then crashing down on a table. He didn't move.

"Is he in a coma?" asked Tanner.

"No, but he's gonna wish he were dead tomorrow." They watched as Parker and William fell to the ground, but with the mass of men on the tables, they couldn't see who did what to whom.

"Parker's near dead. His friend William is alive. Parker was our class-A meth head. He was in and out of here so much they considered putting a revolving door on his cell."

"What about those two big guys, what'd you say their names were? Jeff and something?"

"Trey. Both arms broken. Snapped like twigs. And they're big guys. Takes a lot to do that."

Tanner and Kowalski looked at each other. "Go get Thompson and bring him into the interview room, if you don't mind, before some of your inmates die tonight."

Jake walked through the sterile hallway and into the interview room. Tanner and Kowalski were already there.

"Know anything about what happened tonight, Jake?" asked Kowalski.

"I was sound asleep the whole night. No noise in a place like this can keep me awake. Remember, I was in the military for three years."

"Or more," said Kowalski. "We think you know more than you're letting on, Jake, and we'd just like to know where we stand and how we've come to be the recipients of your graciousness."

Jake looked at the two men. "You sent me here. I asked you to let me out, but you're holding me, without charges. It's late at night, and you've got exactly seven hours to let me go or this jail, you two, the captain, the supervisors, and everyone else even closely involved with the running of this place, is going to be sued." Jake stood to his full 6'3" frame. "And I mean it. I didn't have anything to do with what's going on out there. You even put a camera in my cell, to keep an eye on me. What could I do?" He sat back down.

"Jake, we're trying to understand something here. Four people were killed night before last. Tonight seven seriously injured. Will we lose any more?"

"If you don't let me go, you two may be picking daisies on the side of the road, because you'll be wearing state uniforms and working on road gangs. I had nothing to do with any of this, yet you are keeping me locked up without charges."

"There is that, Jake. You know, you never asked for a lawyer, someone who probably could have freed you on the first night. Know what I think? I think you were sent here, either by your own volition or someone highly placed, in order to kill those four who might or might not be more than we know or knew. Does that sound about right?"

Jake looked from Tanner to Kowalski and back to Tanner. "If I had that kind of power, don't you think I'd also find a way out of here after I committed those crimes? You think I'm Buck Rogers in the 25th Century? You two have me wrong. As I said before, wrong place, wrong time." He sat down.

"Jake, unzip the top part of your prison uniform. Jake unzipped to his waist. "Take off your T-shirt. Jake pulled his shirt up. Tanner and Kowalski leaned in and looked at Jake's upper torso. No scrapes, no marks, no blood, nothing to mark he had been in a fight. They told him to dress and then to show his hands. Jake held out his hands and turned them over, then over again. No blood, no scrapes, nothing.

"Take him back to his cell. We'll deal with this in the morning."

"I'll be out of here in the morning, one way or another," said Jake, as he was being led away.

Tanner and Kowalski walked outside. It was dark; the jail had just gone into lockdown for the night.

Tanner said, "This guy Jake is one master thief or magician or Hoo-di-ni, I don't know which. But if we don't get him out of here, everyone in that jail's gonna end up at the hospital or in the morgue." He turned and got back into his car. Kowalski walked around to the other side.

"Tanner, how about we take him out of here and put him some place where he can't or won't hurt anyone else. Maybe take him back to the State Police Post?"

Tanner thought about it as he drove. "No, if he's a killing machine, I don't want him to suddenly activate inside my police barracks. He'd be shot dead for sure. Or he might kill some of my non-system employees."

"Ghosts can't be shot, Tanner. Didn't you ever watch *Casper*?" The two drove away in silence.

Jake sat down on the edge of the cot in his cell. Four men were dead, and it was being blamed on him. Seven others chose to try and take him on, whether because of a misguided sense of duty or to take out a suspected hit man, he didn't know. What he did know was the four who were found with guts cut, necks and appendages broken, were connected in some way to the Mafia in New York City or the Russian mob, but he didn't care which.

Jake didn't care one way or the other about those four men. They decided to play with fire and they got burned. The other seven, he felt bad about, but figured they had it coming. There shouldn't be any more problems in the jail before he got out tomorrow. Boy, was he wrong.

Tanner pulled up to Kowalski's house. "See you in four days, okay... Ski. I want you rested and ready to go next Monday."

"Yeah, I'll be ready. I might try my hand at fishing or reading, something to take my mind off this craziness that's been going on. This guy gets a walk tomorrow morning, if you can't pin something on him. He's already counting down. See if you can get him on a rifle charge or for killing those four in the jail. But he's some kind of a genius at not being seen. Call me if you come up with something that'll hold him. I can talk to him, as long as he doesn't pull some more of that black magic stuff."

"Pure nuts. That's what I think. Pure nuts," said Tanner. He waved at Kowalski and pulled away.

Kowalski waited for about 10 minutes, standing outside his backdoor, just in case Tanner were to return. He pulled out his phone and made a call to his friend in New York. He talked and listened for about five minutes. Then, he hung up.

Jake lay back down on his bunk. It was now midnight. The staff at the jail in Frankfort, Kentucky, had less than six hours to let him go. The doors to the cells had been closed and the other inmates in his room were asleep. Jake stood and looked out the small window. Nothing moved out in the day room. The guards were back to the 11 PM, 2AM, 5 AM rounds. Jake figured if it was 11:30, he had exactly two and one-half hours to make good his escape. He needed to get on the road to Shelbyville to get his car, then on the road to California to see his little brother.

Kowalski walked back to his car and sat down. This was going to be completely inappropriate, but he saw no other way. He was going to retire at the beginning of next week, if everything worked out that way. Twenty-eight years was long enough, and seeing a man being held the way Jake was, just didn't seem right.

He closed his car door and started the engine, put the car in reverse and backed out. The 10-minute drive to the jail was fraught with doubts, worries, and finally, resolve. He was going to get Jake out and take him to his house. No one would suspect for the next four days Jake was there. They would think he was released after 72 hours and headed out west.

Kowalski arrived at the jail and hit the buzzer. The sally port door was opened, and Kowalski entered. He went to one of the interview rooms and asked for the supervisor.

Donald, the late-night captain, walked into the interview room.

"Hey... Ski. What can I do for you?"

"I need to talk to Jake Thompson again. Bring him in here for me, would you?"

Donald nodded and walked away. In a few minutes, he came back with Jake, who was rubbing his eyes, probably because he had been asleep, thought Kowalski. He motioned for Jake to sit down.

"Are you doing okay?" he asked.

"Good as someone who's in jail with no charges," he answered.

"I think I'm going to take you out of here, before the 72 hours is up. You'd have to go to court and the judge would have to hear what we have, and that might raise more questions, so..."

He stood to go, turned around, looking at Jake, motioning for him to follow. Jake looked back at the sterile hallway from where he had come, then stepped after Kowalski.

The sergeant knocked on the captain of the jail's door. Donald opened the door and looked at Kowalski, then at Jake.

"Whatcha doin'... Ski?"

"I'm moving the prisoner so he can be ready to talk to the judge in the morning. He's only got 72 hours to be held, then he has to be let go."

Donald nodded. "Where are you goin' put him while waitin' for sunrise... Ski?"

"I figured Waffle House might be a good place to wait," said the sergeant.

Donald shook his head. "Gotta have something in writing for me to let him outta here," he said.

"Yeah, I'll get that for you in the morning," said Kowalski.

Donald turned and said something over his shoulder. He then walked out of his office, closed the door, and stood between Kowalski and the exit to the sally port.

"You're not takin' him anywhere... Ski," said Donald. "He'll stay here till mornin' when I can put him in a van and transport him to the county courthouse, where he'll stand before the judge." With that, Donald put his hands on his hips and looked at Kowalski.

The sergeant shrugged. "I know you got formalities and all. I just don't think this is the place for our guy here. But, you're right, and I know it. I'll be back in the morning." Kowalski moved to go past the captain, turned his shoulder, and said to Jake, "I'll see you in the morning. Be ready about 6:00 AM, OK?"

Jake nodded. He turned to walk back down the sterile hallway when he heard a whomp! He turned back and saw Donald lying on the floor, gasping for air.

"Come on!" called Kowalski.

Jake stepped over the now prone body of the captain of the jail. Kowalski pulled the keys off the ring around Donald's waist. He turned and fitted the key into the lock and spun it, opening the door to the sally port.

Cameras were everywhere, and the jail staff could see Kowalski opening the door, Jake right behind him. But, they could not see directly outside the captain's door, so there was initial confusion as to what was happening.

Kowalski slammed the door shut and turned to exit the main side door. The sally port door could only be activated by inside, and he didn't want to draw attention there, so he again inserted Donald's key, spun the lock again, and he and Jake stepped outside.

Kowalski kept Donald's keys as they headed to his squad car.

"Hop in, Jake," shouted Kowalski. "We gotta move it fast or we'll be back inside, both of us this time!"

He started his car, pulled out of the parking space, and hit the gas, hard. Gravel, blacktop, cigarette butts, and other things flew into the air as they pulled away from the county jail.

"We're going to have to find a spot to land, 'cause I think my house is gonna be hot in a bit," said the sergeant. Jake was just holding on as tight as he could to the door handle. He was ready to jump if it got too hot.

Kowalski turned his car down the bypass, headed for Highway 60, just outside of town. He turned on his lights and siren. "No better way to stay concealed than to scream all over the place," said the sergeant. "Everyone's gonna be lookin' for someone trying to sneak away, not for someone running Code 3 through the capital city."

Kowalski took the exit and spun the wheel to the right when he got to the highway. "I've got a friend who owns a house down on the river. I have a key and they're out of town. I head down there from time to time to make sure the place is secure. Tim and Karen won't mind if we lay low there for a day or so." He turned on to a small road from the highway and turned off his lights and siren.

Jake looked at Kowalski. "Why don't you just let me off and let me thumb a ride out west. I want to get to California and see my little brother. I've done nothing wrong and I have no one to answer to, so I'll be in the clear."

Kowalski looked at Jake. "You shot and near killed a state trooper; you killed four people in jail, probably maimed another seven, and then attacked the captain of the jail and broke out. You think, do you really think anyone is going to take your word that you had nothing to do with any of this?" He drove on in silence.

Jake looked down at the floor mat. Then back up at Kowalski. "Why'd you get me out of jail, knowing I probably did all of these things, which I did not do?" he asked.

"Because I know you didn't do most of them, that's why. I've been doing this job for 28 years, I can smell a rat and a rose, and I know the difference between the two."

Kowalski turned right, then headed down a long hill. He turned off his lights and siren and slowed down. They pulled up at the last house on the river before the road ended. Kowalski opened the door and stepped out. He looked back down through the car and told Jake to step out.

Jake pulled his frame off the seat and followed Kowalski into the house. The sergeant turned on a couple of lights but kept the majority off. "Might as well not raise the notice someone is staying here, huh?"

Jake sat on a sofa, put his feet on the coffee table, and closed his eyes. In the interminable time between wakefulness and sleep, there lies a slumber that keeps one from thinking, from processing, and from caring. Jake was in that state when his legs were kicked off the coffee table.

"Wake up. We gotta move," said Kowalski for the third time.

"What?" asked Jake.

"I have to go by my place and grab a change of clothes. I'm gonna take the extra car here so no one knows it's us." He grabbed a set of keys off the entry table as they walked to the door.

The car was a sedan, one seen every day, indistinguishable from other sedans, especially at night.

"How are you going to get into your house?" asked Jake. "It's going to be under surveillance."

"I figure I'll park one street over, crawl over my neighbor's fence, open the backdoor, use my phone light to see where I'm going, get my clothes, and be over the fence before anyone else is any the wiser." He started the car and moved it out of the driveway, and on to the street.

The drive to Kowalski's house took about a half hour. Jake looked at the houses and street corners, the buildings, the trees and the cars parked on the streets. All mostly becoming part of the scenery because it was so dark. His eyes tried to focus but were not able to because everything melded into black as they drove.

Kowalski stopped his car. "You need to stay here. Less noise and all. I can be over the fence and back in less than 10 minutes." He stepped out of the car, careful to quickly close the door so the inside light would be on for the shortest time possible.

"Get some bottled water so we can hydrate, OK?" Jake was feeling pretty thirsty since he was escorted out of jail. Kowalski nodded and moved into the dark.

The problem with the dark is you can never tell if someone is watching you with night vision or not. Jake surmised the police in Frankfort and Franklin County had officers driving by Kowalski's house about every hour. Kowalski was going to have to work his way in quietly in order to not be seen.

Jake reached over and adjusted a switch on the light panel of the sedan, then opened the passenger car door. The inside light stayed off. He moved silently, stealthily, towards where Kowalski had moved just a couple of minutes before. No use staying in the car, a trapped rat in a cage, when he could be on the ground, watching to see if Kowalski needed help, or if he had become reticent about taking Jake out of jail and was now sending officers to surround the sedan parked at the curb.

Jake moved through a backyard, towards a six-foot fence and stopped. He listened at the fence, turning and watching his back, then stood and peered over the fence.

What he first saw was a big pile of debris at the top of Kowalski's driveway. He couldn't make out what it was, or why it was there, but it didn't look natural, so Jake thought it was something Kowalski had piled up over the years.

Jake pulled himself up and over the fence, down to the other side, and laid flat on the grass. It smelled sweet but also like soot. Fire. Ash. Acrid now. Jake's nose was picking up many different scents. He turned his head towards the house and slowly began to crawl forward.

Jake could barely make out the open backdoor. He saw no movement inside, but if Kowalski was shielding his light, it would be almost indiscernible from the outside.

Jake reached the backdoor. He pulled himself up to a crouched position, pressed himself against the back of Kowalski's house, and studied the entrance. It was a standard three-foot opening, the kind made for moving furniture in and out, for carrying in bags of groceries or laundered clothes, or for carrying food from the kitchen out to a picnic table during the summer. He didn't see Kowalski from where he was crouched. But then he saw the door hanging at an odd angle.

His first thought was maybe Kowalski had to kick in the backdoor because he forgot his key, but the noise from that would probably bring whoever was watching the house running, if someone was watching, which Jake assumed they were. What if someone had been waiting inside for Kowalski. He would have run headfirst into a buzz saw, and now, game over. Jake pondered what to do next, but he couldn't leave the house without knowing if the sergeant was dead or alive, or if he had been captured. Arrested? Caught?

Jake slid towards the opening and looked at the doorframe. A wire hung down from the jamb. Possibly a security wire, thought Jake. But most security systems were wireless now, so that thought left as quickly as it had entered. Jake sniffed the wind to see if possibly some sort of Semtex explosive had been used to disorient or disable Kowalski, but the smell from the pile behind the house made it impossible to detect any odor from the door.

Jake turned to enter the house. He crawled forward, not calling out, but sensing something was very wrong. Kowalski should have been in and out by now. Jake began wondering if he had missed the sergeant in the dark, but with the backdoor in the shape it was in, Jake figured only something bad could have happened.

Jake crawled into the back entryway, in through the kitchen, and bumped into something big and doughy. This was not a table or an island or a chair that had been turned over. This was big and prone and human-like. And very dead.

Jake crawled up to the body. He felt for a phone but could not find one. He was sure but wasn't sure that it was Kowalski. He needed to determine what had happened, and then he needed to get out. Someone, whoever killed the sergeant, was going to come in through the back-door, or perhaps they were already inside, and it would be curtains for Jake.

Jake started to back up but heard a noise. He stopped, lay still, and tried to focus his eyes in the dark. He saw a light from a phone coming towards where he and the body were.

"Best get up and let's get going," said Kowalski. He shone the light in Jake's face. That made it even harder to see.

"I knew you would come in behind me. Thanks for the backup, if you wanna call it that." He moved towards the backdoor.

"Who is this?" asked Jake.

"The captain of the jail, Fry, that's who," said Kowalski. "He set some det cord around my backdoor, for what reason I don't know. I crawled over the fence and saw him wiring the doorframe. I couldn't be sure, so I snuck up on him as he was finishing what he was doing. He set the trip wire, you know, to cause it to explode, and I asked him what he thought he was doing. He jumped a mile, and when he did, he pulled that tie wire out. It popped, and the concussion must have killed him. I thought he was a pretty nice guy, but I guess he might have thought you were going to try to get into my house. Instead, he bought the farm. I dragged him in past the kitchen and went into my room and got some stuff.

"Go into the kitchen, open the fridge, and get some water for us. My hands are full." He turned and headed out the door.

Jake crawled to where he thought the refrigerator would be, reached out his hand, and by feeling found and opened the door slightly. The inside door was full of water bottles. Jake hurriedly removed 10 bottles, put them in a plastic bag he found in the pantry by using the same method, and crawled back towards the backdoor.

Kowalski was waiting for him, leaning against the back of the house.

"Head for the fence. I need to try and get this door at least somewhat put back on its hinges. I'll meet you back at the car."

Jake crawled over the fence, through the neighbor's yard, and to the hedge surrounding the neighbor's home. The sky was just starting to turn purple. Dawn was but an hour away.

No movement on the street, not in the bushes, not near the trees in yards Jake could see. He looked for a cigarette glow, a light from a phone, something that would tell him they had found the car and were waiting for him.

Kowalski came up behind Jake. "See anything?" he asked. Jake shook his head.

They duckwalked towards Kowalski's borrowed sedan. No movement. Jake motioned for Kowalski to wait. He felt around the passenger door and motioned for the sergeant to do the same. No det cord. They opened the doors simultaneously and slipped inside the car.

Moments later, they drove away. Just another car, headed for work at the capital, early in the morning.

Jake asked, "Why would the captain of the jail set up such a trap that would kill or maim you?"

"No idea, unless he thought it would get you. But, why not just wait behind what was left of my garage?"

Jake looked at Kowalski. "Was that the pile behind your house? I smelled something that had been burned, but not enough light to let me see what it was."

Kowalski eyed Jake. "We thought that was your handiwork. You had somehow gotten to my house and set up a bomb inside the garage, designed to kill me when I pulled up."

"I was in jail, if I could so remind you."

"Yeah, we put a lot more faith in what we thought you could do than in what you did do." He studied Jake as he was driving. "Tell me about your military experience. And not about the three years. Tell me about your 20 years in. Why lie about it?"

Jake nodded his head. "I get more when I don't tell so much," he said. "Respect, that is. Let's say I had shot the trooper. Then I tell you about the 20 years in the military, about how I was a trained assassin. How I slipped in and out of different countries. Would you have then believed me when I told you I didn't shoot the deputy?" Kowalski shook his head. "So, it has become a point of safety and salvation for me to tell others I only served three years."

"How about you being up for the Medal of Honor? That's what my friend in New York told me."

"Yeah, that was a long time ago."

"And?"

"I helped some guys out of a bad situation. I killed some Taliban members who were going to kill my guys."

"How many did you kill?"

"I don't remember. Maybe 12, 13."

"By yourself?"

"Yeah. No one else was around. But, these medal things take time. Not sure if I'm going to be around long enough to receive the medal, the way things are going now."

"How'd you do it? Did you call in an air strike?"

"No. The Taliban had my guys tied up. I had to go in and take out the bad guys, so I could get my boys outta there. That's what they would have done for me. It was at night, so it was easier. The Taliban guys were all asleep. Someone way above my paygrade wanted to bargain with the Taliban, but they were all already dead when the message was delivered. The president wasn't happy, apparently. Can't help that. Had to get my guys out."

"Are you still in contact with any of them?"

"Well, about that. We consider it only one day in a lifetime. Some of the guys were ready to forget. So, we don't really stay in contact. The others, I hear from them, time to time."

"How'd you kill that camera in your cell?" asked Kowalski.

"Easy. Cameras don't do well in heat. So, I cleaned up my tray with a hot dish towel and then walked back into my cell and wrapped the towel around the camera. Took about 10 minutes for the camera to react. After the fight, I took the towel off and the camera cooled down. I laid down on my bed until they came in and woke me up. No one the wiser."

They drove on in silence. Jake sensed Kowalski wanted to ask more, but he closed his eyes, shutting off the path of communication between the two.

The man in the green sedan had stopped his car in Tennessee. He had found a hotel along the highway. His plans in central Kentucky were not working and he needed to let his bosses know they had to make other arrangements.

He dialed a number from his hotel room. There were a few chirps and whistles as the phone hooked up with the international trunk line under the Atlantic Ocean. A few seconds more and he heard a distant beep, beep, beep ringing sound.

A man answered.

"Da?"

The man in Tennessee spoke with his counterpart for about 15 minutes. He protested a few times, but finally agreed and hung up.

Jake snored himself awake. It was daylight and they had been on the road for the past three hours. They were headed into the sun, so they were going east. Jake didn't have his watch on his wrist, so he had to surmise what time it was by the position of the sun in the sky. He figured it was about 9 AM, but to make sure, he stretched, yawned, and then asked Kowalski.

"It's 9:02," said Kowalski. "We need to stop for some breakfast."

Jake nodded. He was getting hungry and he needed coffee.

"It'd be best if I'm not seen in this jail uniform," said Jake. Kowalski turned and looked at Jake.

"What's your size?" he asked.

"I wear extra-large shirts, 38 waist, 36 length pants, shoes are size 11, and belt is a 40. Underwear, I got. Don't need a T-shirt."

They were coming into a town in West Virginia. Kowalski pulled into a Walmart and parked at the very back of the store. Kowalski told Jake to stay low and not bring any attention to himself.

"I'll get you some clothes and shoes, and be back," he said. He turned off the car and took the keys. "I trust you, but I don't want to walk out here and you be gone. It'd destroy my faith in humanity." He turned and walked towards the store.

"You use your credit card and all the state police in this area of the country will come looking," said Jake.

"I got enough cash. But thanks for reminding me."

Jake slumped down in the seat, low enough to keep from being seen, but with his eyes just above the top of the console so he could assess any threat. He thought about a suddenly righteous Kowalski making a phone call to the state police in West Virginia, but his options were limited at best. If he wanted to run, he'd have to wait for different clothing. Orange jumpsuits sing out escapee in every state.

He needn't have worried. In 15 minutes, Kowalski was back with Jake's new clothes. Jake looked them over, then changed in the front seat, which was quite a job for a man as big as him. It took him more than 10 minutes to get fully dressed. The clothing was itchy, ill-fitted, and looked better on the rack than on his frame. But, the alternative was going back to jail, so Jake said nothing.

The man in the green sedan walked out of the hotel to his car and started it. He pulled out of the parking lot and turned north on I-65. He was 3 hours away from Frankfort. There was a lot to think about in that time. A lot of planning to do. He also needed to talk to his contact in Louisville. There was a lot of cleanup needed in that area.

Jake and Kowalski sat in a 24-hour pancake diner. Jake had coffee and some eggs with bacon. Kowalski ate three pancakes, toast and orange juice. They were feeling tired after having been on the road for the past 4 hours but up for the past 12 hours.

"I need to know the names of the four men who sat at the counter in the Shelbyville diner," said Jake.

"Why do you need their names? These guys are the salt of the earth. Family men. They all like the local and state police. None of them would do anything to hurt my troopers."

"I just need to work this out myself," said Jake. "What's the problem with letting a new set of eyes look at the people who were in the diner with me?"

"You're looking for trouble where there is none," said Kowalski. "I'd trust these guys with my life."

"Well, my life is on the line here, not yours." Jake leaned forward in his seat. "I can't let go of the idea that they would put something on me just because I was from out of town. No one deserves that."

"Alright," said Kowalski. He pulled a small notebook from his left breast pocket.

"Luke Dinkins was the man who sat on the left at the counter. He's a farmer and a deacon at his church. Next to him was Woody Sumner. Woody has been a member of the Chamber of Commerce for as long as I've known him. To his right was Lawrence Douglas. Larry runs the local fix-it shop in town. He's recently widowed. Wife had cancer. Bad thing there. On the far right was Bill Evans. Bill is also a farmer. He's been a coach for little league, an umpire at little league baseball games, and he regularly donates to all kinds of charities. None of these men would do anything wrong to hurt my guys or anyone else, for that matter."

"Nevertheless," said Jake. "I'd like to see more information on all of them. Financials, arrest records, anything you can get me, so I can paint a better picture of all four."

"Why not the six who came in after you, those young boys," said Kowalski. "They'd just as much opportunity to do the shooting or be in on a conspiracy as the four at the counter, right?"

"No," said Jake. "I believe they are innocent parties, just like me. Wrong place, wrong time. They came in after these four, laughing, pushing, and just being kids. I think they'd have to have already been in place, knowing Larson was coming in that evening, for a plan to try and kill your trooper to work. And I noticed the four at the counter kept looking at me and whispering amongst themselves. I figured it was just because I was from out of town."

Kowalski shrugged his shoulders. "The only way we're going to get that information is to head back to Kentucky. Neither you nor I want that right now, I believe. I'm sure they've found Fry in my house, and have probably put out a BOLO for me and you."

"BOLO?" asked Jake.

"Be On The Lookout. It's a cop term, is all. Not an arrest warrant for me, just one of those, 'hey if you see this guy, let us know' kind of thing."

Kowalski and Jake got large carafes of coffee to go and headed out to the sedan they were driving. Kowalski climbed into the driver's seat, and Jake sat in the passenger seat. Kowalski turned the key in the ignition and pulled out of the parking lot.

"We need some sleep," said Kowalski. "I can't drive too much further, and you don't have your wallet."

"I don't need my wallet to drive; I just need it in case I get stopped." They both laughed, more tipsy from tiredness than anything else.

They pulled off the road into a rest stop. Jake climbed over the seat and lay down in the back. Kowalski slid across the front seat and was asleep within five minutes.

The man in the green sedan was nearing Louisville. He was about 50 minutes away from Frankfort.

Jake and Kowalski slept for 4 hours. They awoke when an 18-wheeler roared past, blowing its air horn at a deer walking in front of the truck.

Jake yawned and sat up. It was about three in the afternoon. He peered over the seat at Kowalski, then shook him awake.

"I think we need to head back to Shelbyville and let me talk to those four men," said Jake. "We are in a car no one knows, we won't go to the diner, and we'll slip back out of town if it gets too hot."

"I think it's a rotten idea to go back, but if you're willing to do it, then I'm okay with heading back as well. Everyone's gonna think you've done something with me, when they find Fry, so it's important to see if we can make a united sort of front back in Kentucky."

Jake thought for a minute. "And about that. Why was Fry putting det cord around your doorframe? What could he possibly think he would accomplish if he killed me? I think that det cord was meant for you." Jake climbed back over the seat. "We need to head back, solidify our position, and find out who's doing what to whom."

Kowalski started the car and pulled out of the rest area. He turned around at the next overpass and headed back to the Commonwealth of Kentucky.

The man in the green sedan pulled up to a hotel in Frankfort. He got out, went into the hotel and registered for a room, giving false identification, as usual. He took the key and went to his room. He threw his bag onto the bed, made a local phone call, then settled down to sleep. He would call overseas in a few hours, when it was daytime in Russia.

Jake and Kowalski arrived back in Shelbyville just before dinner-time. They stopped to grab a bite at a fast food restaurant, far enough from the diner to not raise suspicions, but only after Kowalski checked to make sure none of the four counter men were eating there.

"Usually, those four only eat at the diner. It's become kind of a tradition. They all went to high school together; none of them went on to college. They've just kind of made this their little kingdom. They attend the football games together, go see movies together, help each other whenever something needs doing. Good, friendly, salt of the earth kind of people. They've never been in any trouble, and they don't cause trouble. I really don't see why you need to speak to them."

"You said it yourself. You tend to believe in those that are unbelievable, and you tend to doubt those you think you should be able to trust. I'm telling you—these four men, you cannot trust."

Jake got out of the car and they headed inside to grab a bite to eat. Dinner was quick, the coffee was stale, and the bathroom was clean.

They headed out to the sedan a few minutes later. They sat down in the car, and Jake looked at Kowalski.

"Let's do this systematically. The first one we go see is going to call the other three and warn them we are coming. They in turn will call the State Police or the local boys, and we'll be arrested on the spot. So, we have one or two chances at most, unless we do this right."

"You thinking of killing them after we talk?" asked Kowalski.

"No, but I think if we bring them along, we can keep the others from knowing we are coming."

Kowalski looked around. "We need a phone book so I can find their addresses," he said. "I don't know where they live."

"Didn't you write down their addresses in your little book?"

"No, I was more worried about getting you out of the diner than anything else. I was afraid something bad would happen if I didn't move you quickly. I got their names from the waitress after I dropped you off at the jail. But not their addresses."

Jake nodded. "Did you bring your phone with you? You can look up people by using the Internet."

"I brought it, but it's dead," said Kowalski. "I didn't remember to grab my charger."

Jake saw a Radio Shack in the parking lot, and Kowalski went in and got a car charger for his phone. He paid cash for the cord so there would not be a record of him being in the store. He'd have to hope there were no cameras recording the transactions, but if there were, he hoped no one would come looking for the video.

Kowalski plugged in his phone, then unplugged it just as quickly.

"They'll find me if I use my phone. They can ping it and find out where I am, within about three blocks. If I charge this, and they are looking, we're hosed."

Jake thought for a minute. "Can we buy a new phone, one of those disposable ones?"

"Yeah, but they don't have the Internet feature on them. I've got to think of another way to find out where these guys live."

They pulled out of the parking lot and back on to the main road.

"Why not head to the diner and see if the waitress knows their addresses?" asked Jake. "What other chance have you got except to do that?"

"Yep, that's what we have to do. I'll tell them I'm off but just needed to ask some questions of those four. I'm sure she'll give me their names and addresses if I butter her up."

Kowalski turned the car down a side street and headed to the diner. After a few minutes, they pulled on to the street where both the diner and the gas station were visible.

"You get out here, go over and sit under that tree. I'll pull around and find out the information, then swing back and pick you up."

Jake hopped out of the car and headed to an old oak behind the building. It was big and shady and cool, and it was good to be out of the car.

Kowalski pulled around to the front of the diner and walked inside. He saw Annie behind the counter, rolling napkins around silverware.

"Annie, I need to talk to you, just for a minute."

Annie put down a half-finished roll of silverware, wiped her hands on her apron, and walked over to where Kowalski stood.

"Hi, Bill. What now?" she said.

"I need a favor," said Kowalski. "I need to talk to the four guys who were sitting at the counter last week, when Larson was shot. I just need to spend some time with them, asking the usual questions, is all." He shrugged as he said it, trying to make Annie feel as if this were just one more piece of the puzzle to put Jake away for good.

Annie looked at Kowalski for a few seconds, sighed, and walked back behind the counter. She pulled out a phonebook and looked up the names, addresses and phone numbers of the four patrons who had been at the counter, then wrote their information on a piece of paper.

Kowalski thanked Annie and took the sheet from her. He walked to the door and then turned and looked at the waitress.

"Best if my visit is just between you and me right now, Annie. That is, if you don't want to get caught up having to go to jail as a material witness."

Annie nodded and kept folding napkins.

"You were never here, Bill. I never saw you, Bill. Get on outta here, Bill."

Kowalski turned and walked out the door.

He picked up Jake near the tree. The two looked over the addresses.

"This one's only three blocks away, I think. Let's hit it first," said Kowalski.

They drove the three blocks in a little under one minute. They passed the house once to see if anyone was standing outside. They saw no one.

Kowalski turned the car around and pulled back to within three houses of Woody Sumner's home. Both men got out and walked up to the front door. They looked in through the window in the door, but saw no movement.

Kowalski rang the doorbell, but there was no answer. He rang it again, and still no answer.

"Let's walk around the outside of the house. Maybe they're on the back porch, enjoying the end of the day."

They walked around the south side of the house, then the east side, until they were around back. Woody and his wife and their dog were sitting on the back porch, enjoying the sunset. Dead.

The man in the green sedan awoke and went to get some dinner at the restaurant next to the hotel. It was a little hole-in-the-wall eatery, but the food tasted good. The man ate and checked his watch. Still four hours before sunrise in Moscow.

Kowalski stood and looked at Woody and his wife.

"This is terrible," he said. "I can't believe he's dead." Jake knelt and looked at Woody's body.

"No signs of stabbing, torture, anything like that. There's a glass here next to your guy and one next to his wife. Bet anything they poisoned themselves. I guess the dog might have had a drink from one of the glasses." Jake stood and looked around. "Maybe someone came by and talked to them and they figured this was their only way out."

Kowalski shook his head. "Damn shame. I can't even call anyone to come and work this scene because you and I are on the run."

Jake said, "Let's move the bodies inside, so we have more time to talk to the others. And if, as I think, this is going to go bad, we're going to find two others just like this, and one on the lam."

Jake and Kowalski moved Woody, his wife and their dog into the house through the backdoor. They checked around inside to see if there were any clues as to what caused Woody to commit suicide, but nothing was visible. They didn't want to wait too long, in the hope that at least one of the other men at the counter might still be alive.

They headed back to the sedan and climbed in. Kowalski looked down at the list.

"This one's going to be in the next neighborhood," said Kowalski. "It'll take a few minutes to get there because we have to go out and cross over the main drag."

He started the car and they drove in silence. Jake hoped the next guy, Bill Evans, was either still alive or at least not at home. They could wait for him to return home and at least warn him. Jake mentioned this to Kowalski.

"But what if Bill is the ringleader, and he's the one killing the other three? We're gonna have to tread lightly here."

They pulled past Bill's house, stopped the car and got out. They walked up to the front door and rang the bell. No answer. It was starting to get dark outside.

Jake jiggled the front door handle, but it was locked. He pushed on the door to see if it would give, but the deadbolt was thrown. He looked in through the front window and poked Kowalski in the ribs.

"Look here. I see two bodies lying inside," he said. "We need to make entry."

Jake walked around to the back of the house and tried the backdoor. It, too, was locked.

"We're gonna have to break in to see if either of them is alive," said Jake. He walked over to a window and tried to shove it up, but it held fast.

"They might have this place on an alarm system," said Kowalski.

"I didn't see any signs out front," said Jake. "We need to force the door."

Jake walked back to the door and began pushing on it. The handle was locked but there was no deadbolt on the door. Jake used his large frame to push on the door. It moved twice and then broke the jamb.

Jake slipped inside and walked into the living room. There lay Bill Evans, eyes open, transfixed on nothing, with a butcher knife in the center of his chest.

"I guess he wouldn't drink the poison," said Kowalski. He walked past Bill's body to that of Bill's wife. She had been shot once, through the right temple.

"This is getting crazier by the minute. I think we need to contact someone with the state police and let them know about these bodies." He walked over to the phone.

"I don't know if I would do that, Kowalski," said Jake. "I think whoever did this believed they talked or were getting ready to talk. And I think this goes way beyond Shelbyville, Kentucky."

The man in the green sedan pulled back into the parking lot of the hotel in Frankfort. It was nearing 7:30 PM. He could get a shower and shave, have a little dinner and then make a phone call to his counterpart in Russia.

Kowalski and Jake walked back to the borrowed sedan. They sat down heavily and looked again at the list.

"Lawrence Douglas is close. He's the widower. Maybe he wasn't at home. He might have taken the day and headed out to see some sights." He squared himself in the driver's seat, started the sedan, and pulled away from the curb.

"I think we need to pass this guy up and go for the fellow who sat on the far left," said Jake. "He's the one who sold me out the night Larson was shot."

Kowalski stopped the car and they looked at Luke Dinkin's address.

"This is about five miles from here, right through town. I think we'll miss the main road and come to his house from the back side." He put the car into gear again and started driving.

Kowalski turned left and right and drove through the small, back streets. In about 15 minutes, they came to Luke's home. Kowalski stopped about one-fourth mile short of his home.

"If this guy is dead, I am going to a find a payphone and call the police and tell them to go to all these homes. This is nuts." He opened the driver's door. "I wish I had my service weapon. I just feel we are headed into a really bad situation."

"That's amazing," said Jake.

"What, that I'm going to call the local guys and let them know what's going on?"

"No. That you think in the 21st Century, you can find a payphone." He and Kowalski walked down the sidewalk towards Luke's house.

When they were one house short, a car pulled into the driveway and the driver waved to Kowalski. It was Luke.

The man in the green sedan got out of the shower and wiped his head with a towel. He pulled on some shorts and socks, then a T-shirt, and sat down on the bed. He picked up the room phone and made a long-distance call to Moscow.

"Hey, Bill, what're you doing here?" asked Luke.

"Where have you been, Luke?" asked Kowalski.

"Just got back from Louisville, Bill. Went over to see my daughter and her husband. They bought a new house and moved in last week. I wanted to see what it looked like... hey, why the questions? And what's he doin' here?" He pointed to Jake.

"He's with me, and we're trying to figure something out. When was the last time you talked to Bill and Woody, Luke?"

"This morning. Why?"

"Have you talked to Lawrence today?"

"Can't say I have, Bill. He's gone fishing up to Lake Huron in the northeast. Won't be back for a week."

Kowalski looked at Luke. "What made you identify Jake here as the shooter last week at the diner, Luke?"

Luke furrowed his brow. "Cause that's what happened, Bill. I'm not used to being challenged on my eyewitness testimony. This guy walked out to his car, got out a rifle, and shot Officer Larson. That's what happened, and this fella needs to be in jail, not out with you, running across the country. Geez, Bill, I'm telling you, this guy did it." He turned to walk into his house.

"Hold on, Luke. You need to come here," said Kowalski. "I don't want you walking into your house right now. There's been a problem and I want to make sure no one gets hurt."

"Well, I'm calling the police and tellin' them you and this guy are out harassing innocent people." He turned and walked towards his backdoor.

Jake took three long strides and grabbed Luke by the arm.

"You need to listen to what Kowalski is saying," said Jake. "Just stop for a minute and listen."

Luke shook his arm, trying to release Jake's grasp, but Jake held firm.

"Luke, both Bill and Woody are dead, and so are their wives. I think it has something to do with this case, and I'm not going to let you go into your house if, in fact, it has been booby trapped."

Luke looked at Kowalski.

"Are you for real? Both of them are dead?" Luke slumped his shoulders. "I can't believe this. Are you sure?"

Kowalski nodded.

"We've been to their homes and we've seen their bodies. So, now, again, I need to ask you if your story is real, and if it isn't, why did you make it up?"

Luke looked at Kowalski. He bobbed his head for a few seconds.

"We were all such close friends," said Luke. "I just can't believe both of them are dead." He turned and walked back to his car and leaned on the front fender. "Are you sure they're dead, Bill? Are you sure?"

Bill nodded his head again.

"I need to check your house to see if anyone is inside or if your house has been set up to kill you or someone else." He walked towards the backdoor. "Do you use this entrance all the time, Luke?"

Luke shook his head yes and handed Kowalski the keys.

"It's the big key, Bill."

Kowalski took the keys and he and Jake walked to the backdoor. They opened the screen and felt around the edges to see if there were any wires, magnets, or pressure devices on the door. Seeing nothing, Bill cautiously opened the backdoor. Jake stood beside Bill as he loosened the latch and then very slowly opened the door into the kitchen area. Nothing happened. The door had not been compromised. Kowalski nodded his head at Jake and then walked in.

Luke peered around the corner of the door. The house looked the same. Kowalski called to him.

"Where's your wife, Luke?"

She's stayin' with my daughter in Louisville," said Luke. "I'm headed back tomorrow to pick her up and bring her home."

"Why don't you go back to Louisville and stay the night with her and your daughter. I think, for right now, that might be the best thing you could do." Kowalski handed the keys back to Luke. "And I still need to know why you implicated Jake here when both you and I know the shot didn't come from his car."

Luke eyed Jake and Kowalski. A dribble of sweat broke on his brow.

"I'm tellin' you, that's what happened. I'll go to my grave tellin' you that's what happened, Bill." He turned and walked out of the house. "Close up whenever you're finished inside," said Luke.

Jake and Kowalski stood there, watching Luke pull out of the drive, and turn towards town.

"Now if that don't beat all," said Kowalski. "No one ever goes that way to head to Louisville. He'll go right through town and it takes forever. The bypass is so much easier."

"Maybe we better head over to the fourth guy's house, like right now," said Jake. "Luke might be calling him on his cell phone."

"But Lawrence is fishing up north," said Kowalski.

"So says Luke, but do we really know that?"

They jumped into the sedan and headed to Lawrence's house. It took them almost 10 minutes, but they made it. Luke's car was not there, and there was no sign of anyone being home.

Kowalski and Jake went to the front door as they had done on two other occasions, ringing the bell and looking in to see if anyone was moving about. It had gotten dark now and it was almost impossible to see anyone inside. Jake looked at Kowalski and they headed around back.

Jake opened the screen door and looked for any kind of explosive device that had been put up but didn't find one. There was no deadbolt on this door, just like at Bill Evans' home. Jake put his shoulder into the door and it gave on the second attempt. He almost tripped over Lawrence's body.

Jake knelt down and checked for a pulse. Lawrence was still warm, and Jake thought he felt a faint tick in Lawrence's neck.

"I think he's still alive," said Jake. "Let's move him over to the sofa."

They picked up Lawrence and together moved him past the kitchen and into the living room. Lawrence's house was a mess, but not from someone rummaging through the place. He remembered Lawrence was recently widowed and Jake figured he just didn't feel like cleaning his house yet.

Jake checked for wounds, cuts, bruises, anything that would let him know what happened to Lawrence. He couldn't find any. Next, he opened Lawrence's mouth to see if there was any odor of almonds, which would indicate poisoning by cyanide. There was no odor. He looked to see if there was a cup on the floor next to where Lawrence lay, but didn't see one. He then undressed Lawrence to see if there was an injection mark in his external jugular, his antecubital at the bend of his elbow, or the saphenous vein in his leg. Still nothing.

Jake stood and looked at Kowalski.

"I can't figure how they might have tried to kill this guy, and I'm still not sure they haven't succeeded. I see no needle marks, I don't smell any foul odor indicating oral poisoning, and he didn't fight anyone. No marks on his hands, no defensive wounds on his arms or face, nothing to indicate what happened. How do you see it, Kowalski?"

The sergeant looked at Lawrence and shook his head.

"I've got no idea. I guess we need labs and a good ER doc to figure this one out. What say we call 911 from here, let on that I'm Lawrence, and that an ambulance is needed here post haste? We'll split and watch for where they take him, and then we'll figure out a way to interview him if and when he gets better."

Jake saw no other way than to do what Kowalski said, so he walked over and picked up the cordless handset, dialed 911, and asked for an ambulance. He listened for a few seconds, told the dispatcher to send the crew in through the backdoor, and hung up. He placed the phone by Lawrence, beside his left hand, and the two beat a hasty retreat out the backdoor.

The man in the green sedan had finished his phone call. He decided to watch a movie on the hotel's television. He turned on something with Mel Gibson and settled back on his bed.

Jake and Kowalski waited for the ambulance to arrive. When it did, sirens screaming, it attracted a crowd in the early evening. Several people watched as the crew entered the house, found Lawrence, and loaded him on a stretcher. As the EMS crew exited the house, a few tried to give them some information about Lawrence, but mostly it was that he was recently widowed, and his three friends knew more about him than anyone else.

The crew put the stretcher with Lawrence on it in the back of the ambulance, then pulled away. Kowalski waited for a few seconds, then started the sedan and followed the ambulance discreetly.

The ambulance turned on its lights and sirens and raced through the back streets of Shelbyville. Kowalski was having trouble keeping up with it in the sedan.

Jake said, "Hey, don't you know where the hospital is here in town? Or is there one?"

Kowalski shook his head. I think I remember where the hospital is here, but this hasn't been my territory for years. My main area is Frankfort, Lexington, and points east. I go all the way to Richmond, Kentucky, but I don't hang out here much."

They followed the ambulance as best they could, seeing it run stop lights, stop signs, past traffic, until it was out of sight.

"Hey, follow those signs that have the big H for hospital on them," said Jake.

Kowalski turned right and drove down the main drag until he came to another sign telling him to turn left. They worked their way downtown and then back on to Louisville road when they saw a sign for emergency ambulances only. Kowalski turned in and drove up behind the ambulance. The crew had already unloaded the patient and had gone inside. Kowalski turned off the car and stepped out.

"No time like the present to be a cop," he said.

He walked up to the emergency entrance with Jake and tapped on the glass. A nurse opened the sliding glass and asked what he needed. Kowalski flashed his badge and told the nurse he and Jake were investigating a possible assault. The nurse slid the glass door closed and hit a button. A door slid open and Kowalski and Jake entered.

Lawrence had been taken into trauma room one, where a doctor and two nurses were working on him. One nurse looked up at Kowalski and asked if he were family.

"No, state police. We suspect foul play here and just need some information." He picked up a sheet of paper off a table, pulled out a pen, and started writing.

The nurse said, "We don't have anything yet. I'll call the post in Frankfort and give them the lab results if you want."

"No, I think we need to stay here and wait. We don't have any other place to be."

Kowalski and Jake sat down in the trauma room and waited. One of the nurses started an IV, another put Lawrence on a heart monitor, and a tech came in and drew labs. The doctor did a full physical exam, then turned to Kowalski.

"Who found him?" asked the doctor.

"Don't know," said Kowalski. "I was called at home and hurried over here to check him out. Do you think someone tried to poison him?"

"What makes you think poison?" asked the ER doctor.

"Well, I'm not sure why, but there's more to the story that I am not allowed to divulge. Do you think he was poisoned?" he asked again.

"No, I believe he's had a heart attack. But, with the labs we've drawn, we can tell if a poison has been introduced, and if it has been, we can tell what it is and treat it from there. He'll probably need to be transferred to Louisville to their big heart hospital there for further treatment. He may need some stints or even open-heart surgery. Either way, no one is going to talk to him for a while. If he ever wakes up."

Kowalski turned and looked at Jake.

"What say we try to find Luke?"

The two walked out of the ER and stood by Kowalski's borrowed car.

"Imagine that, a heart attack. With the others being killed, maybe the stress was too much for Lawrence? What do you think?"

Jake shrugged his shoulders.

"Not my position to think. But, I know epinephrine can cause a heart attack. Potassium can stop a heart, as well as several other drugs that can also mimic a heart attack. Some of those drugs won't show in a tox screen either."

The doctor came out the sliding ER door and walked over to where Kowalski and Jake stood.

"I'm going to transfer him to Jewish Hospital. He needs more than we can give him. I'm still waiting for the lab results, but we can send those after we transfer the patient. Can you think of any reason he would have suffered a heart attack?"

Kowalski shook his head.

"No idea. He ate really poorly at the diner, like all of his friends, but I didn't know if he had any pre-existing conditions related to his heart."

"No, he was fit and healthy," said the ER doctor. "He had a physical three months ago, including a stress test, and the report shows no heart problems at all."

Kowalski and Jake looked at the doctor.

"So, how do you go from a good heart to a heart attack in three months?" asked Kowalski.

"You don't. Either misdiagnosed or he had an introduction of a foreign substance that makes a heart go bad. Some people have a heart attack from pure fear. I've seen people take drugs thought to be safe and die from a heart-related problem after their first pill. I've seen women have a change in their heart during pregnancy or after giving birth that kills them. I'm ruling out the last two, so I'm wondering, could something have scared him so much, he had a heart attack?"

Without waiting for an answer, the doctor turned, punched in a code at the ER doors, and walked back inside.

Jake and Kowalski turned and looked at each other.

The man with the green sedan finished his movie. He stood up off the bed, reached for his keys and his wallet, and made another phone call.

Jake and Kowalski walked back to the borrowed car. Kowalski shook his head as he sat down in the driver's seat.

"I have to phone in the other two. Wait while I go back inside and give the addresses."

Kowalski walked back into the ER and within five minutes was back.

"State police is gonna send a forensics team to both houses," said Kowalski. "They'll notify the coroner so he can pick up the bodies and confirm what we already know. That Luke Dinkins was somehow involved in their murders."

Kowalski got back into the car and started it. Jake got in on the passenger side and buckled his seatbelt. Kowalski put the car in gear and pulled out onto the main drag and headed towards Louisville. Something nagged at the back of Jake's brain, but he couldn't put a finger on it.

The man in the green sedan drove towards Louisville. He stopped for gas at the station across from the diner in Shelbyville. He filled his tank, got a soft drink, then asked to use the phone behind the counter. He finished and got back in his car and headed west again.

Kowalski nosed the car into a slot for police only at the Jewish Hospital. He turned off the ignition and sat for a long minute.

"Lawrence isn't going to be here yet, I don't think. Why not drive around and grab a bite to eat while we wait?"

Jake nodded his approval, and Kowalski pulled the car back out on to the street, turned on his right blinker, and pulled on to 4th street.

The city of Louisville was like every other big city Jake had ever been in, with one exception. There was a river that marked both the city's boundary as well as the state's boundary. The Ohio River flowed past on the north side of Louisville, bound and determined to wind its way past Paducah to the west and into the Mississippi River.

Kowalski and Jake stopped at an 'all you could eat' diner in downtown Louisville. They ordered burgers, fries, and coffee. As they ate, Kowalski pondered why Luke Dinkins would do something like this to his best friends.

"I don't know, Kowalski. Some people you can never figure out. Money, maybe? Drugs? Someone blackmailing Luke? Maybe he hated these guys all these years and finally snapped?"

Kowalski took a big drink of his coffee. He looked over his cup at Jake.

"Let me ask you something. You're going in to kill someone, some really bad dude. You plan and plan, then you implement your plan. You take out the bad guy, then you leave. Am I right?"

Jake nodded his head in agreement.

"Why didn't Luke leave?"

Jake didn't answer.

"I mean, why did he come back to his house after taking out his three friends?"

Jake remained quiet.

"Look, if it were me, I'd have packed a bag, then popped in to each of the homes and killed my friends and their family dog, then headed out of town, to New York or Vegas, or God knows where, so I could make good my escape. Wouldn't you?"

Jake said, "No, I would have planned it differently. All three would have met the same fate, car wreck, burned in a house fire, robbed and murdered after exiting a movie. But they would have all been together. One kill event, no questions. Too many chances of things going wrong when you have to conduct more than one killing. Who's watching out the windows? Did you make the kill, or in Lawrence's case, did you accidently, or on purpose, leave them alive? What if you had a wreck on the way to number two or number three's house? What if number three was headed to number one's home and saw you leaving and then found number one dead? All these things an assassin has to think of before beginning an operation."

Kowalski thought deeply for a long minute.

"So, is that what you did in the jail? Kill those four, break their arms and legs, disembowel them, and then act like you've done nothing wrong?"

"Let's get something straight. I had no access to any of those guys, and the way I kill, you'd never know it was an assassination. Again, I would make it look like an accident. Not like someone getting revenge on someone else." Jake sat back and looked out the passenger window.

"Sorry, it's just my nature to try and pick a story apart. I couldn't think how you got out of your cell unless you had help on the inside. No way can the inmates open those doors from the inside."

"Or in my case, a guest cannot open the doors from the inside. Remember, I was never charged. By the way, thanks again for getting me out. But if I had stayed, I'd be half way to California by now, what with the 72 hours being up and all," said Jake. "I'd like you to think about this from my point of view. Why would I kill four guys who were already in the tank? These guys weren't going anywhere for a while. I could just sit and wait for them to be released, right? Then I could make it look like a car wreck, or a robbery where they all died. So, no, I had nothing to do with their deaths. Someone was leaving their mark; someone had some real hatred for these four. Who were they—terrorists? Some left or right-wing hate group? Bosnians in a Serbian kind of world? I have no clue, but what are the odds that I got arrested for a shooting that was supposed to be a murder, but the shooter shot too high; then put in with these four supposedly bad guys, kill them without being seen, and then have you help me make my escape? One billion to one, one trillion to one, one googol to one?"

"Yeah, maybe you're right. But, since I've met you, things have been blowing up all around me, and more people have died than in a Cecil B. DeMille movie."

Kowalski paid for their food in cash and they headed out to the sedan. It was getting near midnight and they wanted to see if Lawrence had been transferred to Jewish Hospital yet.

They drove in silence. It took about 10 minutes to arrive at the hospital. Kowalski pulled up into the police only parking area, shut off the engine, and opened his door. The first thing he heard was, "Hey… Ski!" Then a big state trooper walked over and pumped Kowalski's arm in a handshake till it hurt.

"Heard you were out of town, gone fishing up north or some such thing," said the trooper. "Someone said you were giving up after 28 years. Am I hearing this right?"

"Hi, Officer Wise," said Kowalski. "Yep, I was gonna go fishin', but things here took a turn. Wild things are happening, so I'm looking in on them and seeing what floats to the surface. You know how it is, right?"

"Hey, who's the big guy in the car with you… Ski?"

"He's a military guy, helping me figure out what I'm going to do with my life after I leave here," said Kowalski. "He's kinda in retirement planning, if you know what I mean. Hey, Wise, nice to see you and all, but I gotta get upstairs and see about a patient that was brought in from Shelbyville."

Wise nodded to Kowalski, shook his hand, patted him on the back, and said, "We're really gonna miss you… Ski." He walked away towards a state trooper car, got in and left.

"Geez Louise," said Kowalski. "I was afraid he was going to nab us for the breakout. Maybe it hasn't hit the wire yet."

"Don't count on it," said Jake. "I think he's out, rounding up troops, and he's gonna return here shortly and we're both going back in the pokey."

"Well, best we play this out in front of us instead of letting it sneak up on us from behind. Let's head up and see if Lawrence is awake yet. Then, I'll head off the Calvary before they can arrest us. That is, arrest me, and arrest you again."

The two headed inside the ER, found what room Lawrence was in, and then took the elevator to that floor. As they rode up, Kowalski looked at Jake.

"So, if, and I say if, we get out of here without being arrested, where are you headed?"

"Out west," said Jake. "My whole intention was to be in California in three days. To see my brother and spend some quality time with him. He's in some kind of management there in central California. His company provides stuff to movie sets, actors and producers. Not costumes, but essential things they need. Everyday stuff. If a director decides to go to the desert, his company provides two or three motor homes with drivers and EMS crews to accompany them. If an actor needs to work on losing or gaining weight for a role, his company arranges for a trainer. If a producer needs to find the best site for a shoot, his company provides a helicopter to take the producer around to show them where they can shoot. They also help with licensing fees, parking, police—all the things necessary to make a movie go without a hitch."

They walked off the elevator onto a coronary floor where Lawrence had been moved. They headed in the direction of his room when a nurse intercepted them.

"Can I help you?" she asked.

"Looking for a guy named Lawrence Douglas. Brought in by ambulance from Shelbyville." He held up his badge. "My partner and I need to ask him some questions with regard to a criminal case in which he might be involved."

The nurse said, "He's not responding right now, but you can go in and see if you can rouse him. We need him to sign some documents before we can perform surgery tomorrow."

She opened the door to the room 615 where Lawrence had been brought. Sitting inside, holding Lawrence's hand and rubbing his arm, was Luke Dinkins.

The man in the green sedan pulled into a parking space outside of Jewish Hospital. He turned off the ignition, got out, and walked to the main entrance. As he was about to enter, a security guard called to him.

"Hey, there. You can't park your car in this space. This is meant for ambulances and other emergency vehicles. Move it, pal."

The man turned and walked back to his car. He looked at the security guard and opened the driver's door.

"Where do I need to park?" he asked.

The security guard came close.

"There's parking over there, go to that garage. Up to the fifth floor. Plenty of parking…"

The man in the green sedan had suddenly turned and grabbed the security guard by the throat. The guard gurgled, his eyes bulged, and he struggled to get away, but the hand around his neck was like a vise. The more the guard struggled, the tighter the hand got. The guard struggled until he passed out and his heart stopped beating. The big man held his hand around the guard's neck for another two minutes, then picked up the guard, pushed him into the back of the sedan, got back in the car and drove up to the garage.

Kowalski and Jake stopped short and looked at Luke Dinkins.

"What are you doing here, Luke?" asked Kowalski.

"My best friend had a heart attack. I came here to be with him," replied Luke.

"What about your other two friends, Bill and Woody?" asked Jake.

"I've tried giving them a call, but there's no answer." He held up his phone. "I've tried each three or four times, but they don't pick up." There were tears in Luke's eyes.

"I told you they were both dead, them and their wives. Don't you remember?" asked Kowalski.

"I thought you were using that good cop, bad cop stuff on me, Bill. What the hell happened?"

Kowalski sat down and told Luke the story. When he finished, he looked at Jake.

"He's helping me find out what happened to your friends, as well as what happened in the diner. Would you care to tell me the truth about that night now?"

Luke looked at Kowalski and then at Jake.

"We were really scared when Larson got shot. Lawrence, Bill, Woody and me had all just been playing some kind of poker on line. We'd all won big, something like a million, and we kept playing. Then, things went bad, and we lost all that and more. So much that Bill and Woody were going to have to sell their homes to pay. So, we stopped playing, hoping it all went away. Then, this guy comes in and tells us there's gonna be trouble if we don't pay up. Big guy, like your friend here, but kinda with an accent. He gave us until today to pay up. No way Bill and Woody could sell their houses that fast. We begged for more time, but this guy told us there are deadlines.

"When we went to the diner, we saw this big guy and thought he might have been in on the gambling thing, and when we saw a chance, we got him locked up so he couldn't hurt us. I guess we were wrong." He looked at Jake. "Sorry, mister. I never done nothing wrong before, this just got out of hand." Tears began coming down his cheeks. "Now, Bill and Woody are dead, and my best friend, Lawrence, who's been through so much, is hanging on by a thread." He retook Lawrence's hand.

Kowalski asked Luke, "What did this guy look like, Luke?"

"Big as a house, he was. Dark complexion, probably as tall as your friend here, but heavier. Maybe 275-300 pounds. Looked like a fire-plug. And when he talked, you listened. We know we screwed up, but we never figured it would come to this."

"That's okay," said Jake. "I had an issue I had to deal with in the Frankfort jail. I was able to take care of that little problem without having to go on a regular visit."

Kowalski turned and looked at Jake.

"I knew it! I knew, deep in my heart, you killed those four guys from back east. What, did they owe you? Money? Did they give you problems?"

"No," said Jake. "I never had a problem with those four. I told you I never touched them. There's a guy in the jail who wronged my father a few years back. I tracked him down to the Frankfort jail, and I was going to stop by and see him, but I was sure he wouldn't meet with me. We got everything worked out. But those four? Nope, not me. Never would I kill someone like that."

He turned and looked at Luke. "How did you know Lawrence was coming here?"

"I'm listed as his contact, his next of kin. They called me and told me he was being transferred here. I was at my daughter's house. It was close for me to come over, so I did."

Kowalski said, "This guy's still out there, then. And you two are still alive. I need to get someone to come here and stand watch, so I don't have more dead bodies."

He turned to Jake. "Would you be able to stay here with these two? I need to get something set straight, and it would be better for both of us if you weren't involved. You're still a jail escapee and I'm apparently the device you used to get away. I think I can make this work if you aren't with me."

Jake agreed, and Kowalski left.

Jake sat down beside Lawrence's bed. He was tired as well, so he decided to put his feet up and rest for five minutes. He closed his eyes and drifted off to sleep.

Two minutes later, all hell broke loose.

Kowalski walked down to the elevator and hit the down button. As he waited, he looked at the coronary care unit. There were two nurses' stations, with four wings off each one. The unit could hold up to 78 coronary care and step-down patients. Kowalski thought about how many people per day needed to be seen by a cardiologist or a cardiac surgeon. Maybe, he thought, he should modify his diet a little. He was about 50 pounds overweight, but he carried it well.

The elevator door opened and Kowalski waited for a few late visitors to come off the car before boarding. As the doors started to close, the other elevator door opened, and he saw, just before his doors shut completely, a State Police SWAT team enter the hallway.

Jake was somewhere between la-la land and a deep sleep when a noise awakened him. The noise was something moving towards the room in which he, Luke, and Lawrence were. He heard it from down the hall, and whatever it was, it was big. It sounded like a really big man, moving slowly. The sound stopped right outside Lawrence's room.

Kowalski started hitting buttons on the elevator, trying to get it to stop. Each time he hit a floor, the elevator had already passed. He finally hit the STOP button, and the elevator, with alarms screaming, stopped on the 2nd floor. He stepped off.

The big man was standing outside Lawrence's room. Jake could see him because of a convex mirror in the hall. He got a sense of just how big he was. Jake stood up. He was big, but this guy was huge. He was fully 300 pounds if he were an ounce. He looked like a big version of Oddjob, the villain with a killer hat in an old James Bond movie. Only this guy was not Japanese, he looked eastern European.

The man stood in the doorway, not seeing Jake. He could only see Lawrence and Luke, the two dupes who got caught up in the Russian scam for money. It was time to take retribution, and then he could be on his way back to St. Petersburg.

A commotion made him turn his head slightly. Seven men in riot gear were headed towards the room where he stood. They were still at the first nurse's station, making sure they were headed in the right direction. The big guy turned away from the room and walked back towards the stairwell. Jake saw the men in riot gear as well.

Kowalski tried hitting the up button on the outside wall, but nothing happened. The door to the elevator he rode down was still open, the alarm was still screaming, and the SWAT team above must have shut out the other elevator. He turned and ran to the stairs.

Jake knew he was in an untenable situation. The SWAT team was coming for him thinking he was the cause of the death of Captain Fry from the Frankfort jail. He had seconds to find a way out, or he would be going back to jail, this time in Louisville, and there would be no one in the state who could get him out.

Kowalski hit the door to the stairs and started up. He made it to the 3rd floor when a large, eastern European-looking man came down the steps. They bumped into each other, more or less because Kowalski was looking down at the stairs, and the big man was looking behind him. The man ran into Kowalski so hard it knocked him off his feet. Kowalski ended up in a ball in the corner of the stairwell.

"Sorry," said the big guy, in a European accent.

Kowalski knew in an instant this was the big guy who he thought had killed both Bill Evans and Woody Sumner.

"Police! Stop where you are!" called Kowalski. The big man continued down the steps to the 2nd level. The sergeant was torn between following him and heading up the steps to help Jake.

Jake raised a finger to his lips as he looked at Luke. He leaned over Lawrence's bed and picked up a chart. He grabbed a stethoscope from the counter and a thermometer from a bottle by the sink. Luke was wearing a whitish coat/jacket and Jake motioned for him to throw him the jacket. Luke took off the jacket and pitched it to Jake. He pulled the jacket on and he quickly put the stethoscope around his neck as well. It looked like Jake was wearing a kid's coat, but illusions were 99% of the story. He backed out of the room and told Lawrence he'd send a nurse to bring a bedpan. Luke still stared at Jake, but Jake shook his head and turned. He walked away from where the seven-member SWAT team was headed. They were still about 100 feet away, and they were checking each room. Good tactics if you are in hostile country, but this was an exercise in futility.

Jake laid the chart, the thermometer, the jacket and the stethoscope on the far nurse's station, then walked to the stairwell. He opened the door and ran head on into Kowalski. The sergeant grabbed him and pulled him into the stairwell.

"I just passed that big guy, the one we think might have killed Bill and Woody," said Kowalski.

"I know, he was standing outside Lawrence's room when he heard the SWAT team. I think we need to run."

"You run, I'll head them off." With that, he pushed Jake down the steps and opened the door to the stairs.

The big man reached the bottom floor. He opened the stairway door and walked into the lobby of the hospital. Even at this late hour, there was still a lot of activity in the hospital. Ambulances were bringing in and taking out patients, families of loved ones were bringing clothes and things to make them feel like they were at home. Nurses, doctors, techs, chaplains, all moved about the lobby in a choreographed pattern designed to bring the best results to the greatest number of patients.

The big man turned and walked out through the main doors. He wasn't sure where the high rise-parking garage was from this exit, so he would have to walk around the hospital to find it. Military training taught him the first move was to always go right, so he moved to his right, to see if he could locate the garage.

Kowalski stood just inside the hallway of the coronary unit. He could see the SWAT team as they cleared each hospital room, headed down towards where Lawrence and Luke were staying.

"Hey, guys. It's Kowalski. What gives?"

"The SWAT team leader turned and said something to his men, then moved forward till he was about 25 feet from Kowalski. He raised his Heckler & Koch MP-5A2 semi-automatic rifle and aimed it center mass at Kowalski.

"On the ground, on the ground!" shouted the SWAT leader. "Spread your arms out and lie face down, NOW!"

Kowalski looked at the team leader. "Hey, John, is that you? What gives? This is Bill Kowalski. Sergeant Bill Kowalski. From the Frankfort Post. Why are you guys running in here like this?"

The SWAT team leader hesitated for a moment. He was torn between Kowalski's tenure with the State Police and the fact that he was wanted in a criminal investigation. He started to move forward, checking to his left and his right as he moved.

Kowalski stretched his arms out and opened his hands to show he was not armed. The SWAT leader moved closer to Kowalski. He lowered his MP-5, making sure the safety was still on, and let it hang by the strap around his neck.

"...Ski, I gotta take you in for questioning. Fry was killed at your house and you helped a prisoner escape from the Frankfort jail. Are you gonna come quietly?"

Kowalski nodded his head. He made a slow 360-degree turn to show the SWAT team leader he was not armed, then walked towards him.

"Hold on a minute, John. I need to give these keys back to Luke. One of the guys we've been checking on since Larson was shot at the diner. He slowly pulled the sedan's key from his pocket and walked over to the door where Lawrence and Luke were.

"Luke, here's the key to your car. I need to give it back to you because I'm going with these guys to look for the big fella, OK?" He dropped the key on the floor by the entrance to Lawrence's room. He turned and walked towards the SWAT team leader. The rest of the SWAT team had converged with their leader, but there was confusion in the group. Everyone knew Kowalski, as he had trained them in weapons, explosives, and making entry into confined spaces.

"Listen, we don't have much time. There's a big guy running around here who I think killed two people in Shelbyville. He's eastern European, stands a full head taller than me, and he might be armed. He's wearing a long, dark coat and has black hair and dark eyes. He's about 300 pounds. We have to find him. He went down the stairway. I saw him between the 2nd and 3rd floors. He was headed down to the lobby. Can you send your team down and see if you can catch him?"

The SWAT team leader turned and ordered four of his men to hit the stairs and head down to the lobby. The other two stayed with him.

"So, what gives?" asked the SWAT leader.

"Okay, here's the story. I helped a guy who is not involved in any of this leave the jail yesterday. I coldcocked Donald from the jail, so I could get this guy out of there. He was never charged with anything, but I know he has some information we need. Most importantly, I need one of your guys to stay here and guard the two in this room. One's had a heart attack, the other guy just missed getting himself killed by the big fella I described to you." Kowalski filled the SWAT leader in on what had happened the past two days. "I'll plead my case with Captain Tanner. He knows what's going on and he'll clear me. Captain Fry from the jail was hanging det cord around my backdoor when I came upon him. I called to him and he jumped, and the cord went off. The concussion killed him. Tanner should've been able to work this out," said Kowalski.

"Tanner's the one who activated us to bring you in," said the SWAT leader.

Jake stepped outside the hospital. He had no way to travel anywhere. He had no car, no phone, no wallet, therefore no money, and no access to his bank account. He was on the run from the police in Frankfort and was probably being sought by the Louisville police as well.

He turned and tried to blend in with the people moving back and forth from the parking garage to the hospital. As he walked to the garage, he saw a green sedan pull out and turn away from him. He thought he recognized the driver for a split second, but he couldn't be sure. Security drove around in the garage in their little golf carts, so if he was seen by one of the guards two or more times, he would raise suspicion. Jake turned and walked back towards the hospital.

Kowalski borrowed the SWAT team leader's phone and called Captain Tanner. He waited while the phone buzzed three or four times. He heard a click on the other end.

"John, did you nail him? I need you back here ASAP with my sergeant so I can put my boot where the sun don't shine."

Kowalski hung up the phone. He looked at John and shrugged.

"No answer," he said. He handed the phone back to the SWAT team leader.

"We need to find this guy whose goal is to kill the remaining two here on the sixth floor. I need you to call in a favor for me. Get some Louisville police on the way over here and babysit these two. They are in it deep, but they're gonna end up dead if we don't act." He turned to walk towards Lawrence's room.

"Wait a minute… Ski," said the SWAT team leader. "I can't let you go and do your own thing. I have to take you back to Frankfort to meet with Tanner."

"Yep, just let me say bye to these two." He stuck his head in the door. In a low tone, he said to Luke, "You make sure Jake gets these keys, he knows where the car is located. Give them to him and tell him to stay the hell away from Frankfort!"

Jake walked around the hospital. He went from the 2nd floor to the 3rd floor, as if looking for a patient. The night staff paid no attention because Jake didn't look them in the eye. He seemed to know where he was going, thereby not raising any suspicion from the night nurses.

He went to the stairwell and walked back up to the sixth floor. He cracked the door open an inch and peered out into the hallway. The SWAT team and Kowalski were headed back towards the elevator. He only counted three SWAT members, so the fourth, fifth, sixth, and seventh men had to be either in Lawrence's room or outside, looking for him. Either way, he was not going to give them a chance to arrest him.

Jake opened the door and walked to the nurse's station nearest Lawrence's bed. He picked up the stethoscope, thermometer, and coat he had dropped earlier. He also grabbed the chart and turned and walked back to Lawrence's room.

A SWAT team member was sitting on a chair outside the room. Jake nodded at him as he walked into the CCU room as if he were a doctor. He figured bravado and a little magic were all that he needed to get in to see Lawrence.

Luke was still sitting at Lawrence's bedside. He looked sleepy. Lawrence was still out. Jake winked at Luke, checked the monitor, and asked Luke if he had any questions. Luke asked Jake if his friend had made it out of the hospital. Jake said yes, he had made it, but he was being escorted back to Frankfort. Luke pushed the key towards Jake.

"My friend asked me to give you this," he said. "It's a good luck charm." He said that last part a little louder so the guard could hear it. "He wanted you to have it so it could keep you safe for the upcoming operation."

Jake took the key, mouthed thank you, and put down the chart. He walked past the guard, headed to the nurse's station, and dropped off his other tools. He decided to keep the coat because it gave an aura of authenticity to moving around the hospital, even though it was two sizes too small. He headed for the stairs, but looked back before the door closed. The guard was still seated, waiting presumably for relief or to be told to pack it in by his team leader.

Kowalski and the three SWAT members headed to the vehicles used by the SWAT members to get to the hospital. They reached the SUVs and they took off their gear, put their weapons back into the cases after clearing them, and radioed for the other three to head back to the meeting place. The team leader told one member to stay at the room to protect the two men inside. Kowalski climbed into the back seat of the first SUV with a SWAT member seated on each side. The team leader sat down in the passenger seat. They waited for the driver, who had been out on foot patrol around the outside of the hospital to return.

"What were you thinking when you sprung that guy from the jail?" asked the SWAT team leader.

"John, I've been doing this job for 28 years, and something just didn't add up. I went with my gut because I thought this guy was innocent. He didn't belong in there, as much as you or I don't belong in there. Plus, I could keep my eye on him. He's a lifer from the military. Did 20.

He just got out. He was some kind of an assassin. But what he told me made total sense. He couldn't have shot Larson because he was inside the diner when the shooting started. Luke Dinkins made up the story about him pulling a rifle out of his car because he and his friends were in trouble with the Russian Mob. They thought this guy might have been involved with the Russians as well, and if he went to jail, it kept them out of hot water.

"Two of them are dead, and I don't know if the third will survive. Heart attack. I guess from the stress over the Russians. Anyway, Jake helped me to find out where they lived, and we went to their houses to see if they were okay. Obviously, two of them were not. The Russians killed Bill Evan's wife as well as Woody's.

"There's a big guy who's involved in what's happening here. Huge guy. I passed him in the stairwell. 300 pounds, maybe more. Looks like a Russian lumberjack. I think he's doing the killings."

He went on to describe to the team leader what had transpired since he got Jake out of jail. How they had headed east, meaning to go to New York, then decided to return. He didn't tell what car Jake was driving, or where he had gotten the car from; he figured that information might lead to Jake's capture. And that was not what was needed right now. Jake needed to take care of Lawrence and Luke, to make sure the Russians or whoever this guy represented didn't kill them.

Jake went back downstairs and stood on the grounds of the hospital. He waited for a few seconds, then decided he needed, no matter what, to go back to Shelbyville. The end lay there. He could figure out what was going on, get his car, and head to California. His brother was waiting out there for him, but Jake was not due there for another three days.

What Jake needed right now was some money. He now had a car but still didn't have his wallet. It was back at the jail in Frankfort. He was certainly not going back there to try and get it right now. He had to find another way to get some cash for gas, food and clothing.

Luke sat beside Lawrence's bed, still holding his hand, talking to him as if he could hear. Luke told him about the guy with Kowalski, how they'd done him wrong, and how they needed to make it right for the fella. Tears rolled down Luke's cheeks as he begged Lawrence to get better.

Just then, Jake walked back into the hospital room. He was still wearing the coat Luke had passed him. Luke looked up at Jake, wondering what he needed. Jake again put a finger to his lips, nodding his head out the door to the SWAT team member still seated outside.

"I need your wallet. I need all the cash you have, and I need your ATM PIN number, so I can get more cash if I need it. I wouldn't be in this predicament if you hadn't identified me as the shooter. You and your trusty little band of gamblers have gotten a lot of people killed. Hand it over, Luke."

Luke reached into his back pocket and handed Jake his wallet. He shrunk away from Jake as the big man's hand took the wallet.

"My PIN number is 4789. Take what you can get. There's a couple hundred in my wallet. I'm really sorry for getting you involved."

Jake smiled. He kept his voice low.

"I got myself involved, just by being at the diner when the shooting started. Glad no one else got hit. And from what Kowalski tells me, Larson's gonna make it, but he's gonna need a new haircut. Now, I need to get out of here and head back to Shelbyville. Give me the key to your house. I'm staying there tonight. Your wife is here in Louisville, right? With your daughter? You call and tell her to stay there. Not to come to your house. I'll kill whoever walks through the door before morning. Male or female, makes no difference to me."

With that, Jake turned and walked out to the guard seated by Lawrence's door.

"Don't let anyone in. Especially a big, European-looking guy. Big like me, but heavier. And you may have to shoot him to stop him. Do you understand?"

The guard looked at Jake. "I take my orders from my SWAT team leader, not from some doctor that don't know crackers from tea." He sat up straighter so as to make himself more imposing.

Jake smiled. He turned to walk past the guard, then in an instant, grabbed the guard by the neck and pushed him into Lawrence's room. He lifted the guard off the floor and held him in the air as the guard flailed helplessly. Jake applied some tension to the two carotid arteries on either side of the guard's neck, and after a few seconds, he went limp.

Jake took the guard's handcuffs, put one cuff around the guard's right wrist, then took the other cuff and hooked that to the railing of Lawrence's bed. He reached into the pocket of the guard and produced a handcuff key, which he gave to Luke.

"When he wakes up, let him kick and buck a little. Then give him this key. Tell him he's not a very good guard to let someone like me take him down so easily. He won't do anything to you because he'll be really embarrassed and annoyed I got the better of him. Some other guards from Louisville will be here shortly. If they get here before he wakes up, tell them it was the European guy that did this. Got it?"

Luke nodded, gulped, and looked down at the guard.

"He's gonna be pissed," said Luke.

"Yeah, well, better he's pissed when he wakes up than dead."

Jake took off the coat, threw it back to Luke, and walked out of the room.

The man in the green sedan pulled off the interstate and onto Highway 33. He wound his way through town, stopping at a gas station that had no lights on. He pulled up a map application on his phone and checked off two addresses, deleting them from his list. He then studied the other two addresses, found one to be closer than the other, set that address in his phone, and started driving.

Kowalski sat between the two men, as they passed the diner just off the interstate. Kowalski turned and looked at the restaurant, and for a split second, he could see Annie, the cook, and the manager, taking care of the late-night guests. He turned back and faced forward. No further words were spoken on route to the State Police Post in Frankfort.

Jake got to the car Kowalski had borrowed, noticing it had not been touched while in the police lot. He figured security knew better than to mess with the police or their vehicles. Just as he opened the driver's door, another car pulled up. A tallish officer from Louisville stepped out of his car, an unmarked Louisville Metro unit. He looked at Jake for a short moment.

"Do I know you?" he asked.

"No, don't believe you do. I'm doing government work for the military. Investigating a criminal matter. From here to Moscow kind of stuff, if you know what I mean."

The Louisville officer nodded his head as if he understood. He closed and locked his door.

"Have a nice evening, ah, what's your name?"

"Jake. Jake Thompson. Working from Washington, D.C. What with budget cuts, they don't even give out a military car anymore. They flew me in and told me to rent a cheapo, so this is what I get. See you later."

The Louisville officer waved his hand as he disappeared inside the hospital.

Jake climbed into the borrowed car and started the engine. The fuel gauge showed a half tank of gas, so Jake figured it would take him back to Shelbyville. He turned on his right blinker, just as Kowalski had done earlier in the evening, and headed to the on-ramp of I-64 East.

The big man in the sedan pulled up to one of the houses. He pulled in behind so no one would see his vehicle. He turned off the lights, opened the driver's door, and stepped out. The stars were shining brightly as he turned towards the backdoor.

The caravan of cars, minus the one team member left at the hospital, turned off the interstate and onto Highway 127. They drove the three miles to Post 12 and pulled into the parking lot. Team members got out and began carrying weapons and gear inside. The SWAT team leader beckoned for Kowalski to step out. They walked to the Police Only entrance, which led directly to Captain Tanner's office. Tanner was inside, on the phone. When he saw Kowalski and the SWAT team, he begged off the line and swiveled in his chair.

"What the hell kind of police officer and police work are you trying to pull here... Ski? Have you gone completely mad?" He stood from his chair. "Bring him over this way," he told the SWAT team. "I'm gonna plant my..."

"I know, I heard you on the phone," said Kowalski. "But before you kick my butt, you need to hear what I have to say."

"Say it and head to jail, for all I care. You killed a guard, for Pete's sake. A guard? How mad do you have to be to kill a guard... Ski?"

Kowalski looked at his captain.

"Listen, firstly, this guy Jake is not guilty of shooting Larson. Secondly, two of the boys from over at the Shelbyville diner are dead, the third fellow is in the hospital. I left a SWAT team member to look after him and the fourth guy. They are safe, for now. But we are going to have to find the guy who killed the first two, and that'll lead us to whatever else is going on."

"How did Captain Fry end up dead at your house... Ski? There's no way I can cover you for this." He turned to the SWAT team. "You guys go ahead and write up your report. I'll read it tomorrow. Then head home and get some rest."

The team headed out of Captain Tanner's office. The captain turned back to Kowalski.

"You know, this is going to go really hard on you... Ski. Never, in all my 35 years with the Kentucky State Police have I ever heard of something this strange.

"We're going to drive over to the jail, where I'm personally going to drop you off so the guards there can deal with you, if you don't start talking some big words to me, right now!" He slammed his fist down on the desk for emphasis.

Kowalski looked at Tanner.

"Captain, I think, somehow, not sure, but I think Fry was in on this thing with the Russians. There's some big gambling con going on, which the four from Shelbyville somehow got involved in, and now two of them and their wives are dead. Fry was stringing up some det cord around my backdoor when I went home to get some clothes after springing Jake. I really don't think Jake's involved. I think, again, just supposition, that Fry and maybe some others are involved in the deaths of those four inmates. Can't prove it yet, and I may never be able to prove it, but if you send me over there, with what I know, I'll be dead inside of 24 hours. Believe me, Cap, I never would have done this unless I thought, beyond a shadow of a doubt, that this guy Jake was not guilty."

Tanner shook his head in disbelief. He turned and sat down in his chair.

"Take a seat… Ski." Kowalski did as he was asked. "You know why I want to kick your butt from here to the jail and back again? Because Fry was a friend of mine. I can't believe he would be involved in something like this."

"You know my motto, Cap," said Kowalski. "I tend to believe the ones who are not believable, and I tend to doubt those who I think I can trust. Maybe you should do the same."

Tanner got up and poured himself some coffee.

"Want some… Ski? No? Okay, here's how it's going to play out. You and I are going over to the jail. We're gonna sit down and have a face-to-face with Donald, the guy at the jail you conked over the head. We're gonna see where this leads, and if it leads to you going to jail, then so be it. Any questions?" The last comment was not made for Kowalski to answer. It was notice that this conversation was now officially over.

The big man in the sedan pushed open the backdoor. He walked inside, through the kitchen and into the living room. He pilfered through the mail on the table, looked at some pictures that were on a secretary desk, then sat on the sofa and turned off the light. He was asleep within five minutes.

Jake turned off at the first Shelbyville exit. He drove slowly, as it was dark, and he had trouble remembering where to turn. He finally found the house he was looking for. It was pitch-black from the front. He parked two houses down and across the street. Kowalski's vehicle would not seem odd to early risers parked here.

He stepped out of the vehicle and walked towards the driveway. The stars were still twinkling as sunlight had not started to filter the sky. He walked up the driveway towards the back part of the house. He stepped past a parked car and walked up to the backdoor.

Tanner and Kowalski drove silently to the jail. It was nearing 4 AM. The night watch would still be on duty. That meant Donald would still be working.

Tanner pulled his service vehicle up to the sally port. Both men exited the State Police vehicle. Tanner buzzed the button beside the sally port door. In answer, the big door began rising on its rollers.

Tanner and Kowalski walked through the large door and waited for it to close. The second, inner door buzzed, and Tanner pulled it open. Fry's right-hand man met them. He glared at Kowalski.

Jake silently opened the backdoor. It was dark inside the house. He listened for a long moment to see if anyone, the State Police, jail staff, a random homeless person looking for a place to sleep, was inside the house. He heard nothing.

Donald led Tanner and Kowalski to one of the interrogation rooms. He sat down behind a desk and motioned for Tanner to do the same. He neither looked at nor motioned to Kowalski.

"How's your head, Donald?" asked Kowalski.

He didn't answer.

Tanner said, "Donald's head is fine. You'd have to hit him a lot harder to make a dent in that crown."

Donald looked at Tanner.

"If it were my call, Kowalski'd be locked up under the jail right now. As it is, I want him brought up on assault and battery charges, on aiding and abetting an escapee, on fleeing with intent, and on being a real jerk, just on general principle."

"You'd have the County Sheriff here right now, if you were thinking of pressing charges," said Tanner. "As it is, be glad that big guy Jake didn't hit you. You'd be in a coma or worse if he'd been the one swinging at your head." He looked at Donald. "Kowalski's got some information I'd like you to hear before you think about charging my sergeant." He turned towards Kowalski. "How about it… Ski. What do you want to say to Donald?"

Jake didn't turn on a light in the room. He preferred it to stay dark and let the sunlight slowly work its way into the house. He found a recliner and racked it back to the sleeping position. He made sure no one could see him by looking in a window, but he could see if anyone tried to come in through the backdoor. He was asleep in just a few seconds.

Kowalski looked at Donald. The captain of the jail's right-hand man was seated behind a desk—Kowalski had sat in that same seat just a few days ago. He had known Donald for a long time. He never considered him in any manner other than as a professional, in the same genre as himself. 'To Serve and to Protect'. That was a great motto, thought Kowalski. He wondered if Donald ever thought about those words.

"Donald, I know something's going on in here. Captain Tanner and I need to get to the bottom of this. Those four men killed in the jail were from back east, right?"

Donald took a moment. "I think you're right. Seems I heard some talk about them being from New York, New Jersey, some place on the east coast."

Kowalski nodded his head. "And I think they were involved in some kind of gambling scam, am I right on that? Is that what they were in here for?"

Donald shrugged his shoulders. "Not sure. I'll have to look at their files."

"I would have thought you'd have looked at their files right after they were killed."

"But we're not the investigative party here. The county Sheriff's office is the lead in this, along with the State Police," he added.

"Curiosity didn't get the best of you?" asked Kowalski.

"No, it didn't," answered Donald. "Look, I'm not the guilty party here. I'm just a night guy, doing my job here at the Frankfort/Franklin County jail. I wasn't in on their murders. No way. You need to be looking at that big guy, that Jake fellow you took out of here. He's the one in my book."

"You say you weren't in on the murders. Did you know they were going to happen?"

Donald looked from Kowalski to Tanner. "Look, he's putting words in my mouth. I had nothing to do with that, I knew nothing about their murders. I don't have a clue as to who would've done this," He said, his voice raising as he spoke the last four words.

"I think you do," said Kowalski. "I think you've known about this for a long time. And I think you're in on the gambling scam as well."

"Are you gonna sit there and listen to him bad-mouth me?" asked Donald. "I won't stand for this, not at all!" He stood. "This little talk is over. I want to press charges against Kowalski, and I mean now!"

Tanner said, "You need to call the Franklin County Sheriff's office, if you want to prefer charges against my sergeant. They'll want you to write up a report. Did you file a report last night when he took the big guy out of here?"

"No, but I will."

"I wonder why you didn't file anything. And if you hadn't called me, I would never have known Kowalski had taken the prisoner out without due course. I wouldn't have sent the state SWAT team to Louisville to look for Kowalski and the other guy, either. I think you'd better rethink what you are planning on doing in this case."

Tanner continued. "We have a man who has not been charged with anything, held here in jail for almost 72 hours, amid some serious circumstances, in which I think your staff is far more complicit than this fellow, Jake. I think both you and the State Police put him in a very dangerous situation by placing him here without charges. I accept full responsibility for doing that. Will the jail accept responsibility as well?"

Donald sat up. "Not without talking to the county attorney, I won't. And neither will anyone else here. You two can get on out of here, and I don't care if you come back or not."

Donald stood up, scooted his chair back with his calf muscles, and walked out of the room.

Tanner looked at Kowalski. "I think that means we can leave."

Both men stood up and walked to the exit door to the sally port. Tanner turned and looked at the camera. The door buzzed, and they walked through. The sally port door was already opening, which was a complete violation of standing orders not to have both doors open at the same time, but Tanner figured Donald wanted them out and off the premises as quickly as possible.

Tanner sat down in the driver's seat of his car. Kowalski walked around to the passenger side and opened the door.

"That was the strangest conversation I think I've ever had. How about you... Ski?"

"There's something happening inside the jail, and I don't know what it is. I need to talk to the Sheriff in the morning."

"No, you're off duty till Monday, remember?"

"Yeah, about that, I'm not going fishing. Too much to do around here."

Tanner turned on the ignition and pulled the car out of the sally port. He looked in his rear-view mirror as the sally port door slowly closed behind him.

The sun had just started depositing its beams on the long night that had gone by. Jake awoke, sore, tired, and hungry from his makeshift bed. He wandered into Lawrence's kitchen to see if there was anything he could eat. The refrigerator was close to bare, but there were the ingredients for coffee and a real BUNN coffee maker on the counter. Jake filled the coffee urn with water and poured it into the top of the coffee maker.

He filled the basket with a coffee filter and extra grounds, as he liked his coffee strong. Luke's cell phone chirped in his pocket. He pulled it out and the descriptor on the front said, THE WIFE. Jake dropped the phone back in his pocket. He was sure Luke had talked to his family by this time, and he was in no mood to answer questions before his third cup.

The big guy from the sedan was also waking up. He stood in Luke's living room and looked at the surroundings. Luke and his family had not come home last night. Perhaps they had been warned. Nevertheless, the big guy needed to call Russia, and he couldn't use the house phone to make that connection. Too easy to trace back to Russia, and then compromise both his boss and him. He decided to wait for another 30 minutes to see if anyone would show up, then head out to find a phone.

Tanner pulled back in to the State Police Post #12 on Highway 60. He and Kowalski got out of his vehicle and walked inside. Tanner's desk was strewn with papers and files that needed to be put away. He pushed them aside and sat down at his desk.

"Where's this Jake guy right now?" he asked Kowalski.

"My guess is he's holed up somewhere, waiting for daylight. He may have found a place to sleep in Louisville, but my guess is, he headed back to Shelbyville or he might have gone to my house. And I don't have any way to contact him."

"Well, he can't go far, and your house is still being watched. The jail has his wallet and keys, so he can't leave and head to, where is it he's going? Somewhere out west? Colorado?"

"California. He's got a brother out there. He stopped to get a bite to eat in Shelbyville, and then he was heading on to Points West."

"Yeah, well, he sure stepped into a hornet's nest, didn't he?" Kowalski nodded.

Jake took a long draw on his cup. The coffee was a generic brand, but it was hot and good and what he needed to clear his mind. He studied the house a little more closely in the sunlight. Just to see if there was anything he could find that might indicate how and why and what and who was behind the gambling and subsequent killings.

He noticed some letters from a couple of collection agencies, but they did not indicate huge amounts of cash that could be tied to any gambling debts, whether legal or not. One was for a late car payment, the other from a medical practice, both numbered in the hundreds, not hundreds of thousands of dollars. Both bore the name Lawrence Douglas.

Jake pushed the papers aside and opened a few drawers, looking for something that would both clear him and incriminate the two remaining men from the restaurant. Jake did not want them to take a hard dive, but they were willing for him to take a fall, and he did spend three days in the slammer, so it made no difference to Jake if the men got clipped by collection agencies or not.

Post #12 on Highway 60 West was just beginning to come alive. Those going off duty were checking in before heading home, those coming in for first shift were arriving, giving their shoes one last shine before roll call. Kowalski had been asleep in Tanner's office for almost 2 hours. Tanner himself, still in street clothes, went to the bathroom to shave. He was dog-tired, but he kept spare uniforms on the back of his office door just in case this ever happened. And it happened often.

Tanner dragged a razor across the stubble of his beard and washed the shaving cream from his face with a small towel. He brushed his teeth and put on his uniform. On his worst day, Tanner looked ten times better than any recruit or first year officer. He looked in the mirror and made sure the gold on his collars were straight. His tie, a real one, not a clip-on, was square and perfect; the Full-Windsor made the uniform. He lifted the tie to make sure the gig line was straight, but he knew, by years of experience, it was perfect.

Tanner walked past Kowalski, still asleep on the couch, and made his way out to roll call.

The big man in the green sedan walked out of Luke's backdoor. The sun was coming up over the roofs of the houses adjacent to Luke's backyard. The man sidled out to the green sedan. He slid in behind the steering wheel and started the car. It caught after 3 cranks. He drove out of the subdivision and back on to Highway 60. He turned left and headed towards Louisville. The route took him through east Louisville, Jeffersontown, Middletown, and finally, downtown.

Louisville lies on the southern bank of the Ohio River. It's a great place to drop a body or a car or whatever someone with nefarious undertones needs to absolve themselves of in a trying time.

The man took Exit 3 on Interstate 64, the east and west interstate through Louisville, Lexington, as well as Ashland and Shelbyville. He parked in an open lot near an old paddle-wheeled steamboat. One can hide in plain sight anywhere along the road, except when that one is an oddity. Someone with a second head, four arms, or who weighs 300 or more pounds might not disappear as easily as most, but the man in the green sedan had not lived so long and done so much living by the odds.

Jake pulled out Luke's phone from his pocket. The power bar, the little indicator that showed how much juice was left, was almost gone. Jake looked around the kitchen for a plug, found one, but could not make it fit. He opened the phone, which was not password protected, and looked to see if Kowalski was a friend of Luke's. He thumbed back and forth through the phone list but did not see Kowalski's name. Jake was not sure how to look at past calls, but he was sure he could reach one person. THE WIFE.

He pushed the button that said, CALL BACK. He waited for a few seconds as the phone connected.

"Hello?"

"Is this Luke's wife?" asked Jake.

"Yes, who are you?"

"I'm the guy your husband tried to frame. I need some help, but I also want to make sure you do not come back to your house. Two of Luke's friends are dead and someone out there is trying to make sure Luke and Lawrence fall into that category as well.

"I need you to find a number for me. This phone is going to die soon, and the faster you can get that number, the better for both of us."

"I need to know who you are and why this is happening."

"I can tell you later, but this phone won't last. Look up State Police Post number twelve in Frankfort, Kentucky. The man's last name is Kowalski. Give him this number and have him call me."

"I need to know somethin—"

Jake hung the phone up while she was still talking. No use trying to explain over a near dead phone. That would help no one.

Jake needed to contact the Shelbyville Police Department and tell them about his suspicions. He picked up the house phone and dialed 911.

The big man with the green sedan finally found a phone booth, one of the very few still available, and called a number he had memorized years before. He didn't want to use his cell phone if at all possible. It rang three times and was picked up in Moscow. He talked for a few minutes and listened for a few minutes, then hung up. He turned and walked back to his car. He looked at the steamboat. It was named *The Belle of Louisville*. It had a large paddle wheel on the stern of the boat. The big man figured it was used for daily or nightly cruises up and down the river.

He sat in his car and turned on the ignition. The motor started up and he put the car in drive.

Jake waited for the phone to be answered and then directed to the Sheriff's office. He spoke with the desk sergeant at the Shelby County Police Department. The officer knew of the deaths of Woody, Bill, and their wives, that the state police and the coroner had removed the bodies, and that there was an investigation opened, but that was about it. Jake mentioned he had some inside information, but that he was not able to speak about it right at that moment. He needed to talk to a detective as soon as possible. The sergeant asked for his phone number. Jake knew the phone he dialed from appeared on the screen in front of the sergeant, and that he probably was having the call cross-referenced to Lawrence's address. Jake told the sergeant he would be in touch with a detective when he could find a secure place from which to talk.

He hung up the phone and headed out the backdoor. The car was still parked down the street, and Jake walked quickly towards Kowalski's vehicle.

He opened the door and sat down, crouching low with his eyes just above the steering wheel.

About one minute later, two Shelby County Sheriff Deputies pulled up in front of Lawrence's, pulled out their service weapons, and made entry into the house. About 10 minutes later, the local newspaper and TV trucks from Louisville rolled up to the scene.

Jake turned on the car and drove away slowly. Unlike Kowalski, stealth was the key to Jake's safety and freedom.

He pulled out onto I-64 and headed for Louisville. Everything seemed to point in this direction now. He had to finish up there, find this big guy he saw the night before, and head out to California to see his brother.

The big man in the green sedan drove past Jewish Hospital. He didn't need to go there now, with all the security probably inside. They would be looking for the dead guard now. He was still in the back of the big man's sedan. He hadn't started stinking yet, but it had been nice and cool all night. Today would be different. He would have to dump the body where no one would see, and where no one would think to look. He headed back to the paddle wheel boat. But first, he stopped at a sporting goods store and bought two anchors, a tarp, and some chain. He paid cash.

Jake drove into the city and found a place to park. He shut off Kowalski's car and dropped the keys into his pocket. He needed to eat and the diner where Kowalski and he had eaten the night before had had good coffee, so he decided breakfast there was probably a good choice as well.

He pushed himself out of the seat of the car and right into the faces of three young men. All three were armed with knives, and the business ends were pointed right at Jake.

"Big man, don't move, don't do nothin' stupid," said the one on the left. "I'll cut you and then take your money and your car."

He waved the knife close to Jake's face. The young man stood about five and half feet tall, and he was the tallest. The second and third young men stood about 5 feet three inches tall. And between the three of them, they weighed maybe 250 pounds. Jake was just behind at 230. But, they had six arms and three knives.

"Just reach slowly into that back pocket, mister, and we may let you—"

The young man suddenly was lifted off his feet by Jake's left arm and thrown over the car next to Jake's. He landed head first on the pavement. He didn't move. The other two young men were frozen for a few seconds, and then they turned to run.

Jake grabbed the closest one by the arm that was holding the knife, nearer the wrist than the elbow, and shook the young man's arm up and down, hard. The knife flew out of his hand and his collarbone snapped as the young man's shoulder separated. He let that young man's arm go, and he fell to the ground, screaming in pain. The third young man disappeared around the side of the restaurant.

Jake fished the keys out of his pocket, slammed the car door, started it and gave chase. The young man was just crossing the main street beside the diner when Jake cut him off. The young man slammed into the side of Jake's car.

Jake exited Kowalski's car and grabbed the young man before he could run again. He used an arm bar and dragged him around to the driver's side of the car and pushed him into the vehicle. The young man was sitting on the center console, and Jake had a death grip on his arm.

"Let me go, man, I didn't do nothing!"

"Like putting a knife in my face is nothing?" asked Jake. "We're gonna take a drive and if you answer me correctly, you'll get out of here with no broken bones, get me?"

The young man nodded.

"What's your name?"

"My name's Sparky," he said.

"Not your street name, a real name." He gripped tighter.

"Ouch! My name's Dwight Watt. Watt, you know, like a light bulb. That's why they call me Sparky."

"Okay, Dwight, here's how this goes down. I need some help. Your friends are no good to you now, as in they are hurting, but I need some eyes and ears, got me?"

Dwight nodded.

"We're gonna go to another diner, one where there aren't any holdup guys trying to take money from someone like me, okay? I'm going to get some food and I'm going to feed you as well, and we're going to sit like we are father and son, older and younger brother, cousins, friends. Got it?"

Dwight looked at Jake. "But we ain't the same color, dude."

"My name's Carl, you call me that, like we're real friendly, and I promise I won't break any of your bones, you hear me?"

Dwight nodded again.

They drove down the main street, Jake driving with one hand, holding Dwight's arm with the other.

"Man, you cut the circulation off to my arm. Let me go!"

Jake let go of Dwight's arm and elbowed him in the side of his head with his right arm, knocking him out completely. Dwight fell over on to the passenger seat and didn't move.

The big man in the green sedan drove slowly back to the dock where *The Belle of Louisville* was moored. He pulled into a parking lot that edged right up to the water. There was a pier, tires and water. The big man surmised the water was about 20 feet deep. He looked around to see if there were any cameras located on poles overlooking the boat and the dock, but didn't see any.

He opened the backdoor of the vehicle and took the tarp and wrapped it around the security guard. Then he tied the chains and anchors to the body.

The big man stood back up and looked around. There were no workers on the boat, no one else in the parking lot. The guard had weighed about 165 pounds, including his uniform and radio, and now the chains and anchors made him about 250 pounds. The big man picked him up like a light suitcase and flung him out into the Ohio River.

The body made a splash, bobbed for a few seconds as the air left the tarp, and then sank out of sight. The big man closed the backdoor of the car and climbed back into the front seat. He started the vehicle up and pulled out of the lot.

A construction worker on scaffolding under I-64 noted the car and the last three numbers of the Georgia license plate and called 911 to report a suspicious person throwing something into the river. He was on the phone for about 2 minutes. Police officers from the city of Louisville were dispatched to the pier. Two hotels overlooked the pier, and both had cameras pointing out to the river.

Jake pulled into another diner, drove the car around to the back, and parked. He shook Dwight until the young man woke up.

"Geez, mister, why you hit me like that?"

"I told you I wouldn't break any of your bones if you cooperated. I still mean that. I need you to be on my side for just a few minutes, then I'll let you go. Do you understand?"

Dwight nodded, but didn't say anything.

They stepped out of the car and walked to the front door of the diner. Jake opened the door for Dwight. As he started to enter, Jake leaned in and said in a low voice, "You make any move, try anything, and I break every bone. Your body has 206 bones in it. I'll make you feel every single one as I break them. Sit back, eat, and we make friendly chitchat."

He and Dwight headed in and a waitress seated them.

Two Louisville police officers walked over to the hotels and had the managers play back the video that overlooked the pier. Both cameras showed the big man, the dark green sedan, and the body wrapped in a tarp. The officers captured stills of the car, the license plate, and of the man when he had turned to look for cameras. They called Louisville dispatchers and had an All-Points Bulletin broadcast, along with an alert for a possibly armed and dangerous killer.

The big man in the green sedan pulled his car into an underground parking garage. He drove down three levels and parked the car in between two SUVs. He backed the car in, exited the vehicle, and removed the license plate. He placed it in the small of his back and walked towards the exit.

Jake and Dwight sat down in a booth away from most of the traffic, next to the bathroom. Dwight kept rubbing his arm and the side of his head.

"What you need me for, mister?"

Jake smiled at Dwight.

"I need an alibi. I need people to see me and know I am just a nice, quiet guy who never does anything wrong. I need you to tell the cops when they pick you up that I did nothing wrong. It was another guy that did this. Not me. Got it, Dwight?"

The young man nodded.

"Cat got your tongue?"

Dwight shook his head. Jake could tell he was nervous, but Dwight's street smarts started kicking in.

"Man, I got your back, dude. I know how to play the game, so you just sit over there, and I just sit over here and now we bros." He picked up a glass of water the waitress had dropped off, took a sip, and smiled at Jake. His teeth gleamed. White and gold teeth reflected the lights in the restaurant.

"I need to go to the hospital in a few minutes. We're gonna eat and then you're going to go with me to the ER. I need a way to get in unseen."

"What you gonna do, man?"

"It's not what I'm going to do, it's what you're going to do, dude." Jake grabbed Dwight by the shoulder and smiled. Dwight shrunk back, not sure what was going to happen, but sure whatever it was, he was not going to like it. He was not going to like it at all.

Kowalski stirred on the sofa, sat up and looked at the time. It was after 9 AM. His clothing was appropriately rumpled. He got up, used the facilities, and went out to the day watch area. Tanner was seated at a table, going over some old cases.

"Hey, Cap. I'm gonna run home and change. Be back in about an hour." He turned to head to the exit.

"No, the heck you're not. Your house is a crime scene. I've got it taped off and I have a car parked out there day and night. Did you forget Fry from the jail died there?"

Kowalski turned and looked at Tanner.

"No, I didn't forget. But I have to get my razor, new clothes, a tooth-brush, toiletries, you know, stuff."

Tanner shook his head.

"We'll run to the store and see what we can get you for the time being. Your house is off limits till further notice."

The driver of the green sedan took the license plate and threw it into a dumpster. He walked away from the river, south, under Interstate 65. Traffic was light, and the big man walked down the side of the street, as there was no sidewalk.

He walked past a restaurant that was 24 hours. The police and the fire department were on scene tending to what appeared to be two young men. Both had been loaded onto stretchers and were being placed in the back of two ambulances. Several people were standing around, watching. The big man stopped and stood with the crowd. Hiding in plain sight.

Jake finished eating. Dwight was not as hungry, seemingly, as he only pushed his eggs around his plate.

"You need to eat," said Jake. "You're going to need your strength in just a little bit."

"What you mean, dude? You gonna hurt me?" His voice rose and his eyes grew wide.

"I told you I was not going to break any bones in your body. I promise you I won't do that. I just need a way to get into the hospital. I have a friend in there I need to see."

"Jes walk in the front door, dude!" Dwight looked like someone who had come up with the perfect plan. "You don't need me to help you do that, dude!"

Jake laid a 20-dollar bill on the table. He motioned to the waitress. She nodded her head and made her way over to where Jake and Dwight were seated.

"That's all for the two of you?" she asked.

"I think that'll take care of us. Dwight here's got a doctor's appointment. We're going to run over to the hospital and get him looked at. He's been running, ah, a low-grade fever for the past few hours. It makes him nervous and edgy."

The waitress nodded, smiled, and made some comment about how she knew, that she had three kids, and that's why she had to work, and they were sick all the time, and they had doctor's visits as well..

Jake and Dwight got up from the booth and headed for the exit. Dwight was now looking scared. He knew he couldn't run, and he was truly afraid of what the big man was going to do to him.

"Dude, just let me go!" he said, as they walked out the door. "I been good to you, I didn't tell no one and I won't talk. Jes let me be!"

He tried to pull away from Jake, but his arm was again in a vise-like grip. In fact, vise grips were sissies compared to the grip Jake had on his arm. They walked around to the back of the restaurant and got into Kowalski's friend's car. Jake opened the driver's door and pushed Dwight in, and made him sit on the console again.

Jake pulled out of the restaurant and headed towards the hospital. He waited as two ambulances screamed through the intersection, headed towards downtown Louisville.

"What you gonna do to me, dude?" asked Dwight. "Man, let me go!"

"I told you I'd let you go when I was finished with you. I mean to keep that promise."

The lights on the road to the hospital were timed so Jake didn't have to slow down. He kept a steady pace of 23 miles per hour, holding the wheel with one hand and Dwight's arm with the other.

They pulled into the police parking area, near the Emergency Room entrance of Jewish Hospital. There were no police cars present, but an officer was standing out near the ER entrance, looking bored. Jake turned off the car. He looked at Dwight.

"I told you I was not going to break any of your bones, like I did your buddies. I mean to keep my promise. And as an added bonus, here's some money." He pulled $100 out of Luke's wallet and handed it to Dwight. "Man, you gonna kill me, ain't you?"

Jake shook his head and grabbed Dwight by the neck. Dwight's eyes bugged out of his head as Jake tightened his grip.

"I just need to get back into the hospital without being seen, Dwight. You're my ticket."

Dwight passed out in about 10 seconds. Jake felt for a pulse. It was still strong at the carotid arteries in his neck. He would be out for 5, maybe 10 minutes at the most.

Jake picked up Dwight in his arms and headed for the ER entrance. He nodded to the officer, who came over to see if he could see what was happening more than lending a hand. Jake stepped on the mat but the door didn't open. He saw a doorbell beside the sliding glass door and reached out his left arm and rang it.

A tech opened the door and Jake pushed past and called loudly.

"I'm a police officer. I've got a suspect here. Think he's gone into some kind of cardiac arrest. Need a bed, fast!" He made as if he was doing compressions on Dwight's chest while holding him in his arms.

A bed was pushed from a spare room and Jake laid Dwight on the bed.

"I think he's started to breathe again. I'll notify Louisville Metro and have them come down and deal with him. He's being held on suspicion of strong-arm robbery. His name is Dwight Watt, but he goes by Sparky. I have another suspect I have to transfer to jail."

He turned and walked out of the ER past the officer and into the hospital. He needed to get up and see Luke.

The big man left the scene of the two would-be robbers Jake had put down, though he didn't know Jake had been responsible. He continued walking towards downtown, towards the hospital where Lawrence and Luke, and now Jake, were.

Kowalski grumbled, as he put on some new clothing in the men's dressing room at Kohl's. Tanner had given him his credit card and was waiting outside the dressing room.

"Everything fit?" he asked.

"No, I need some bigger pants or a smaller butt."

"Bend and flex, Kowalski. Get those on. I need to get back to the Post."

Kowalski came out, dressed in new clothing, with two new pairs of pants and some shirts, two bags of underwear, two bags of T-shirts, a 10 pack of black socks, a toothbrush, toothpaste, hairbrush, deodorant, and a new electric razor. He had torn off the tags on his new shirt and pants but decided to keep the same belt he had on earlier.

They went up to the register and Tanner paid for Kowalski's things. The bill came up just short of $350.

"You can pay me when you can get back into your house," said Tanner.

Kowalski nodded and smiled. A real, you are one of the good ones, smiles. He picked up the purchases and they left.

"We need to get back to the Post and I need to check on our patient at Jewish Hospital," said Tanner. "I still have guards there, Metro is doing me a big favor."

"How many?" Kowalski asked.

"I think one or two, not sure. I can call and find out."

Kowalski nodded but said nothing. He was wondering where Jake and the big man were right now.

Jake was walking up the steps to the ICU right then. He opened the door and peered down the long hallway. The clock on the wall above the nurse's station said 11:23 AM. It was a digital clock using military time, therefore it read out in 24-hour increments, so the AM was not technically necessary. Jake felt it was probably for the uninformed patients and families who passed through the ICU each day.

The stethoscope and chart Jake used were gone from where he had laid them the night before. He scanned around to see if others were available, but nothing caught his eye. He could just make out a chair outside Lawrence's room, although he could not tell if anyone was sitting in it.

Jake walked up to the nurse's station nearest him. A nurse or a tech or a respiratory therapist, he didn't know, was seated, writing some documentation.

He waited until she saw him.

"Can I help you?" she asked.

"There's a guy down the hall, room 615. Name, Lawrence Douglas. I need to see him. Government matter." Jake leaned over the counter as he said it, both to inform the person at the nurse's station it was a private matter, and to use his height as an overpowering advantage.

"I'm Doctor Tatum," said the person sitting at the station. "I've been given strict orders from the police to not let anyone into that room. Now I'm calling security because I don't believe a word out of your mouth."

She reached to pick up the phone but was stopped when Jake's hand covered the handset.

"Listen, there's a guy trying to kill Lawrence. A big guy…"

"Like you, big?" asked Doctor Tatum.

"Bigger, way bigger, dark complexion, dark eyes, 300 pounds if an ounce. He'll kill anyone who gets in his way. Both your patient and his friend in there are in way over their heads. I am here to make sure they don't die."

"There's a police officer in there right now. I'm sure he can handle anything that comes his way."

"Small, wiry guy, wearing black clothing, helmet?"

The doctor nodded, and Jake shook his head.

"What, are you implying the police can't do their job?"

"No, doctor, I'm saying there's going to be three dead in that room within the hour if you don't let me go down there and talk to them."

"I'll accompany you down there. I need to check on him for surgery anyway."

"Alright, but if something starts happening, get back to this phone and call 911, and I mean in a big hurry!"

The big man walked up to the entrance of Jewish Hospital. The structure was huge at night; it looked even bigger in daylight.

He walked into the main entrance, one he had not used the day before, and asked where the ICU was.

The clerk on duty asked, "What do you need, Sir, trauma ICU, med ICU, Cardiac ICU, ENTC-ICU, Neuro ICU, Peds ICU?"

"I don't know," said the big man with a thick Russian accent. "My friend had heart attack or was sick or something. I don't know. He's on 6th floor of one of these buildings."

"Well, Peds is in the second building back, to the left. ENTC-ICU is the third building back on the right. Trauma ICU is housed in our emergency room area, and that's four buildings back, on the left. Med ICU is upstairs, but that's the seventh floor. Cardiac ICU runs from 10 to 12 on the last building on the right, but there are overflow rooms down four floors. Any of that help?"

The big man shrugged his shoulders.

"His first name is Larry, I think."

You have to have a last name in order for me to be able to find the patient in the registry. Do you know his last name?"

The big man again shrugged his shoulders.

"I'll try to find it using phone. I'll check back. *Da,* I'll check back."

He let a little Russian out, hoping the clerk would think of something that would be useful. The clerk just looked past him at the next person in line.

Jake and Dr. Tatum walked into room 615. The SWAT officer was sitting there, with an MP5 slung loosely over his right shoulder. The officer looked first at Dr. Tatum, then at Jake, and a small, incendiary device in his brain went off and he recognized Jake as a wanted man.

"Stop right there!" he shouted, as he tried to move the weapon to a ready-on stance. "Police officer! I need you to get down, now!"

The officer made the move with the MP5 to about port arms when Jake grabbed the barrel and forced it down. Jake surmised, he didn't know for sure, but he surmised the officer would have the weapon locked and loaded, meaning it would be in safe mode.

As the officer tacitly protested and continued to try to bring his weapon to bear, Jake began talking in a slow, soothing tone.

"I'm not here to hurt you or the patients. You need to stop and listen to me."

The officer continued to struggle, but Jake's grip on the barrel, combined with his other arm pushing the weapon down towards the floor, left the officer no choice but to listen.

The officer quit struggling, and Jake released some of the tension off the barrel, but kept it pointing down.

"The biggest thing you need to know is I am one of the good guys. I've not been involved in anything bad here, but there's a big guy coming, maybe already here, who wants to kill these two, and will stop at nothing to complete that agenda."

Luke was sitting next to Lawrence and had been a rapt listener for the past two minutes.

Luke interjected. "This guy's for real. He saved my bacon. I got no reason to lie. He saved Lawrence's life, too. Give this fellow a chance to tell you what's going on, please."

The officer nodded. Jake let go of the MP5 and stood back. The officer didn't put his weapon in the slung back position, but kept his hand on the stock so he could move it to a ready stance quickly.

"There's a big fellow, eastern European, maybe Russian. He's killed four people I know of, maybe more. He's bad medicine and he's here to take down these two for an online gambling debt. Their friends were the recipients of his wrath, and he has no desire to stop until they, and anyone associated with them, are dead.

"We have to work quickly, because I think he could be here in the hospital like he was last night. He could squeeze all our necks together without breaking a sweat. I need you to call your superiors and have them give this place a once-through, looking for him. Any chance you could accomplish it?"

The officer nodded.

"My name's Rick. Rick Chaffee. Louisville PD. And from what I've been told, you're the one killing everyone here, not some big Russian."

Jake shook his head. "I have no reason to hurt anyone here. I could have killed the SWAT guy last night, but I just choked him out and left him handcuffed to the bed. There's a young man in the ER who I used to get in here. I choked him out and pretended he was having a heart attack. Gave him $100 for his part. He may be telling on me, but I think his street smarts are probably kicking in about now. He doesn't want to lose that money. What say you and I work to protect these two as well as you and me?"

The officer tilted his head one way and then another. He looked at Luke and Dr. Tatum.

"Alright, tell me what you know and what you think you know, then we go from there. If I don't believe you, I'll put you in cuffs and have Louisville Metro pick you up and haul your butt downtown. Got it?"

He tried to emphasize the last two words, more for his own benefit and of those around him than as a threat to Jake.

Jake nodded his head. "I'll make sure you have all the info you need so when this giant comes up here, you can make sure the cuffs go on him. If I can't make you believe me, I'll help you put the cuffs on me."

Jake started from the beginning. The restaurant, the State Trooper being shot. Kowalski taking him to the jail in Franklin County. The jailer being killed by det cord. Luke and Lawrence and their friends' involvement in a gambling scam. His thoughts on some of the jailers working for the Russians, and being in on the gambling scam, along with the four who were killed at the jail.

The officer listened intently, making mental notes. He stopped Jake a few times to ask questions, but otherwise remained silent.

Jake finished and turned to Dr. Tatum.

"What do we need to do with Lawrence? He's in grave danger here. I think this big guy is coming back to finish what he started. He won't stop until everyone in this room is dead or he's dead. That means you, me, this officer, your patient, and Lawrence's friend here are all on a hit list. And maybe the nurses and techs on this floor as well. He may not come with a gun but with some kind of device to incapacitate us until he can conduct the kill. That's how I would do it."

"We need to move him to pre-op. It's protected by security doors. We can put his friend and the officer in there as well. No one gets past the OR clerk. She's the clerk from hell. Shoot, I have trouble getting in."

Dr. Tatum called from Lawrence's room to see if a bed in pre-op was available. She gave the room number and asked for the clerk to call her back as soon as possible.

Jake leaned out the door and looked up and down the hallway. "When's your relief coming?" he asked Rick.

"Not for another three hours."

"You need to call for backup, set up a perimeter on this floor, and then move it to pre-op. You need to get hospital security in on this and make sure they are surveying each floor for this guy. He's big, he's bad and he's coming."

Kowalski called Jewish Hospital and asked for room 615. The phone buzzed and buzzed but there was no answer. He called back and asked for the same room. Still no answer. He called a third time and asked for the nurse's station on the 6th floor. After a few rings, the phone was answered. He identified himself and asked what happened to the patient in room 615. The person on the other end asked him to hold. Tanner came into his office and saw Kowalski on the phone. He mouthed what's up and Kowalski told him he was waiting for an answer from the hospital. In a few seconds, the phone clicked back on.

"Dr. Tatum here. May I help you?"

"Hi, doctor, this is Officer Kowalski from the State Police, Post #12, Frankfort, Kentucky. You have a patient of interest there in room 615. I have police protection on him and I need to make sure he is in good care."

The doctor hesitated one second. "I'm sorry, Sir. Mr. Douglas passed away this morning. His heart gave out. He was scheduled to go under the knife, but he was borderline being able to survive the surgery. I'm sorry to have to give you that information over the phone." She asked if he had any more questions. Kowalski told her no and hung up.

He turned to Tanner. "We lost our boy at the hospital. Died before surgery. Just talked to the doctor and she gave me the news. I have to call Luke and make sure he and his family are still okay."

Tanner agreed it was best to let the family know because the hospital didn't have Lawrence's information. Kowalski thought about Luke and told Tanner he needed to call the hospital again to check on the fourth involved in the gambling scam.

Kowalski dialed the number and asked for the sixth-floor nurse's station again. The same person answered the phone. He identified himself once more and asked about Luke.

"Are you talking about the man who was here with my patient?" she asked. "He left the hospital to make arrangements for Mr. Douglas. I'm not sure where he went after he left his friend."

Kowalski thanked her again and hung up. He looked at Tanner.

"I think something's fishy at the hospital. We need to get there pronto. They never give out information to anyone over the phone."

Tanner agreed, and they headed out the door. Kowalski turned to the on-duty desk sergeant and told them to give Tanner a call if any information came in from the guy named Jake. They hopped into Tanner's car, turned on the lights and siren, and headed for Louisville.

The big guy walked from building to building. Nothing looked the same. He was confused more by all the people than by the different locations. He finally turned and walked outside to see if he could find a way into the hospital that would get him back to the building and the floor he needed. It took 10 minutes, but he found the exit he had taken the night before. He walked past two unmanned Louisville police cars as he opened the door.

Jake looked back at Rick, the Louisville Metro police officer.

"Are you ready where you are?" he asked. Rick nodded. He had barricaded the room in pre-op and had two officers stationed near the pre-op nurse's station. The head clerk would not leave her desk, despite several admonitions by the Louisville Police.

"I've been through tornadoes, crazy patients, out of control family members, every kind of storm you can imagine. One more loon doesn't scare me away!"

She sat, arms crossed, staring down the two officers. The officers looked at each other, then at her, and then sat down in ready positions.

Both held MP5s, they had also holstered Sig-Sauer P-226 9-millimeter sidearms, plus they had two concussion grenades apiece. Rick also had a Heckler and Koch 9-millimeter USP in a chest holster. They had cleared all patients from pre-op and moved them to different floors. They had contacted the fire department, and Louisville had sent three engines, a ladder, two medical units, a battalion chief and a district chief. Those units were stationed three blocks away from the hospital, in a ready staging area.

The officers had also alerted the Louisville SWAT team, and members had set up two perimeters. One team set up inside the hospital, and the other team set up outside the parking garage. All members were in their traditional SWAT gear, but were laying low, keeping themselves out of sight and out of mind from the general public.

The big man was in the stairwell, the same one in which he ran into Kowalski the night before. He was standing between floors 4 and 5 when his phone rang. It was his contact in Russia, calling him back.

"*Da*," the big man said. He listened for a few seconds, then disconnected the phone. He turned and walked back down the steps to the ground exit. He opened the door slowly. There was no one visible. He checked high and low to make sure he wasn't being watched.

He moved out the exit and towards the street. There was a small amount of traffic, but not like a big city should have at this time of the day. Something ticked inside his head, and he made for the street, flagged down a cab, and got inside.

The phone at the Pre-Op desk rang. The Pre-Op clerk answered the phone on the first ring.

"Pre-Op, may I help you?"

The line was garbled, and so, the voice on the other end was garbled as well.

"I need to speak to Mr. Lawrence Dugless," the voice on the other end said.

"Who?" replied the clerk in Pre-Op.

"Mr. Lawrence Dugless. He has problem with heart."

"We do not have anyone with that name on this floor," the clerk said.

"Yes, I know he is there in hospital. I need to give him message. Tell him heart attack is almost over."

"Sir, there is no one here by…" The line went dead.

The clerk turned and looked at the officers. "I think someone knows something. I don't know how they know, but that guy on the phone did, and he spoke with an accent. He said the patient's heart attack is almost over, whatever that means."

Tanner and Kowalski drove at over 100 miles per hour west on I-64. The tires tore up the interstate at more than a mile every 45 seconds. The distance from Frankfort to the big hospital in Louisville was 46 miles, give or take one or two, depending on which exit Tanner took. He was able to keep the speed up for most of the distance, which meant the trip took only about 22 minutes, plus the time to navigate around the hospital grounds.

Tanner pulled into the Police Only area and turned off the lights. It was just after 1 PM. The day had been rough so far, due to lack of sleep, but standing up out of the State Police squad car gave both Tanner and Kowalski a new lease on life.

The big man asked the cab driver to turn down an alley in west Louisville. They had just passed Seventh Street. The driver turned down West Oak Alley.

"That'll be $7.50, senor. You can hand it through the window."

The big man reached into his pocket to get some money out.

"This is not the kinda place you probably need to be, so if you want, I will wait," said the cab driver.

"No, is OK. Thank you."

The big man reached through the window and handed the cab driver $20.00.

"You keep rest, is OK?" said the big man.

"Wow! Thanks! Best tip of the day!"

"No, one better for you. Trust no one."

The big man still had his hand through the glass, and he grabbed the driver by the right arm. The hole in the glass was almost too small for even an average-sized person to get one arm in, let alone two, but the big man's powerful hand held the driver tightly.

"Ouch, let me go, senor!" said the driver. "You're hurting my arm!"

He pulled away from the big man and tried to open the cab's left front door, but the big man held on.

The driver then reached with his left hand and pulled out a pistol from under the steering wheel. He fired a shot into the big man's forearm.

The big man howled and released the driver. The driver jumped from the vehicle, still carrying the gun and ran, screaming.

The big man pulled his arm from the hole, bleeding profusely. He removed a handkerchief from his coat pocket and wrapped it tightly around the wound, staunching the flow of blood.

The big man stepped from the rear of the cab and slid into the driver's seat. He turned off the available sign on the roof of the cab, put the car into gear, and pulled out of the alley.

Jake let out a sigh. He motioned to Rick.

"I guess this guy isn't coming today. Maybe never, now that we know who he is."

Jake turned to the clerk. "You can call security and tell them to stand down, for now. Apparently, our Russian fellow's not going to grace us with his presence."

Rick picked up his microphone and called down to the SWAT teams to see if they had seen anything. He learned no one matching the big man's description had been seen, but there were a few holes in the cordon they had set up, and perhaps he slipped through their web.

Kowalski and Tanner entered the hospital and headed up to the cardiac floor. There they found Lawrence, Luke, Jake and the officers had been moved to Pre-Op. They headed to meet up with Jake and the police to formulate a plan.

Kowalski walked through the door and almost ran over a small, demure woman.

"Pardon me," he said.

"What do you want in here, this is no place for visitors," said the Pre-Op clerk.

"State Police, ma'am. We're here…."

"Let me see some I.D., sonny," said the clerk.

Kowalski reached for his wallet and looked up to see the clerk armed with a huge hunting knife.

"What the heck?" said Kowalski.

"You pull that wallet out real slow, mister. I'm small but I pack a big punch."

She continued to hold the knife at Kowalski's stomach as he pulled his wallet out of his pants pocket with his right arm. He flashed his badge to the clerk, and only then did she pull the knife away.

"Sorry, but I can't take chances. Who's the guy in the uniform with you, sonny?"

"That's my Captain. His name is Tanner."

Rick stepped forward and indicated to the clerk that both men were with him. As they walked away, Kowalski looked back at the clerk, now ignoring the three of them, filing paperwork in and around her desk.

"We sure could've used her on the force, eh Cap?" Tanner just shook his head.

The big man drove the cab out of Louisville, east on Interstate 64. The bleeding had stopped, as the bullet wound had not hit any major blood vessels or bone, but the pain was great and seemingly getting greater by each passing minute. He drove the cab to an Outlet Mall directly off the interstate and parked it in the farthest lot behind the building.

He didn't want to go into the mall but needed to find a way to get back to Shelbyville to see if he could get another car. As he walked the lot looking for the right car, his phone jingled in his pocket. It was difficult to pull the phone from his pocket with the bullet wound to his arm, but he managed before the phone stopped ringing.

"Da?" He listened. "I am at a building off interstate. West of Louisville. Come to pick me up, please. Bring bandages." He listened again, looked at his watch, and answered. *"Da."* He named the mall where he was standing, which was an outlet, and the address of a storefront, hung up the phone and walked back towards the cab, but not too near to raise suspicion. He then noticed several people standing out near the street, looking as though they were waiting for rides. He moved near them, looking to the left and right to see if his ride was coming, in the same way the others were looking for their rides. It was hot, but

he kept the coat buttoned and kept his right arm protected so no one could see his arm.

Kowalski met Jake in the Pre-Op waiting room.

"No-show, huh?"

Jake shook his head.

"Not sure if and when this guy will show up. My guess is he's getting reinforcements. That's what I'd do."

"Well, you're not some Russian guy trying to off two or more people, then, are you?" He turned and talked to Tanner.

Tanner ordered the SWAT teams back to usual duties. He also asked for officers to be on alert on both Luke and Lawrence's homes, as well as Lawrence's daughter in Louisville, but then changed his mind.

A brown sedan pulled up behind the outlet mall in Shepherdsville, Kentucky. The driver pulled the car up to where the big man stood.

"*Zalezay,* comrade." said the driver. "Get in." The big man climbed into the front passenger seat. He turned and looked at the two men in the back. One man reached beside him and lifted a medical kit over the seat to the big man.

He unbuttoned his coat and pulled his right arm out of the sleeve. He loosened the handkerchief and applied some triple antibiotic to the wound entrance and exit. It wasn't really necessary, as the bullet's speed most likely sterilized the wound area.

He applied three 4 x 4s with some gauze and taped it securely. He reinserted his arm into the coat and pulled it back to his shoulder.

"*Vesti Mashinu,* comrade. Drive the car."

Jake walked into the waiting room outside Pre-Op. Kowalski, Tanner and Rick were all there, whispering in soft tones.

"Kowalski, I need to talk to you."

Kowalski turned and nodded at Jake. He left the group and walked over to where Jake stood.

"Still need to get some things cleared up here, Jake," said Kowalski.

"Like what, Kowalski?"

"Like I want to know how you would assassinate people when you were in the military, Jake. What would you do to pull off something like you said, so no one would know you were targeting the perps?"

"Car wrecks, mostly. It's a wait and see game, so I have to get all the players in one car—that could take days or weeks—and then, I would set off a little device that blew the left wheel off their vehicle when it was traveling at a high speed. I would plant the device at night, when no one was around. Usually some interdiction into a closed area, a garage maybe. In and out in about 1 minute. Then I would wait until the right time to blow the device, like in a curve. The government handed those explosive devices out to me like candy. I would follow discreetly and after they wrecked, if anyone were still alive, I would break their necks. Not hard after they were traumatized by the accident."

Kowalski shook his head.

"So, you weren't a sniper?"

"Far from it, Kowalski. Snipers sit back and wait for their target— usually only one—and it may take the better part of a day for that target to get into a position to be sanctioned or sanitized, whatever you want to call it. Sometimes, in the heat of battle, a sniper could take out as many as ten or more, who are hiding in a building, firing at our guys. I just called in a jet to bomb the building they were hiding in, I wouldn't wait for a sniper to get on site, set up, and take that shot. But, a sniper's job was not my specialty. I was deep undercover most times. Like when I was upstairs with Lawrence and Luke, and the SWAT team came in,

I acted and looked like a doctor. Not hard when people are not looking for what you have become but what they think they know you are."

Kowalski shook his head. "I never would have suspected you if I had met you on the street, away from the diner."

The car with the big man and the other three Russians rolled slowly off the ramp in downtown Louisville. Other cars sped past them, most drivers glaring at the near-stopped car, a couple giving the one-finger salute before hitting the gas and slewing around the Russian's vehicle. The big man pointed towards the left.

"*Povernut' nalevo.* Left... turn left, here!"

The driver spun the wheel to the left and the car crossed three lanes and onto West Market Street. Four cars piled into each other trying to avoid the Russian driver. The four drivers got out and began arguing with each other.

Another person, an off-duty Louisville police officer driving his personal SUV, noted the license plate of the car the Russians were in, pulled out his phone and called dispatch. He then began following the car.

Kowalski nodded.

"I knew a couple of guys at State Police with military experience. They were clandestine characters. But that was during Viet Nam. They were leaving as I was coming on. They talked about what they did, like capturing a North Viet Cong general after following him for three or four days. Took a lot of guts to do what they did, seems like."

Jake shrugged his shoulders.

"Anyone can do this if they're trained well enough," said Jake. "I once met a guy in another company who was in Nam. He and his group crawled through a field, following a small unit. They had to watch while the unit killed everyone in a village, thinking that village was sympathizing with the U.S. soldiers. He said they were looking for the leader, some VC general. They captured him and killed the rest of the unit. Told me people like that deserved to get themselves killed.

"I never tried to make it personal, myself. Bad guys doing bad things get themselves killed ngay bay gio." Jake used the term he had heard soldiers returning from Viet Nam use that meant 'right now'.

Kowalski said, "I've heard that term, too. Couple of cops from Louisville also used that. Me, I never served in the military. Too late for Nam, too old for Desert Shield, Desert Storm." Kowalski's phone rang. He turned to pick it up.

The car with the four Russians in it pulled into the hospital-parking garage in downtown Louisville. The big man told the driver to stay with the car, while the other three stepped out and headed for the entrance the big man knew.

They walked into the hospital and started up the steps. The big man stopped on the second floor and pointed them to the door. He talked to them in low tones and then they opened the exit door and went out into the hospital. The big man continued up the steps. The off-duty Louisville police officer pulled past the stopped sedan and into a parking slot one level up. He opened the trunk of his car and pulled out his jacket that said "Louisville Police" on the back and slid it on.

"We're gonna head back to Frankfort," said Tanner. "This is a no-show. Guess they've probably headed back to Russia."

Jake looked at Tanner then at Kowalski.

"He's going to keep coming back, Captain."

"How do you know, Sir?"

Jake leaned back on a desk. "Because that's what I would do."

The big man opened the door to the sixth floor. He stepped in and let the door shut behind him. He took a quick look around, then headed to the room where Lawrence was. As he walked down the hall, he noticed there were no nurses, no doctors, no patients in the hallway. He got to the room and peered around the corner. Empty.

The captain of *The Belle of Louisville* was in his early 40s. Not many sailors or seafarers wanted to take a job as a party boat captain, but Lucas Jenkins didn't mind. He got to go home every night, although late, and did not have to be back to work until afternoon the next day, unless there was a special cruise on the Ohio River.

His crew was cleaning, sweeping, stocking, readying the boat for that evening's twilight cruise. Two crewmembers were hanging over the side, giving *The Belle* a new coat of paint. As the older one rolled paint on the port side of the paddleboat, the roller slipped from his hand and fell into the water. The rollers were attached to the crewmembers' belts by safety lines, so he reached down and grabbed the line and began pulling the roller back up. As he did so, it snagged on something in the water.

The big man turned and headed back towards the stairway exit. He opened the door and heard talking from above. He hesitated, then pulled the door back, almost shut, but where he could see who was coming down the steps.

Captain Jenkins looked over the rail as Harlan kept hold of his safety line.

"Not sure what it is, Cap, but it's heavy. I don't think I can pull it in by myself."

"Fouled on some flotsam, you think?"

"Yeah, could be. Throw me a rope and I'll tie off my safety line and maybe we can pull it up from the deck."

The off-duty police officer walked down a level and stepped over to the passenger side of the vehicle he had been following. As he passed the trunk of the car he pulled slightly on the lid, but it was locked tight. He leaned forward and tapped on the passenger's window glass.

"May I talk to you, Sir?" he asked.

Captain Jenkins passed a rope down to the deckhand below. The hand deftly tied a bowling knot using a figure eight on a bight and handed the lead back up to Jenkins. The captain quickly passed the rope around a stay on the davit and began pulling on the rope, paying it around the stay as he pulled.

"*Da?*" asked the driver. "I no speak English."

The officer asked the driver for some identification, but the driver acted as if he could not understand what he was being asked. He kept shaking his head and lifting his shoulders. The officer pulled out his wallet, pointed towards the license in the window, and looked back at the driver, straight into the barrel of a GSh-18.

Jenkins kept pulling on the line. The deckhand kept feeding him more, and then a tarp broke the surface.

"Hey, Cap. It's a tarp, wrapped in chains. Want me to pull it on in?"

"No, tie off right there. I'm going to call the Coast Guard."

The officer hesitated one second too long. The bullet entered the officer's right eye, through the pupil, through the skull and into the cerebellum. At least part of the bullet entered the cerebellum. The bullet broke apart after hitting skull bone. One piece sliced through the temporal artery, one through the cerebral artery, and the third lodged in the bottom of the medulla oblongata after darting around the cerebellum. The officer would have liked to have known where each one ended up, as his wife was pre-med and studying neurology. He was interested in that kind of thing, but he was already dead before he hit the ground.

The driver pulled his car forward, stopped the vehicle, pulled the trunk release by the seat, and opened the driver's door. He stood up, scooped the body, and put it in the trunk, then slammed the lid.

The Coast Guard pulled up next to *The Belle of Louisville*. They threw a line to Captain Jenkins, who tied it off. The bosun's mate made the line fast on the Coast Guard boat, then jumped over to the deck of *The Belle*. Another crewmember pulled out an iPhone, hit the video button and started recording. The first Coast Guard member, a seaman, second class, pulled out a knife and started slitting the tarp.

"We got a body in here," he said. "Get me Louisville Police here and also the coroner."

The Russian driver parked the car in a slot one level up, right next to the police officer's car, though he didn't know it. He turned off the vehicle, left the keys on the seat, got out and closed the door. He then called a number on his cell phone.

The big man waited until Tanner and Kowalski passed him, passing from the sixth floor down. Just as he stepped out on to the stairwell landing, his phone rang. He reached behind him, opened the door, and stepped back inside the sixth floor.

"*Da?*" He listened. "Call the others. We have to leave. Now."

The Louisville Police pulled up in a van to where *The Belle of Louisville* was docked. The officers got out of the van and pulled out various pieces of equipment. One of the officers surveyed the situation, another set up tape that said, 'POLICE LINE: DO NOT CROSS'. Another pulled on a wet suit, buoyancy vest and flippers.

The police diver, a man named Vickers, slipped into the water under the tarp, tied off a rope onto the chains and anchors, then gave a thumbs-up to the Coast Guard man on *The Belle*. Jenkins and the seaman tied off the lines on the anchors and chains, then started pulling on the line to the tarp. They pulled the tarp up to the deck, laid it out, and the seaman sliced open the tarp the rest of the way.

One of the officers turned to Jenkins. "Better let the owners know this boat is closed down tonight and maybe tomorrow night. This is going to be a murder investigation."

The big Russian walked down the empty sixth floor hallway towards the elevators. He pressed the button and waited for the doors to open. While waiting, he pulled out his phone and called the other two to tell them where to meet.

The driver sat on the bumper of the police officer's car, waiting for the other two. As he waited, he thought he heard a phone ring. He looked around, but could not see where it was coming from. It stopped, then started again.

Tanner and Kowalski made it down to Tanner's vehicle. They stood there for a couple of minutes, then Kowalski shook his head.

"I sure thought we would find our guy here, boss. Jake felt like it was going to happen today, and it sure seemed like it would."

Tanner said, "Hey, where is that guy, Jake? Did we just let him slip out of our hands while he put on a ruse, a misdirection?"

Kowalski shrugged. "Not sure. I'll run back upstairs and get him and ask. I sure don't want to think he duped us, boss."

The strange cell phone rang again, but as it rang, the three Russians approached the vehicle. The driver started to get in, but the big Russian stopped him.

"I think we need different car, no?"

"Officer is in trunk, possible he has key to other car?"

"Open and check," said the Russian.

The driver popped the trunk and felt the pockets of the dead officer. As he did so, he heard the same ring he had been hearing, coming from the dead man's hip. He pulled the phone out. He hit the button on the front and the screen lit up. There were 10 missed calls and a number of unreturned messages. He threw the phone onto the ground of the parking garage and smashed the phone with his heel. He then found the keys to the officer's car, hit the door-open button, and all four turned when the locks on the officer's car, parked right next to them, opened.

The big Russian smiled. "Is okay. St. Petersburg smiling down on us." They all laughed as the four men climbed into the officer's SUV and pulled out of the garage, heading west on Interstate 64 towards Indiana.

Kowalski walked out onto the eighth floor and almost got bowled over by Jake.

"Hey, I was just coming up here to get you."

"And I was just coming down to find you. I think, not for sure, but I think this guy's not alone."

"What makes you say that?"

"Just a hunch. He doesn't seem like a loner. Being so far away and all, I think he has to have some support."

Kowalski shrugged. "We gotta get going. We need to head back to Frankfort." Kowalski's phone rang, and he turned away to answer it.

Jake turned to Luke. "You think Lawrence is gonna be okay?"

"I sure hope so. I lost half of my best friends and I don't want to lose him. Is this big guy going to keep coming until... until either we are dead, or he is?"

"That's about it, Luke. Oh, here's your wallet. I took out $300 from the ATM. I also took $100 from your wallet and gave it to a kid, so I could get back in here. I don't think you'll be getting it back, but he doesn't know anything about you, and I think he doesn't want to answer any questions, anyway."

Luke thanked Jake again, and went back and sat by Lawrence.

"Hey, Jake," called Kowalski. "There's been a shooting in Louisville. A cab driver is claiming he gave a ride to a big guy with an accent and that person tried to rob him. The cabbie pulled out a gun and shot this person, not sure where, but he said the fellow howled like a cat that's been run over. I'm gonna head over with Tanner and we're gonna talk to this guy and see what's up. Need you to come along and give me a hand." This last part was a lie, which both Jake and Kowalski knew, but it did keep the onus off Jake for the moment.

The four Russians drove for about an hour on Interstate 64 west, well into Indiana, then pulled off at a gas station. They drove around the station to the back side and the big Russian took off the license plate and put it under his coat. The station was one that catered to both cars and big trucks. The four walked into the station and back into the area where drivers could take a shower. One truck driver named Clem had just finished undressing and was running a load of clothes in the wash. He stepped into the shower and turned on the water. The big Russian searched through the man's clothing quietly, found his truck keys, and the four headed out of the showering area and into the parking lot.

Tanner, Kowalski and Jake found the cab driver sitting in one of the Louisville police substations near town. The cab driver had come in to report his cab stolen. He had been afraid to go to the police since he had been working without a green card. Someone in his family told him he needed to get this straightened out, and the owner of the cab told him he was going to fire him if he didn't find the cab or at least file a stolen car report.

The man, named Rolando Gutierrez, from Guatemala, had driven in Louisville for several years, always under the radar, but things had been getting harder over the past few months. He mostly had been giving rides to other Spanish-speaking people, a kind of sub-culture for illegal aliens that had been taking place over the past decade or so.

Kowalski asked him, "What did this guy look like?"

"He was beeg as a truck. Take up my whole back seat."

"Did he say anything to you?"

"He tell me to keep the change, after he give me $20. I told him *gracias*, best tip I had all day. He tell me one more thing. Trust no one. Then he grab my arm. I thought he was going to break it off. Really hurt. I pulled out my pistola from under the steering wheel and I shoot him. In the arm, I think. He let go, really quick, *que sabe?*"

"Why didn't you report your cab stolen earlier, Mr. Gutierrez?" asked Kowalski.

"I let my green card run out. I afraid, but *mi jefe y mi esposa* both tell me to come down and tell what happened. I really scared, but I hope you can find him before he does thees to another cab driver."

Kowalski got the information for the cab, including the number on the trunk and called the Louisville Police Department to add details to the story the cab driver told him. It took a few minutes to get the information out, but when he hung up, he noticed Jake talking to the cab driver. He walked up and listened in on the conversation.

Jake asked, "Did this big guy say anything else?"

"No, *senor*. He only asked me to drop him near Seventh Street."

"Where did he get in?"

"Right by the hospital," answered the cab driver.

Jake looked at Kowalski, then at Tanner. "Need any more information?"

"I think we have enough." Kowalski's phone rang again. He pulled it back out of his pocket. Jake watched as his face turned ashen, then bright red. He hung up and turned to Jake.

"One of Louisville's police officers is missing. He was supposed to report to work this afternoon. They have been trying him on his cell and got no response.

"He had called in to Louisville dispatch and reported a car with four men inside. They pulled up to the hospital a little while ago. They had caused a wreck downtown and he followed to see what was going on. He told dispatch they had pulled into a parking garage, and he was going in to see what, if anything, happened. That's the last they heard from him."

Tanner said, "Call dispatch back and have a team head to the parking garage. Geez, which one?"

Kowalski said, "I guess the one by Jewish Hospital where the two from Shelbyville are right now."

The three left the police substation and got into Tanner's car. They drove back to the hospital.

Tanner said, "I've been here so often in the last three days I think I need to pay rent." The other two laughed, but there was no humor in any of their eyes.

The four Russians started up the big truck and pulled it out of the parking lot and headed east on Interstate 64. They had cover now, and they started formulating a plan. There were several trucks parked outside the hospital, including an MRI truck the big Russian had noticed. He had no idea what MRI stood for, but the truck they were in had no writing on it at all. It would be a great place to set up observation and a great place to hide out while at the hospital.

Tanner pulled his vehicle into the parking garage closest to Jewish Hospital. The Louisville Police Department had just arrived, and were putting up yellow police 'Do Not Cross' tape across the entrance, but let Tanner's vehicle in under the tape.

Tanner, Kowalski and Jake jumped out of the vehicle and walked up to the officer-in-charge.

Kowalski nodded to the officer, and said, "Hey, Bill. Anything?"

The officer replied. "We found his cell phone. Crunched up here by this car. No sign of his vehicle. City's bringing a dog out, so maybe we'll get a break. I hope so, for his wife."

Kowalski and the officer talked some more. Jake walked over to Tanner.

"I don't think... I know, these Russians will keep coming back over and over again. They don't give up."

"They did in Afghanistan. They did in East Germany. Why do you think they won't stop here?"

"Because this is not politics. This is someone's money. It's a scam I've seen before, nothing I've ever dealt with myself, but I've heard of these happening overseas. These Russians won't give up. It's not completely about the money, either. It's about control. If someone plays and loses, and they don't pay up, and these guys let it go, the intimidation is over.

"It's the same reason—on a much larger scale—why we didn't have a nuclear war with Russia. We intimidate the Russians and their pact; they intimidate America and our pact, and no one pulls the trigger. But these guys, they pull the trigger, big-time. And they're not going to stop."

The Russians drove the truck east and pulled into a truck stop about ten miles short of the border of Indiana and Kentucky. There were more than 100 trucks parked in the huge lot, so the truck they were in blended in with the others. The big Russian sat in the sleeper because of his size, while the other three sat across the bench seat in the front.

The driver got out of the truck and headed in to get some sandwiches and drinks. The big Russian pushed his way out of the sleeper and stepped on to the blacktop, stooping and stretching his sore back.

He looked into the cab. "Too many years in small cars," he said to no one in particular. The two others grunted but otherwise did not answer.

The driver walked out of the service station and started towards the truck. The big Russian saw him walking out with two bags in his left hand. He was about 50 yards away. The big Russian was walking towards the truck when two police cars, lights flashing, pulled up between the Russian and the driver. The officers stepped out of their cars, guns drawn. The big Russian stopped where he was, and the driver looked at him, then at the police, then dropped his bags and reached into his coat.

"Freeze, freeze, don't move!" yelled the police. The driver never stopped. He pulled out his GHs-18 pistol, pointed it at the police, and died.

The police, it was later proved, fired a total of seventeen rounds into the driver, who never got off a shot. The big Russian watched the event unfold in a matter of seven seconds. He turned around, went back to the truck where the other two had not seen what happened, climbed in the driver's seat, started the truck, and then turned it off. He looked down under the driver's console and found a tracking device.

"Groviand!" he cursed. He wrenched the tracking device out of its holder and threw it on the ground, started the truck again, and ran over the unit, crushing it completely.

"Gennadi will not be back with us. He's being questioned by the police. We have to leave."

"What did he say?" asked the second man.

"I don't know, but there will be holes in his story, I am sure."

The big Russian pulled the truck back on to the highway headed east to Louisville. With so many trucks moving in and out of the lot, the police missed the stolen truck. They didn't find the smashed tracking device for over an hour. They put out an all-points bulletin for the truck and trailer, but the Russian would change the license plate just after they crossed back into Kentucky, and the truck would not be found for another month, long after what was soon-to-be called 'The Louisville Incident' had come to fruition.

The Louisville Police dog handler and his dog, Shasha, arrived in the parking structure beside Jewish Hospital. The dog was a scent tracker, but there had not been a scent laid because they could not find where the officer's last known position was. The officer opened the backdoor of his vehicle and Shasha jumped out. She heeled when commanded, then whined and sat down.

"That's strange. She hasn't even been given a command and she's already hitting on a scent," said the handler. He commanded the dog to find, and Shasha walked 12 feet and sat down beside a sedan.

The police convened on the car and that's when they smelled that odor every police officer, doctor, nurse, fire fighter and paramedic knew. The smell of rotting, decaying flesh is easy to remember, hard to forget. The police pried open the trunk and found the off-duty police officer's body stuffed around the spare tire. People said afterwards, it was the biggest funeral the city had seen since Mohammed Ali passed away. More than 3,500 police officers from around the country attended the funeral. It was broadcast live on all the local television stations and simulcast on the radio stations. The entire city would stop for a full day in remembrance.

Tanner, Kowalski and Jake got back into Tanner's car, and drove back to the police sub-station. It was getting dark and none of them had slept much in the last 96 hours. Jake found a chair and slumped down. He was asleep in about one minute.

Tanner and Kowalski walked back into the squad area, where an officer handed Tanner a black band to put over his badge. Tanner slid the band across his badge and patted it to make sure it stayed in place.

"I've had to do this too many times," he said.

Kowalski nodded. He didn't have to say anything.

The two sat and talked to the Louisville Police officers in the squad room. The officers told them they had found another body, this one pulled from the Ohio River. The body had been identified as a security guard with the hospital, who had been missing for a couple of days. They explained how the workers from *The Bell of Louisville* had pulled the body up from the river.

Tanner shook his head. "All of these have to be interconnected. I've not seen this many dead bodies since two women killed five people in one night in Lexington. Turner referred to Tina Marie Hickey Powell and LaFonda Fey Foster, who had been found guilty of killing five homeless people in one night in Lexington, Kentucky. Tanner had just started with the State Police and was assigned to the Frankfort Post as a new officer. His investigation along with that of the Lexington Police had helped to break the case and convict the two women to death. Their sentences had been overturned and they got life in prison, but that seemed like so many years ago to Tanner.

Jake's chair shook as Kowalski kicked one of the legs. He opened his eyelids and looked at Kowalski through two slits.

"Wake up, Jake. We're heading back to the jail in Frankfort."

"I told you I was not responsible for any of these things that happened. I'm not going back to jail."

"You're not going back to jail, but I would think you'd like to get your possessions back. Your wallet, your car keys?"

Jake nodded and stood. He stretched his arms and legs to get circulation back as he slept with his legs under his seat and his arms folded across his chest. He always slept like this when in a chair, as his long legs and arms tended to get in everyone else's way.

"I need some food, first. I've got to eat. And there's still that big guy out there. He's not going to quit."

"He's not your worry anymore. We're sending you on your way. Should have done that two days ago. You don't need to be here, fighting our fight. We've got the whole Louisville Police Department and The Kentucky State Police who are gonna take this guy down, as soon as we find him."

"Figure on at least two more, maybe three more. No one works alone, especially this guy."

The three of them headed out to Tanner's vehicle. They got in and Tanner started it up. He noticed he was low on fuel, so he headed to a gas station that took state credit cards. He stepped out and began fueling the SUV. He didn't notice a semi-truck pull past and head towards Jewish Hospital.

The big Russian pulled the truck on to a side street one block from the hospital. There were several trucks parked there, so he pulled in behind the last one. He and the other two got out and walked among the trucks, making sure there were no parking permit tags on the windows, the dash or the sides of the trucks. There were none. The three pulled the pin on the trailer, dropped the steady wheels, and pulled the truck forward.

"Now we have transport, no?" said the big Russian. The three got back into the truck and pulled away, but not before the Russian unscrewed a license plate off the back of another truck and attached it to the back of their stolen rig. Invisible again.

Jake rode in the back of Tanner's vehicle on the way to Frankfort. There was no hurry to get there and the conversation in the front was muted, so Jake watched the scenery but mostly slept. They pulled into the sally port and Tanner used the radio in his SUV to call for the door to be opened. The roll door moved up on its tracks and Tanner pulled his vehicle inside. The door closed behind them and the three got out and waited to be buzzed in through the jail entrance door.

The Indiana State Police finished working the scene of the shooting, had called the coroner, and had pulled up the police tape they had stretched across part of the parking lot. The police officers had their personal cameras on, so they had recorded the shooting and the service station had cameras positioned all over the parking lot up to and including the entrance to the station, so it had also recorded the event.

The Indiana Police Department had already reviewed the videos of the police officers and had asked their attorney to subpoena the video for their records. The police ran a check on the dead man's fingerprints, but they did not come up in the database. Since the man had no identification papers on him, they also requested the FBI and Interpol to lend help in finding out who the guy was and what he was doing in Indiana.

Sixty-eight miles away, in Frankfort, Kentucky, Jake was about to get his life back. The jailer Kowalski had conked out was off until late in the evening, and both Kowalski and Jake figured it would be better if there was no face-to-face with him right now. The assistant jailer processed Jake, which was really hard, since there were no records to help, in fact they had not even taken his picture when he first arrived, which breeched protocol, but this was completely different in all aspects.

Jake got his wallet, his keys, and his clothing, which he had signed for when first taken to jail almost a week ago. He pulled some money from his wallet and handed it to Kowalski.

"That's for the clothes you bought me, remember?"

"No, I'd completely forgotten. Thanks," said Kowalski.

"Thanks for getting me out of this mess. I'd probably still be here if it wasn't for you and Tanner."

"Wasn't me," said Tanner. "I'd have let the chips fall, were it up to me, but I'm also not retiring in just a few days."

"Well, I'm glad that didn't happen. I'm ready to head out to California tonight, if I can get back to Shelbyville to get my car."

"…Ski here can take you back. He's off work, so he has the time to run errands. Me, I have a department to run. Someone will lend him a vehicle, so he can get you back to Shelbyville to get your car." With that, Tanner nodded both to Jake and to Kowalski, and walked to the exit, calling for the door to be opened on his personal radio. Jake heard a buzz and watched Tanner pass through the door and then heard it slam shut.

The big man drove the truck to a small, out-of-the-way eatery on the east side of Louisville, away from Jewish Hospital.

"We need food, *da?*" he asked the other two. They nodded and climbed out of the truck and headed into a Mexican food restaurant.

They went inside, were seated, and ordered food.

"You carried out mission well," said the big Russian. "You killed two of four. Our job to take out other two. You two can then go back to St. Petersburg, *xopowo*? Hurry, okay?"

One of the men cocked his head. "We have killed no one except the man by the car."

The big Russian shook his head slightly. "I thought you went to the peoples' houses and killed them, no?"

"They were already dead when we got there."

They ate mostly in silence, as they worried someone might pick up on their accents.

Jake sat quietly in the right seat of the borrowed car, as it headed back to Shelbyville. Kowalski talked about a few things, mostly cop stuff Jake didn't understand, but he nodded as if he knew what Kowalski meant.

They pulled up to the driveway of the diner in Shelbyville, where Jake's car still sat half-in, half-out of its parking space. The police tape around his vehicle was gone, but orange cones marked the four corners of the vehicle. It put a 'do not touch' vibe around Jake's car. Kowalski got out and picked up the cones, put them in the trunk, then got back into the borrowed squad car.

Jake turned and held out his hand to Kowalski. "I'd like to thank you for getting me out. I'd like to thank you, but I'm not going to. Let's just shake hands and I'll be on my way," he said.

Kowalski pushed his hand into Jake's. They shook for a second, then Jake slid out of the seat. Kowalski pulled away as Jake walked up to his vehicle.

The waitress brought the three Russians their check and laid it on the table. She had drawn a smiley face at the top of the receipt. She had been told it brings a better tip, and she had included her name, Tiffany, on the top as well. Classes she took had told her the personal touch is what brings bigger tips.

The big man nodded and picked up the black guest check presenter. The bill came to $34.89. The Russian pulled out two twenties and put them into the black folder. He held up the check presenter for Tiffany to see, but she had gone to wait on another table.

Just then, they saw a police car pull into the parking lot. An officer got out and headed inside, with his wife and their two kids.

"Best we go now," said the big Russian. "Go out the side exit."

The three stood and headed away from the officer and his family. They opened the side exit and walked towards the truck. Tiffany watched them go from the front window. As the officer and his family walked up to the check-in podium, Tiffany waved him over.

"See those three right there, officer? That great, big guy? Well, my boyfriend's a clerk with the Louisville Police Department, and he said there were some Russian guys around. And those guys were speaking Russian. I took a year of it in college. We're taught here at the restaurant to pick up on little hints, like if a child has been kidnapped and such, ya know? So, I just was thinking, this might be the guys who were doing the bad things here. Can you call it in or whatever?"

The officer, Milton Valder, looked out the window but didn't see anyone. "What did they look like?"

The waitress described the three men as best as she could, taking special account of the big man in the overcoat, favoring his right arm.

The officer turned and looked out to the parking lot but saw no one. His view of the road was partially obscured by a truck without a trailer driving past. He didn't see the men, but he pulled out his cell phone and called the shift supervisor.

Jake sat in his car for a long moment, then began putting things back in the glove compartment. It had been stripped by the forensics team, looking for clues of what had happened when Larson was shot. He had almost got everything back in place, when there was a loud knock on his driver's side window. He literally jumped, then turned his head. He saw Kowalski's waist. Jake rolled down the window.

"We just got a clue about some Russians leaving a restaurant on the east side of Louisville. Wanna see the end of this?"

Jake nodded, held up his index finger, indicating one moment, started his car and pulled it back into the space he had vacated so many nights before. He turned off the engine, pocketed the keys, and climbed out of the vehicle.

The Russians headed back towards Jewish Hospital, where the trailer was parked. It was dark outside. They pulled in, then backed up, almost touching the trailer, but not quite. If they had to move fast, they didn't want to be tied to a box. The truck itself would be easier to dump than a whole truck/trailer combination.

The big man shut the truck down, but not before looking at the fuel gauge. It read ¾ full. They could still drive to another city and catch a flight to Europe and then make their way back to Mother Russia. There were no pictures of them, and the Russian entities who were in the know of their work in the United States had scrubbed them from all databases, so Interpol could not pull up their pictures.

Jake and Kowalski rode in silence back to Louisville. They turned off at the 264 Waterson Expressway exit and headed north towards the Mexican food restaurant.

They pulled into the parking lot where three police cars now sat, including Officer Valder's squad car. Kowalski parked next to Valder's vehicle and left the motor running. He and Jake stepped out and walked up the officers standing outside the restaurant.

"May I help you?" asked one officer. Kowalski pulled out his badge, complete with the black band across the number.

"Sergeant Kowalski, State Police. This is my partner, Jake Thompson. What's going on? Any word on those Russians?"

The officer shook his head. "We have a description of the men, mostly, but the best we have is of a big guy, maybe 275 -280 pounds, wearing an overcoat and a hurt right arm."

"Three hundred, more like it," said Jake. "The big guy. Three hundred pounds, at least. After a meal here, I'd say he'd go 315, if he had bottom-less chips."

"We're waiting to see if they have anything on their cameras, but I'm looking for any other businesses that might also have a video of them leaving. We need to see what they're driving."

The Indiana State Police were at a rest stop 64 miles west of Louisville, interviewing a truck driver who had his rig stolen.

"Jerks came in while I was takin' a shower. Stole my keys an' my wallet. Never saw them."

The Indiana State Police filled out their paperwork and then had the rig operator fill out a complaint, describing the rig, the license plate and any marks on the truck. The rig operator finished writing and gave the paperwork back to the police officers.

"I hope you get the guy who did this," he said. "That rig cost me $400,000 dollars and I'm an owner/operator. That's my home." His voice creaked, and a tear came to his eye. "Please, I hope you can get it back."

"We'll do our best," one officer said. "This information will help."

They turned and went back out to their cars. One officer typed in the vehicle information on his MDT and asked for a BOLO for the truck and trailer. Then they pulled out of the lot and went back on patrol.

The big Russian sat in the driver's seat. He talked to the other two, giving them directions to the 6th floor. He emphasized the importance of killing the other two.

"Make sure they are dead. I saw them both in the room. *Yben nx!* Kill them!"

The two got out of the truck and headed towards the main entrance of the hospital. The big man watched them go, then climbed into the bed in the back of the truck. He was asleep in minutes.

One of the Russians looked at the other. "*Na kokam ethaze on skazal?* What floor did he say?"

"*Ne bespokoyites. My nadem ikh.* Don't worry. We'll find them."

The only camera working in the area of the Mexican food restaurant had a view down the street, not of the restaurant. It showed five vehicles leaving the restaurant at about the same time. The police asked for a copy of the video to take to their video experts back at the forensics department. In 15 minutes, they had a flash drive loaded with the five vehicles. It took 15 minutes because no one could find a flash drive at the car dealership. One mechanic finally found a GM flash drive that had some truck parts loaded on it and gave it to management to use. The police officer put the drive into his pocket, got into his vehicle, and drove downtown to headquarters.

Jake and Kowalski got back into the borrowed vehicle and headed to Louisville Metro Police Headquarters. The main station was located on Jefferson Street, near the Ohio River. Kowalski wanted to see the video and if the Russians were driving one of the five vehicles the camera had captured.

They pulled up and Kowalski parked in a spot for 'Police Only'. He and Jake stepped out of the vehicle and walked into the main entrance. A woman with a headset on was seated behind bulletproof glass, talking into the microphone. She stopped, looked up and saw Kowalski, and a slow grin passed across her face.

She hit the voice box so someone on the other side of the glass could hear. "...Ski, you son of a buck! How many years has it been? Last time I saw you was in Frankfort! My, my, my, you've put on some weight! Look at that belly. Looks like you havin' a baby!" She rolled back in her chair, took off her headset, and walked around the corner, opening the door. She reached out and gave Kowalski a long hug, then punched him lightly in the stomach.

"You look like a prizefighter what ate too many fish samwiches! How you been, buddy?"

"Well, Doris. You look great yourself. Not a day over 75 years old, and not a pound over 800."

Doris turned sideways, rubbing her hand over her stomach and cocked her head at Kowalski.

"I'm not a pound over 180, and my last birthday cake had 52 candles on it, you old coot. Say, when you gonna retire?"

"Well, I have 28 years in, but I'm turning my paperwork in next week, so it looks like I can go anytime." His face turned from a broad grin to a stern look. "My partner here is Jake Thompson, he's from the military and helping me on a case. We're looking into those Russians, who we think killed about four or five people. Louisville Metro brought in a flash drive, and we want to see if they can pull anything off, license plate, marks on the vehicle, whatever. Can you direct us to the forensics office here?"

"Sure thing, honey. Let me get you some badges, so they won't bother you." She turned, nodded to another worker behind the glass, and the door buzzed. She crooked her head in indication for Kowalski and Jake to follow her through the door.

Once on the other side, she had both sign in on a visitor's register and gave them clip-on passes.

"This pass allows you access anywhere in the building, hon. But, let me get someone to take you there, so's you don't get lost. Hate to have to come find you, an hour after lunch, and you ready to shoot yourself cause you's so hungry." She tossed her head and laughed out loud, then grabbed her headset and pressed a button. She spoke into the mic, and in about a minute, a recruit opened another door and motioned that the two should follow him.

They passed through the door, down a hallway, and into an elevator. The lift took them up three floors. The recruit held out his arm indicating they should step off the elevator. The three walked down another long hall, turned right, and through another door. This door was marked 'Louisville Forensics. Absolutely no one admitted without prior authorization'.

The recruit led them past a couple of tables, into a dark room filled with computers. A technician was bent over an editing system, and he was shuttling a video back and forth. The video showed five vehicles, four cars and a truck, leaving from the area of the restaurant. The technician kept shuttling the video, then stopped on each vehicle when the light and angle were the best, and captured the license plates by hitting a store button on a computer.

The tech turned and looked at the three.

"Can I help you?"

"Sergeant Kowalski, State Police." He held out his badge. "This is my partner, Jake Thompson, from the military. We need to see what you have on those vehicles from that Mexican food restaurant."

"I'm pulling them up now. What we can't do is what they show on TV. A long distance shot that's blurry and when they zoom in, it suddenly becomes clear. We actually have to do some detective work to see if we can decipher the letters and numbers on the plates. I've got a computer that can fill in that information. It recognizes patterns and tries different sequences, and then fills those in and gives us several different choices. So, it's not perfect, but it sure cuts down legwork and guesswork."

The technician hit a button and three sheets of paper ran through a printer. Of the five vehicles caught by the camera, there were 38 choices of license plates.

"I'll go have one of our new people run these through the National Database. The National Crime Information Center, has all of the license plates loaded, and so, it only takes a few minutes to search all of this information. Follow me." He stood and turned away from the bank of computers and video monitors.

Kowalski turned to Jake. "That's the NCIC. It's a data base that has all vehicle license plates loaded on it. Like when you get stopped on the highway, the officer can run your plate through this." Jake nodded his head.

The two Russians walked to the front of Jewish Hospital's general entrance. The same lady was there who had talked to the big man two days earlier. They asked for a man who had had a heart attack and had been brought in by ambulance. Again, the lady asked if they had a last name. The two shook their heads, but they were having trouble understanding her, so they made up a name.

"I tink name is Grover Cleveland," said one of the two Russians. The clerk looked at the register and shook her head.

"No Cleveland here at this hospital. Could be at Norton across the street." She turned towards the next person in line.

The two Russians moved past and headed towards the elevators. They hit the 'Up' button and waited. The hospital was full of visitors, so it took a while for the doors to open. The men, along with several other visitors, doctors, nurses and techs, stepped inside. One of the Russians hit floor two by mistake. The doors closed and then opened again. The two men stepped outside. They were on a surgery floor. The doors had closed by the time they could read and understand the descriptors on the wall. They turned and hit the 'Up' button and waited.

Kowalski, Jake and the two employees of Louisville Metro walked down a hall, through a stairwell door, and down a flight of steps. They entered a room with eight dispatchers at consoles, all wearing headsets, speaking to the police, fire department and EMS over radios. The tech walked up to the one who looked the least busy and asked her to run all the plates on the three pages. The dispatcher unplugged her headset, took the pages from the technician, and began entering the plates one by one.

Of the 38 plates, four had no match, meaning they had been junked, had not been renewed, or were incorrectly identified by the computer. Three more had moved out of state and had been transferred to the appropriate state licensing county. That left 31 plates.

It took about 20 minutes to run all the plates and identify the vehicle owners. Five vehicles had been positively identified. One was a worker at the Mexican food restaurant, heading home to rest on her split shift. One was an employee at the GM car lot. The third was an elderly woman in her 80s, who apparently took a wrong turn and was headed back out to the main street. The fourth and fifth vehicles held some hope. One was a large sedan, capable of holding three big people. The windows were darkened. The fifth belonged to a green truck, an over-the-road tractor built by Kenworth. But the plate didn't match the vehicle.

"Think that's the one?" asked Kowalski. "A plate that doesn't fit the vehicle. How many can there be like that?"

The dispatcher hit some keys on her keyboard. The computer whirred, and several windows popped up, which, in turn, opened more windows. Finally, one last window opened with a red flashing warning above the license plate number. The dispatcher turned to Kowalski and Jake. "That plate was reported stolen earlier today at a truck stop in Indiana. Possibly, that's the one you're looking for."

"Put that out as a BOLO. And make sure everyone knows the occupants are armed and extremely dangerous."

The Russians finally re-boarded the elevator that was headed up. It was crowded with three doctors in white lab coats, two nurses wearing scrub hats and two other visitors. One of the visitors was extremely tall. The other was shorter, a little rotund, and looked to be about 55. Or at least he seemed elderly. One of the Russians looked at the other.

He spoke in Russian. *"O Chem nas preduprezhdal nas tovarishch?* He the one our comrade warned us about?"

"Da, ya tak dumayu. Yes, I think so."

Both Russians pulled out their GSh-18 semi-automatic pistols. Starting from left to right and right to left, they deftly and quickly shot all the riders in the elevator. Each pistol held 18 rounds of ammunition. Each victim also received one shot to the head.

The elevator doors opened, and the two Russians exited as well as copious amounts of nitrocellulose gas that had been expended from the GSh-18 barrels along with the bullets. The doors to the elevator closed.

The Russians walked to the closest stairwell. They walked back down the steps to the lobby and out the front doors. Without stopping, they walked left and headed towards the parked truck.

Julius Frenquava, a security guard from Jamaica, was on duty in the hospital. It was his fifth hour into a 12-hour shift. It was Julius' job to float from the first floor to the top floor, just enough so staff could see him. He also had a set of keys, a radio, and a pouch for handcuffs. The hospital had never given him cuffs, but he was hoping, one day, to be able to acquire a set.

After midnight, only one set of elevators remained busy. Julius should have taken that set, just to be visible. However, he had decided a long time ago, invisibility was next to Godliness. So, he took the third set.

The doors opened to what looked like a scene from a Halloween murder movie. Julius' first thought was he was seeing things. He rubbed his eyes. Next, he pulled out his radio from its holder, and immediately dropped it. The radio bounced across the floor and into the elevator, right into the middle of the bodies.

Julius started coughing, and then threw up. He heaved up Subway, McDonald's and Five Guys. Everything he had eaten in that day came up. Julius turned and started running. And screaming. He screamed, 'I quit, I quit', in Patois, the second language of Jamaica. He ran to the stairwell and down the steps, ripping off his security belt and his badge. He ran through the now-empty lobby screaming, crying, wide-eyed and unintelligible. No one stopped the security guard because there was no one in the lobby.

Jake and Kowalski walked out the door of the Louisville Metro Police Station and towards Kowalski's borrowed vehicle. Jake slid into the passenger seat and Kowalski hefted himself into the driver's seat.

"My rump is tired of riding around in cars all day and night. Wish I had a vehicle I could stand in. Know what I mean?"

"I spent about 12 years standing up in Humvees. I never have enjoyed a seat so much."

Kowalski backed out and headed to an all-night diner in downtown Louisville, near Jewish hospital.

He pulled into a slot and put the borrowed vehicle into park. Jake and Kowalski stepped out of the vehicle and headed inside.

The Russians reached the stolen truck and knocked on the passenger door. It took the big Russian more than a minute to get out of bed, crawl from the back to the front, and open the door.

The Russian looked at the two men. They nodded their heads. "*Eto bulo zaversheno.* It has been completed."

"*Khorosho. Zalezay.* Good. Get in."

One man climbed into the passenger seat while the other walked around the front of the semi and pulled himself into the driver's seat by the steering wheel. He started the truck and moved forward. The big Russian lifted his hand.

"*Nam nuzhno poluchit' treler chtoby nomernoy skyrt nomernoy znak.* We need to get a trailer to hide the license plate."

The driver looked in the side view mirror at the trailer they had dropped, but the big Russian shook his head. The driver stepped on the gas and the truck pulled away from the curb.

Jake and Kowalski sat down in a booth at the back of the diner. They picked up menus and nodded to the server when she held up a carafe of coffee.

The server dropped off rolled cutlery and pulled out her pad after filling both coffee cups. Jake ordered bacon and eggs while Kowalski ordered grits, a waffle and sausage.

Jake took a long drink of coffee. It was hot, black and deep. He looked at Kowalski.

"How long am I going to have to stay here? I want to be on the road to California. My brother is expecting me to show up any day."

"You don't have a certain day you need to be in California?"

"It was supposed to be in two days from now, but nope. When I show up, I show up."

"Your tautology is showing," said Kowalski.

"Gee, you know the English language!" Jake moved back, as the server set food in front of both of them.

Jake and Kowalski ate in silence. Jake chased his scrambled eggs around the plate with a strip of bacon, while Kowalski ate the last of his grits. Kowalski looked up as he took a bite of sausage.

"I don't guess we need you around here much longer. We gotta get you to your vehicle and set you pointed west on I-64. Let's finish eating and I'll take you to Shelbyville. I've also got to get my car I left in Woodford county."

Jake nodded and motioned to the server for more coffee by holding up his cup. The server filled his cup and then dropped off their check. Kowalski picked up the check and waved it in front of Jake.

"State of Kentucky would like to feed you one last time," he said. "Let's finish and I'll drop you before I head home. I still have a report I have to write to make sense of all this. Can you—"

Kowalski's phone rang. He pulled it out of his pocket and pressed the answer button. He listened for a minute, nodded his head as if the person on the other end could see him nod, then hung up the phone.

"Well, I'm not heading to Frankfort and you're not heading west. At least not today."

Jake crooked his head.

"Multiple victims at Jewish Hospital. Security guard found them and then he left. Ran out of the hospital screaming. Police found him huddled in the parking garage, vomiting." He handed a state credit card to the server. "You mind hanging out with me for just a few more hours?"

"In for a penny, in for a pound." They drove back and picked up Kowalski's friend's car and headed to Louisville.

The hospital was on lockdown, and it took several minutes for Kowalski and Jake to navigate the halls and elevators. When they got to the floor, Kowalski walked over to the Louisville medical examiner. He was kneeling down over one of the bodies. Jake hung back.

"I know you've let others know what happened, but mind going over it one more time?" said Kowalski.

The medical examiner stood and took off his glasses.

"Mindless execution, all I can figure," said the examiner. "Looks from the shells to be a 9 mm. Lots of shells here, so at least two firing, or one guy with two guns."

"Anybody see what happened?" asked Kowalski.

"Haven't started to ask questions. Thought I'd leave that to the locals and state constabulary."

"Okay, I'll start."

Kowalski turned and started looking for people to question. Jake walked up and stood beside him.

The big Russian and his two men found a trailer parked by itself. It was unmarked and dirty. The perfect subterfuge for those wishing to stay under the radar. It only took five minutes to hook up to the trailer. They started driving towards Lexington and Interstate 75. Atlanta lay eight hours south. A couple of plane rides and they would be standing in St. Petersburg Square.

"How did you kill them?"

"They were in the elevator. The big man and the old man. Also, some doctors and nurses. We shot twice each, then head shots."

The big Russian nodded. "*YA by sdelal to zhe samoye.* I would have done the same."

Kowalski talked to several nurses who worked at the other end of the floor. None of them saw or heard anything. He turned and walked back to the elevator where the medical examiner had finished his preliminary investigation.

"This looks like a hit to me," said the examiner. "I've seen several of these this year, but always on the street. Never in a hospital."

Kowalski shrugged his shoulders.

"Maybe some foreign intervention?"

"What are you thinking?" asked the examiner.

"Just musing, is all," answered Kowalski.

The medical examiner motioned for the interns from the Coroner's office. They moved in and started placing bodies in black bags, then lifting them on to stretchers for transport to the Coroner's wagon.

"I'll get these bodies back to my office and start autopsies." He turned and moved out of the elevator towards the interns.

Kowalski nodded his head to Jake. Jake walked over to Kowalski.

"You thinkin' what I'm thinkin?" said Kowalski. "I think this was meant for you and me."

Jake bobbed his head up and down.

"I agree. A really big guy and a guy in his 50s, looks to me. I feel bad about this right now. All these dead because they probably think it was us. But I'm also really pissed off. This is more than personal. This is now a grudge match."

Jake walked over to where the interns were finishing loading the now-bagged bodies on to stretchers. Jake turned and walked back to the medical examiner.

"I got a question for you."

The examiner looked at Jake.

"And you are?"

"Just a fly in the ointment, a rusty chain," said Jake. "How do you think they were shot?"

"With guns, I guess," answered the medical examiner. "Not trying to be a smart aleck, but what's your point?"

"Can you tell me if they were shot by one person or by two? And how many bullets per person?

"I really can't tell you that until I get the bodies back to the office."

"It's important to tell me if they were shot two or more times each and if they had time to react. Did any of the victims have time to turn and try to get out of the path of the bullets?"

"I can tell you each body was shot at least two times and it looks like they were each shot in the face as a final *coup de grâce*. Whoever did this, didn't want anyone talking."

Kowalski walked up to Jake's side.

"Hey, doc, can we meet you at your office?"

"Sure. You know where it is. See you there."

The medical examiner walked on to another elevator, which had been turned back on by the maintenance staff.

Jake turned to Kowalski.

"Ski, I think this was a deliberate hit by the Russian. This goes way further than a gambling ring, if you ask me."

"That's funny, Jake."

"Why? You don't think it was deliberate?"

"No, I think it was very deliberate. I think it's funny you feel familiar enough with me to call me '...Ski.'"

The two walked to another elevator and hit the 'Down' button.

The Russians hit the Interstate 64/75 Interchange and turned south. Atlanta was six to eight hard driving hours ahead of them. Louisville was an hour behind to the west. The big Russian laid back down in the sleeper. It was just after midnight. He sat back up quickly.

"We need to change truck, one more time." The other two nodded. A sign for a truck stop was up ahead, on the southbound side of I-75. The driver took the exit and turned into the parking lot.

The Lexington Police Department had more than six hundred officers, each working an eight-hour shift. The most senior officers got the best slots available. Lieutenant Brad Barker had nineteen years with LPD. His plan was to go out at 25 years, after buying five ghost years, which would give him a total of 30 years of service. But retirement was still almost six years away. With his seniority, he could have taken a day shift, but he liked the solitude of the night. There was comfort knowing he had to handle situations by himself while also not having the brass breathing down his neck.

Barker sat at the on-ramp of the Athens-Boonsboro entrance road, watching for southbound speeders. It was 12:20 in the morning. The lieutenant had always had a sixth sense about things. He was never sure where it came from. Neither his mother nor his father had ever had that same feeling like he had when something was about to happen. Maybe it was a grandparent or a great-grand who had that feeling instilled in them. He tried not to think about it much, but sometimes it hit him hard. Like it did tonight. He just got a feeling.

There were always trucks moving up and down Interstate 75. It was the most heavily traveled road in the United States. If Barker sat and counted southbound trucks on his fingers and toes, he would run out in about 30 seconds.

A truck pulling a trailer passed the entrance ramp doing the speed limit, but the marker lights on the trailer were not on. This was a clear violation, and he would have notified the State Police, but Vehicle Traffic Enforcement only worked during the day. Lucky people, maybe. Maybe unlucky.

Barker turned on his headlights and pulled off the shoulder onto the entrance ramp. The truck was just passing over a small hill, so Barker hit the gas and topped the hill at about 90 miles an hour. There were several trucks ahead of him, but he quickly spotted the one without markers. He slowed down and glided in behind the truck and ran the trailer license plate. The two vehicles kept moving south. Barker waited as the NCIC whirled. NCIC came back with information that the trailer belonged to the Cotash Development Group out of Cedar Rapids, Iowa. Barker had never heard of that company, but with no running lights, the truck should have been stopped between Iowa and Kentucky at one of the many weigh stations.

Barker flipped on his lights and tapped his siren. The truck slowed and pulled off the interstate onto the shoulder of I-75 south.

Kowalski and Jake pulled into the lab in Louisville. It was attached to the Metro Police Department's building on West Jefferson St. Many bodies had moved through the metro building, living and deceased, civilian and civil servants, arrested and free.

Kowalski opened the door for Jake, and the two walked into the Louisville Metro Lab. Kowalski hit the 'Up' elevator button and they rode to the seventh floor.

Barker stepped out of his vehicle and walked up to the passenger side of the 18-wheeler. The passenger window rolled down. Barker stepped on to the hi-step, grabbed the bottom of the right mirror, and hefted himself up.

Kowalski and Jake walked into the Office of the Medical Examiner. Dr. Tracy sat at his desk, looking through some files. He looked up and saw the two enter. He pushed his papers aside.

"Hey, …Ski. This one puzzles me a lot. Not gang-related, nothing that screams a Chicago-style hit, nada."

Jake stepped up to the medical examiner's desk and peered at the papers.

"Any way to tell who the shooters were?"

"No, there's just no way to tell because there's no DNA evidence."

Jake shrugged. "I really think this might have been meant for Kowalski and me."

"What makes you say that?" asked Dr. Tracy.

"Just by looking at the bodies. There was one older, just about Kowalski's height, and a big guy, like me."

"But killing five other people just to take out two?"

Kowalski cleared his throat. "We think there's some Russian influence going on here. Not sure how, who or why, but we think the Russians have designated central Kentucky as a ground zero for some nefarious dealings."

Barker looked at the three men in the truck. There was a big guy in the middle and the driver and passenger were smaller. All looked nervous, but most drivers had that, 'what did I do now?' look when he stopped them, especially at night.

"Driver's license, proof of insurance and bill of lading, please."

The driver nodded and reached for his wallet while the passenger opened the glove box for the insurance card.

Jake and Kowalski left the office of Dr. Tracy and went back to a meeting room in the police department. Two other officers came in and asked both the men to take seats.

"What happened at the hospital?" asked Officer Johnson.

"Why are you asking us? We weren't there," said Jake.

"I know you weren't there. Why are you here, now?" said Johnson. "Why aren't you heading out west, to your brother's house in Los Angeles?"

"Every time I start to head out, something else hits the fan. I get caught up in it more and more. Like molasses, I'm stuck. And how did you know I was going to be headed out west?"

Johnson shook his head. He turned to Kowalski.

"This guy has got to go. He's not an officer and he doesn't belong in this fight."

"I know, I know," said Kowalski. "Three times I've started to take him back to his car, and something else happens. I don't have time to drop him off. So, he rides with me."

"That stops right now, …Ski. We don't need a citizen involved in a police matter."

Jake stood up. He reached over to where Johnson was standing. He held out his hand to the police officer. Johnson reached for it. As Johnson grasped Jake's hand, Jake pushed Johnson's arm down, spun the officer to the left, and wrapped his other arm around Johnson's neck. It all happened in less than a second. Johnson was helpless to do anything. The other officer tried to stand but Jake shook his head.

"Listen to me and listen good. I've been telling everyone for the last five days I had nothing to do with the officer's injuries at the roadside diner. I was put in jail and have dealt with some real Podunk deputies. One died while trying to set up a trap to kill Kowalski here. Kowalski's alive because he's smart and that other guy was stupid. I've had more people pull weapons on me here than all the time I was in the military. You put me in this position. Your police force is a bunch of jerks that think they know what they are doing."

Johnson tried to break Jake's hold, but Jake's grip was too tight. Johnson literally couldn't move. Jake continued.

"There's some really bad guys out there, that, I am sure by their actions, are Russians. At least two people have been killed by them and they have been trying to kill two others. Maybe those at the hospital were killed by them as well. They are possibly laying low somewhere in this area, but you're worried about my safety. My safety? No way. You don't want me here because you don't want to deal with the Russians. This is America. You don't kick someone out of your state because you're worried about their safety. That is anathema to your 'Serve and Protect' statement written on your cars." Jake squeezed Johnson's neck tighter. "Get this and get it good. I'll leave when I'm ready, not before." Jake released his hold on Johnson and shoved him towards the other officer.

Johnson bent over, took some deep breaths, and rubbed his neck. Kowalski stood and looked down at Johnson.

"Think you better make a friend of this guy instead of getting on his wrong side. I've found him to be most interesting. He's an asset to the State Police, and his knowledge of the Russians is better than any information your department or mine has available right now. But we're wasting time arguing about whether he leaves or not. We've got some bad guys out there that want their money back, and they're willing to kill for it. Shelbyville is not your worry, but it sure as hell is mine. Jake stays with me."

Kowalski turned and started walking towards the door. He turned and looked at Jake.

"Coming?"

Jake walked past Johnson, bumping shoulders with the officer. Jake stopped at the door.

"You have no idea what you're dealing with right now. But I do. I've studied the Russians for years. They'll send more to get their money. This mob is nothing like you've seen before. Death is commonplace for them. They're willing to take the life of those who owe them money. They kill, we arrest. Big difference. Learn it or you too can die, by their hands."

Jake walked through the door with Kowalski. They got into Kowalski's car.

"I think Johnson is right. You do need to head west. You've been here too long."

"I'm staying to make sure Lawrence and Luke survive. Let's head back to the hospital where Lawrence is."

Kowalski started the car and pulled out of the police lot. They drove in silence.

Barker handed the information back to the driver, whose name was Jones. He told Jones to stop at the next southbound truck stop and get the marker lights fixed. Barker wrote Jones a warning, which technically was not the best thing to do, but it was 12:45 in the morning and time for Barker's coffee break.

The big Russian and the other two sat in a new truck and trailer. The big Russian had moved out of the sleeper. Again, they had waited for a trucker at a truck stop on Interstate 75 south near Lexington to use the shower. They had to wait for about 20 minutes, but finally they saw a truck that would work. They quickly picked the lock on the locker he put his belongings in, took his keys and wallet, and walked out to where he had parked his truck.

They chose his truck because it was nondescript, like the other truck and trailer. No identifying marks. No name on the tractor, and this one also had a sleeper. One of the men stole a license plate off another truck and put it on the back of the trailer. He also changed the plate on the truck, which was a feat unto itself and required some skilled machinations to reach the screws with the trailer hooked to it. The big Russian crawled into the sleeper but did not lie down. He sat up because the truck was more uncomfortable than the last one. The license plate thief started the truck and pulled out of the truck stop, after making sure there was no tracking device in the cab.

Officer Barker had turned under the interstate and got back in the northbound lane. He headed towards the truck stop that was on the southbound side of I-75, what officers running traffic called doing the loop. As he pulled in, a nondescript truck pulled out in front of him. The truck failed to stop as it left the lot and moved on to the feeder road. The officer had to slam on his brakes. Barker shook his head. Truckers, he said, under his breath. He pulled into the truck stop, turned off his lights, thought about it again, then pulled out after the semi.

The big Russian turned to the driver.

"Did either of the losers say anything before they died? Did they beg for mercy?"

The driver looked at the passenger.

"We killed the big man and the fat, short one. We thought that was who we were supposed to kill."

"*Nyet!* No, no no! You were supposed to kill the two in the hospital! Now we have to go back and kill two more. We will need to buy stock in a bullet factory by the time we are finished in America!" The big Russian slammed his fist on the bed in the sleeper. The driver pulled the truck out of the parking lot and went under the freeway. He then headed north on I-75. They failed to stop at the stop sign before pulling out. Barker noticed, fell in behind, and turned under the freeway as well.

Jake and Kowalski walked out to ...Ski's car.

"Jake, what say we go to my friend's place and get my car back. I think Johnson is right. You should be headed out to California."

"No, the State Police got me involved in this and I'm going to see it through. More people are going to die if I don't help you with these Russian creeps."

They got into the car and Kowalski started the engine. Kowalski pointed the car east and they headed towards Frankfort.

The driver of the stolen truck looked in his side view mirror.

"We have company," he said. The Big Russian tried to adjust his head, so he could see out the side mirror, but it was a function in futility. Each time he got his head just about right, the truck bounced and moved his head. Trucks weren't meant for comfort, at least this stolen one wasn't.

"Keep your speed low, and don't run any red lights, *khorosho?*" The driver nodded and kept the truck moving towards downtown Lexington.

Officer Barker tried to move his vehicle beside the truck, but the truck's license plate was obscured by the following trailer. Barker thought about lighting up the truck, but it was coffee break-time, and the IHOP in Lexington was a probably a little slow, so he moved to the left lane, and kept pace with the truck.

Jake's head lolled back and forth as he fought sleep. He had been up, more or less, 20 hours a day since he was arrested a week ago. And the anxiety of knowing there were bad people out there made his sleep even more difficult.

Jake sat up suddenly. "We need to go to the hospital. Right now."

Kowalski turned sharply, as Jake sat up. "Why? You having chest pain?"

"No, I need to talk to Lawrence and Luke. There's something that's been bothering me, and I couldn't put my finger on it until now. If I'm right, we've been wrong all along, and this is deeper than any pit you thought about falling in."

Kowalski headed to an exit on I-64 and pulled under the overpass. It was about midnight.

The police car pulled past the Russians and sped ahead. The driver sighed noticeably. The big Russian shook his head and laughed. "Kill too many police officers and there's a special place in hell for you, comrade?" The big Russian continued to laugh. The driver laughed nervously, took an exit, and drove into Lexington.

"What are you thinking, Jake?" asked Kowalski.

"I'm thinking we've been sent on a wild goose chase, that's what. And if I'm right, then everything we've been looking at the whole time has been wrong."

"I don't get what you mean," said Kowalski.

"You go to a magic show, knowing magic is not real. Magicians can't really make things appear and disappear, although it seems they can, right? So, we get a story told to us about some kind of Russian gambling outfit that comes to Kentucky. Why here? Why not New York City or Los Angeles or Dallas or Chicago?"

"Cause we're not as smart here?"

"No. You're plenty smart, and I think I've led you and the State Police on a real Statue of Liberty play. If a magician wants you to believe in something, they have to use sleight of hand in order to fulfill that imagery. But, you have to accept the premise they can make something disappear when in reality you know they can't. Right? We know a magician has a hole in the hat on the table or is palming cards, but we accept the imagery that the illusion is real. We know mirages aren't real, but driving down the highway in the summer, with heat rising off the road, makes it look like it's raining ahead. This is what keeps people in the desert moving forward, because they believe something is there that isn't real, but they're thirsty enough to go ahead and disobey their brain because of the need to believe in something."

"Man, that was a long explanation for something you could probably have said in one sentence. How about the short version this time?"

"I can't make dollars appear from nowhere, right? Neither can the Russians make a gambling scam seem easy pickings unless they use imagery. Got it?"

Kowalski shook his head. "I don't understand any of what you just said. Maybe I'm too old to be using my head for anything more than a hat rack."

Kowalski turned the steering wheel and pulled his vehicle back onto I-64 West.

Officer Barker pulled into the IHOP on North New Circle Road and parked behind the building. Shirley was behind the counter. She was 74, flirty, and had the worst set of teeth he had ever seen. But, she kept the coffee hot and the strawberry crepes were to die for.

Barker sat at the edge of the counter, so he had a view of the room. No one could walk up behind him and he had a good defensive position, in case he needed it. The door to the kitchen was just behind him, and beyond that door and the cookstove was the back exit. Two ways in; two ways out. Good cop strategy.

Shirley filled his coffee mug with strong, black coffee.

"Crepes this morning, dear?"

"As always, my love!"

"Coming right up. HEY, WALTER, CREPES FOR A COP!" she shouted to the kitchen, as if the place were packed. It wasn't. The cook yawned, nodded and threw a pan on the stove.

Jake and Kowalski pulled into the hospital. Kowalski turned off the car.

"You're going to have to tell me what's happening before we go up and confront these guys. You think they are in on the scam?"

"Unfortunately, yes, and unfortunately, I think they've been scamming us for the past two days," said Jake. "We've been chasing rabbits, and Bugs Bunny is right in front of us."

They climbed out of the car and walked into the hospital.

Officer Barker used the 10 code on his portable to let dispatch know he was taking a break. The 10 code was not really authorized since 9/11, but local municipalities still used the codes unofficially. He told dispatch he was 10-5, meaning he was eating a midnight snack. 10-5 meant the same thing during the day, but those officers called it lunch. Shirley brought the strawberry crepes and set them down in front of Barker. She refilled his coffee cup from a carafe and turned away.

The truck pulled through town and stopped on the side of the road at an all-night diner. The three Russians got out and went inside. They found a table in the back and sat down. The waitress brought coffee for all three. The men ordered off the menu and began to talk amongst themselves.

Jake and Kowalski walked to the elevators. Kowalski pressed the button for the proper floor.

"I don't know, Jake. I'm just not sure about this. Could Lawrence and Luke really be smart enough to fool the Russians?"

"They don't need to fool the Russians... just us."

The elevator doors opened, and the two men stepped inside the car.

Sometimes, in the still of the night, voices can be heard. Words are not usually detected, but the staccato and speed of the diction can be interpreted. The English language has a distinct, smooth-flowing meter. The more crowded a room, the harder it is to hear fully what others are saying. Shooting guns on a regular basis, even with hearing protection, can also cause a loss of audible function. The language has to be so different, so confounding, that the brain, even when not consciously working, can decipher the grunts and guttural complications of said language.

It was after the fourth bite of strawberry crepes that Barker detected a foreign language he knew was Russian. He picked up his coffee and sipped to the low, growling sounds of the three men in the room. He slipped a cell phone from his pocket and dialed a number.

Jake and Kowalski hit the button for the 8th floor and rode up in silence. The doors opened and they walked down the hallway. They entered the room where Lawrence was bedded. Only the bed was empty. No sheets on the bed, no heart monitor in the room, no wires, no pole with an infusion set up, no beeps, no nothing. It was as if Lawrence had never been in the room.

Kowalski turned and walked out of the room. He stopped at the nurse's station.

"Kowalski, State Police, where's Lawrence Douglas, the guy who had a heart attack?"

"Checked out this evening. No heart attack. All clear. That's all I can tell you. Sorry."

Kowalski turned and walked back into the room where Jake was still standing.

"What in the hell?" said Kowalski. "How did you know?"

"Intuition, detective work, and a whole lot of luck," said Jake. "Think back to what they told us. When they identified me as the BIG GUY who was looking for them, how did they know? How did they know who was coming for them? They were playing Russian poker electronically. Every one of those machines has safeguards. Ever read about those who supposedly won some money and then the computer kicks in and they didn't win at all? The computer programs are written and re-written so the game manufacturers don't lose money. And if they did lose, whose fault is it? Would Russia really send someone here to kill four people who mysteriously won and then lost some money? It's probably cost whoever sets this game up more than a million to put these Russians here. No, we've been played like flutes, you and me. And it took us running all over Kentucky for me to figure that out."

Jake turned and walked out of the room. Kowalski started walking behind him, then stopped.

"Wait, why then did those Russians kill two Shelby county men and threaten two others? And those two knew they were being threatened, as well. There's something so much deeper here, I just don't know." Kowalski shrugged his shoulders to emphasize his opinion.

"What's here in Kentucky? Manufacturing wise?"

"Bourbon. They make Bourbon here," said Kowalski. "And horses. They race horses here and in Lexington."

"No, deeper."

"They have vehicle assembly plants in Georgetown and here in Louisville."

"Think illegal."

Kowalski rubbed his chin. "Counterfeiting? Illegal alcohol? I don't know."

"Think about drugs. What has been happening in the drug market? Pills, heroin, fentanyl—what do those and these four have in common? Any ideas?"

Kowalski shook his head. "I am at a loss."

"Douglas came in with what appeared to be a heart attack, right? And now he's gone, no heart attack, right? What mimics a heart attack?"

"Drugs can do that."

"Right. So, either Lawrence Douglas is a member of some big drug ring in central Kentucky, or someone gave him some really bad stuff when he is used to the tame stuff. Any ideas?"

"We have drugs coming in from north, south, east and west. Interstates 64 and 75 intersect in Lexington. Pills come from down south in Florida, meth comes from the west, middle part of the country. Fentanyl comes from the north and heroin comes from the east.

Interstate 75 was the funnel for pills from the south, mixes of different kinds. We called it Hillbilly Heroin, whatever it was. It's gone out of favor now. Ebbs, flows, then ebbs again. Like different restaurants. People go to them like crazy, then the restaurant loses favor for some other eatery. Don't know why."

The two walked back to the elevators. Jake hit the 'Down' button.

"I'm going out on a limb here. I think the Russians are here because of some big drug deal. That's in the hundreds of millions of dollars. I think our four from the diner on I-64 are way in deeper than even we know. You got any contacts with the drug enforcement entity?"

"You mean the DEA? Yeah, I do, but it's too late to call about it now. I'll have to ring them up tomorrow. And you don't need to be here anymore, if you want to hit the road."

"They put me in jail, I figured this all wrong, four people in jail are dead because I figured this wrong. Two of those four at the eatery are dead, because I figured this wrong. And their families. Seven people in the hospital are dead because I figured this wrong. I want to see this big Russian dead. And whoever is riding around with him. And they're going to stay until they can get their drugs—or whatever it is they are doing—running again."

The elevator doors opened and the two stepped inside.

Barker spoke into the phone in muffled tones. He pushed his strawberry crepes from in front of him and walked back to the kitchen.

He nodded to Shirley. She stepped up to him.

"You and the cook head out back. Get in your cars and drive away from here. Go two or three blocks away. I'll come looking for you. Just get low, real fast, okay?"

"Shirley opened her mouth to say something, but Barker put his finger to his lips, then pushed Shirley back. "NOW," he grimaced through clinched teeth.

Shirley motioned to the cook and they headed out the backdoor, got into their cars, and pulled away. Barker stood looking through the kitchen serving window at the three men. He kept his radio low and turned his ringer off.

The elevator doors opened, and Jake and Kowalski stepped out. Waiting to get on to the elevator was Johnson from the Louisville Police Department. The two nodded to each other, but as the doors began to close, Jake stepped back to the elevator and put his hand in between the doors.

The doors stopped closing and opened back up. Jake stepped back inside so he was in the middle of the door path and stood in front of Johnson.

"Why the sudden rush to get rid of me, Johnson?" asked Jake.

Officer Johnson started to say something, but Jake cut him off.

"I'm talking to Kowalski here, and suddenly, I think this is not a gambling ring at all. I think this is a drug ring and it's not just four guys from Shelby county that are involved.

"I asked myself while I was talking to Kowalski how these four could get so far without anyone being the wiser, and I think I know now. I think there's local police involved in the drug running, like in the 1980s in Florida. You got any clue what I'm talking about, Johnson?"

Officer Johnson shook his head. "You are definitely barking up the wrong tree here, mister. I lost a brother to drugs three years ago. I take umbrage at what you're saying to me. I think you'd better do what I said earlier, and head out of town. Go visit your brother, before it's too late."

Johnson pressed the door close button while Jake still stood inside the elevator car. Jake stared at Johnson for another second, then stepped back. As the doors closed, he again stuck his hand in, caught the door and shoved them back.

"What are you doing here tonight, Johnson? Why are you here? In this hospital. Same one Douglas is in. Or used to be in. Any ideas you can pass to me?"

Kowalski caught Jake's arm and pulled him back.

"Let him go up, Jake. Let's go get some coffee."

Kowalski turned and walked away. Jake stared at the elevator doors as they closed. He then turned and followed Kowalski out of the hospital and to Kowalski's friend's vehicle.

They sat down in the car and Jake shook his head.

"I'm still not sure what in the heck is going on around here. First gambling, then drugs, but I still think I'm way off."

"Well, I can't think without coffee. Let's go to the late-night diner and have them give us an urn. At least one. Maybe two."

"You had me at one," said Jake.

Kowalski started the vehicle. Jake continued to fidget in the front seat. Kowalski looked at Jake.

"Look, man, I think I need to go up the ladder a few rungs if this is drug-related. Let's get something to eat as well, then we'll find a place to sleep for a little bit. Sound okay?"

"Yeah, but I need to find out where Lawrence and Luke went. And why no notice from the Louisville Police? You saw no uniforms sitting outside. They disappeared as well. This is just getting deeper and deeper."

"Alright, we get some grub, rest up some, then I'll help you find out what weirdness is going on, okay?"

Jake nodded, and Kowalski pulled out of the parking space.

Barker continued to watch the three men from the kitchen. Something just didn't ring right in his head. He'd contacted his captain and told her of his suspicions. She told him to wait and watch. One minute later, Barker was in the fight of his life.

Kowalski pulled into the diner closest to Jewish Hospital. It was the same diner where Jake had fed the young would-be robber, Sparky, two days earlier. Jake closed the car door and looked over the top of the vehicle.

"I am rethinking my idea of drugs. I just don't think Russia is the kingpin in this case. Too much comes from China, Afghanistan, Pakistan and Mexico. Russia is a late player."

"My drug of choice is coffee. Let's get some."

The two men walked into the diner. They sat down in a back-corner booth. Jake had to stretch his legs under the bench seat where Kowalski was sitting. He turned sideways and rested his upper body against the side wall of the diner.

Kowalski picked up a cup and waved it to a server nearby. Both cups were quickly filled.

"I thought you were sold out on the drug idea. What changed?"

"Johnson changed my mind. Let me digress. When I was in the military, we had a problem with some of our soldiers using drugs in the field. Officers sometimes covered for them. It was accepted as the norm. The ends justified the means. Life was hard, so drug use was accepted. It was worse in Vietnam.

"But, somewhere along the way, the government stepped up and started testing soldiers. I noticed a look among those who used. You know what they call the 1,000-yard stare? Soldiers who had been in war got it. We know it now as Post Traumatic Stress Disorder or PTSD. The look stays with them even after they leave the battlefield. It's always there. Maybe not visible to the non-military, but I see it. Johnson didn't have it. That is, if he were a drug user, he would have it, but he said his brother died of an overdose."

Kowalski took a long draw on his cup. "What else could it be? Not alcohol, gambling, or drugs. What else is there?"

"I can't think right now. I need sleep. Let's eat and then catch some zzzzs."

They ordered and continued to talk and drink coffee.

Barker turned and looked out the backdoor to see if his lieutenant was coming through the kitchen. He turned and looked down the barrel of a 9mm SPS, the choice of weapon by the Russian KGB. It had a 4.7-inch barrel and fired at a rate of 40 rounds per minute. It carried armor piercing bullets that could fly through 32 Kevlar plates. It had an effective range of 218 meters. It was six inches from Barker's face.

"Comrade, keep your hands in view. My friend here is really, how you say, nervous?" He waved the gun in front of Barker. "Slowly, pull your gun out of the holster and give it to me."

Barker's mind thought for a millisecond. Years of training came down to one move. When a semi-automatic pistol is discharged, the barrel of the pistol reacts to the concussion. A left-handed shooter will notice the pistol pulls to the left, a right-handed shooter pulls opposite. The man holding the SPS 9mm was right-handed, and it seemed his right arm was somehow disabled, meaning the pistol reaction would be greater.

Jake and Kowalski's food came and they began to eat. Jake stirred his eggs under his bacon and used his toast as a bulldozer, pushing the eggs onto his fork. As he lifted the fork to his mouth, he saw the server coming towards their booth. She had a cell phone to her ear.

As she stepped up to the booth to refill their coffee, she said good-bye and slipped the phone into her pocket.

"Sorry, guys, problems at home, ya know?" She poured coffee into the nearly empty cups and stood back.

"All good? Need anything else?"

"Yeah, Doris, what's going on?"

"Oh, the usual. Drama at home. This is the only place I can go to, where I make the drama. The rest of my family takes over at the house. Four kids, a lazy husband and a sick dog. That's my life, ya know."

Kowalski laughed. He knew Doris' husband. He worked 80 hours a week at a big box store as a manager. Doris only worked so she could get out of the house. Her kids were nearly grown.

Jake sat up. He took a draw on his coffee.

"Doris, right?" he asked. She nodded. "How many kids?" Doris held up four fingers. "All good?" She nodded. "Great. Always good to hear that a happy family is at home."

"Happy? Ha! They all think they should be doctors and lawyers. They don't apply themselves at all. They sit at home and watch Jerry Springer."

"Doris, if one of your kids went missing, would you look for them?"

"Are you serious? Of course, I would. Now, I always told them when they were young that I could have more if they went missing, but my kids... No way. Hell and heaven would be moved so I could find them. They all have phones and they keep in touch with me and their dad."

"Have any of your kids ever gone missing? Stayed out too late?"

"Sure. What kid doesn't? Why?"

"Not sure. Just asking."

"Well, you need more coffee or more sleep, one."

"That's for sure. Just keep the java coming, will ya, Doris?"

"That's me. All walk and no talk." She turned and sashayed away.

Officer Barker knew his life hung in the balance. He looked past the end of the gun at the face of a huge man. He was 325 pounds, at least, but he was favoring his right arm. As if the arm were hurt. He looked past the big man, which was hard to do, because he was so big, and he saw the other two standing behind the big guy.

"You need to put that away and put your hands up. You're under arrest."

The big man laughed. "Arrest?" He turned to the other two. *"Arestovyvat! On govorit, chtoby podnyat ruki.* He says to put your hands up."

The two men stood still. As the big man turned back to Barker, the officer's training took over. Knowing a pulled trigger from the right hand would mean a kick to the right, the pistol would move to his left, as he looked at it. Barker dove right, pulling his service weapon as the big man's SPS barked flame.

The bullet grazed Barker's left ear. Barker landed on his right, his semi-auto in his right hand, and he began squeezing the trigger. Fifteen rounds spit out the end, mostly hitting the ceiling and the counter above his prone body.

The big man tried to lean forward, but Barker's bullet fusillade as well as his sore right arm prevented the Russian from hitting Barker. The three men turned and exited the front door and headed to the truck.

"What was that about, asking if Doris would go looking for her kids?" Kowalski asked. Jake shrugged. The cop added, "You indicated she probably didn't care about her offspring, you know that, right?"

Jake shook his head. "I think anyone would go looking for a family member or friend. That's what we do. We had a couple of guys get lost in Afghanistan. We turned over every rock looking for them. Who wouldn't do that for a member of their family?"

"Yeah, so why those questions?"

"I'm not sure. Just testing out other ideas."

"On Doris? She'll gut you with a steak knife, Jake." Jake grinned.

"I guess I'm sleepy. Food in my stomach. Let's find a place to sleep."

The two drained their cups, left money for their meal, and headed towards the exit.

Barker held his ear while he reloaded his Glock, which was no easy task. It took placing the service semi-auto in his left hand, lolling his head to the left so his ear touched his left shoulder, staunching the bleeding, reaching into his belt for another magazine, keying the mag lock to drop the empty, and shoving the new mag into his weapon. It took all of about 2.5 seconds, but he feared for what was on the other side of the wall.

Barker reached for his mic. In the melee, it had fallen to the ground, and he was lying on top of it. Barker moved to his right and then to his left, as he pulled on the mic cord. The microphone popped out from underneath him and slid across the floor. The officer pulled the cord and the mic homed in towards his right hand. Barker switched hands, moving his weapon to his right hand while picking up the mic with his left.

"Shots fired, shots fired!" he called into the mic. "Officer hit! Three men. One of them a really big guy. Armed and dangerous. I'm at the diner on North New Circle Road. I need backup and an ambulance, fast!"

Jake and Kowalski left the diner and walked to the car Kowalski had been driving. Jake stood at the passenger door as Kowalski moved to open the driver's door. An SUV pulled out of a parking stall near them and rolled towards the exit. The lot was busy with three or four other cars moving in and out.

"That was good, sir. Now I'd like to get some sleep, if I could."

Kowalski nodded. "I'm good to just pile into the vehicle and snooze. Not too hot nor too cold tonight. Could get three or four hours before sunup."

Jake nodded and moved towards the back-passenger door, just as the front passenger door glass shattered.

Jake dropped to his knees, looked around, knelt under the vehicle so he could see if Kowalski had seen or heard anything, and saw the officer lying face down on the pavement.

Jake raised his head up slightly, then quickly ducked again, as two more shots rang out. They were sitting ducks in the parking lot and Jake couldn't return fire.

"Kowalski!" Jake whispered. No answer. Jake ducked down low again, but this time Kowalski was gone. Jake shook his head, then raised up again. More cars moving around in the lot, but no more shots fired.

"Kowalski! Are you hit? Are you okay?" No answer.

Barker headed out the backdoor, pistol in his right hand, mic in his left. He leaned out the window, looking left and right, then stepped out. He heard sirens in the distance. Nothing moved but two trucks, one a food delivery truck, the other a big, non-descript 18-wheeler. Barker turned around and assessed his situation in the restaurant. No one was at any booth or table, no one in the kitchen, no one in the restrooms. He was in the building by himself. He walked through the kitchen and stopped in the dining area. He picked up a dry dish rag and pressed it to his ear.

Flashing lights caught his attention, and he turned as three officers came through the double front doors, weapons drawn. They lowered their sidearms as Barker motioned to them all was clear.

The lead officer, Captain Gibson, was the one he had spoken to before all the excitement. She walked up to Barker.

"Well, you know how to draw a crowd, huh?"

Barker nodded his head. "Yes, ma'am, I guess I do." He was sweating and shaking a little.

"I'll get a team here from State Police to help us. Who were these guys?"

"Russian, by the sound of their voices. Couldn't hear real well, but that's what I think. Yeah, I'm gonna go with Russians, or at least eastern Europeans."

"Did you see them drive away?" Barker shook his head. "Give me your gun. You're on a desk for a while." She turned to the other two. "Look outside to see if there's any blood on the sidewalk or in the parking lot. And see if there are any witnesses to what just happened, alright?" She turned to Barker. "You need an ambulance? Well, I'm calling one, just to make sure." She leaned her head over and talked into the mic on her shoulder. Barker tried to tell her he had called for one, but maybe in the melee, the need for an ambulance went unheeded.

Jake stood up, looked back and forth, then walked around the borrowed vehicle to find Kowalski squatting behind a tire. The sergeant looked up at Jake.

"You hit? No? Good. No idea what that was about. Good thing you moved when you did, or you'd have a through-and-through right there." Kowalski pointed to Jake's chest. "Did you see anything at all?"

Jake shook his head. "I moved to get in the back seat and the front window shattered. I saw pavement and the bottom of your friend's car. By the way, he's gonna need some new window tinting."

Kowalski walked around the back of the car. "Don't know what that was all about. Someone doesn't like us, I think." Jake nodded his head in agreement.

Kowalski pulled out his phone. He called Captain Tanner and told him what had just happened. The captain told him to call the Louisville Police. He also told Kowalski to stay there. He indicated he was on the way from Frankfort.

"Let's get some more coffee. My boss is on the way. I'd rather wait inside than here where they—whoever they were—could come back around and shoot again."

Both men turned and walked back into the diner, but they looked over their shoulders as they made their way to the front doors.

Captain Gibson turned off her phone and dropped it into her front pants leg pocket. She looked at Barker.

"You've got a nasty cut on your ear that's gonna need stitches, but nothing that won't heal soon. Any clues as to what happened?"

"No, just running my night shift and decided to get some dinner. I sat over in the corner so I could have a good look at the room. These three came in. Didn't see what they were driving."

"What started the shooting?"

"I don't have a clue. It was just a suspicion. We had that all points bulletin on three or four guys, one of them big. They fit the profile. They were talking in low tones. I went into the kitchen and told the waitress and the cook to head out the backdoor. Told them to get in their cars and drive about 3 blocks away. I looked out the backdoor and turned to look into the barrel of this big guy's gun.

"What kind was it?"

"Some eastern European, I think. Not really sure. Could be a 9mm or a 40, but my guess would be a 9mm."

Captain Gibson looked at the floor. There was a lot of brass by where Barker had shot at the big guy. The big guy's brass was on the other side of the order window. Gibson ordered police to put up police tape around the entire property and then sent someone out to find the two diner workers. She stooped down and picked up a shell from where the big Russian had stood.

"It's a nine," she said.

Kowalski pulled his cell phone from his pocket. He called Louisville Metro and told them to send a unit for the shooting. Four Metro Police cars pulled up within a few minutes. Officer Johnson was one of the first to arrive.

Kowalski and Jake sat in the diner. Doris had refilled their cups. Officer Johnson approached the two.

"What happened, Kowalski?"

"No clue. We had finished eating and were headed to find a place to crash when a shot rang out. We ducked, then two more shots. Not sure about the direction. We didn't see any car pull away fast. It didn't seem like a gang shooting. No one else was around. An SUV was driving past, but it seemed the windows were up."

"You see anything, Jake?" asked Johnson.

"No, my back was to whoever shot at us."

"Could be some random shooting? Someone had a misfire?"

"Three times?" said Kowalski. "I don't think that ever happens. Not even with a full auto does it happen like that."

Jake looked at Johnson.

"You were the first officer here. Were you in the area?"

"Yeah, I had just left the hospital when I heard the call."

Jake stood up.

"Were you visiting family at the hospital? Friends? A suspect?"

Before Johnson answered, Jake reached out and spun Johnson around so he was between him and the other officers. He felt Johnson's service weapon. It was cool. Jake released Johnson with a push.

Johnson stumbled forward and turned around to look at Jake. He put his hand on his service revolver.

Kowalski stood and put his hand on Johnson's hand.

"Relax," said Kowalski. "Not sure what is going on here, but we're a little jumpy right now. No one needs to get hurt, okay?"

Johnson relaxed. He looked at Kowalski and then at Jake.

"Get him outta here, now! I want him gone from this city. He has no reason to be here. He's not an officer, he is not involved in this, and I don't want to be responsible if he gets hurt." He looked at Kowalski. "And neither do you."

Johnson spun on his heels and walked back to where the other officers were standing. They all turned and looked at Jake and Kowalski while talking to each other.

"Let's sit down and wait for Tanner. We're not going to get any place by arguing with these guys."

He and Jake sat down.

Barker waited until the cook and the waitress came back in. He and Gibson asked the two what they saw. The cook was obstructed by the wall. The waitress said she didn't really notice the three, and they didn't talk to her except to order something to eat. She said she treated them like any person passing through who didn't speak English as a first language. More sign language than anything else.

Gibson headed out to her car. Forensics had shown up and she told Barker to head to the ER. When someone is involved in a shooting, they have to be seen by a healthcare professional as well as take a drug test. Barker was going to need stitches in his ear.

Barker headed to his squad car as an ambulance pulled up. Gibson waved Barker over.

"Give me your keys. Take a ride in the ambulance. I'll meet you at the hospital in about an hour." She put Barker's gun belt in the trunk of her squad car.

Barker nodded and climbed into the ambulance. In a minute it screamed towards the University of Kentucky Hospital. Gibson pulled her phone out and made a call. She talked for about three minutes, looking puzzled, then hung up. She headed to her car after talking to the forensics people.

Jake and Kowalski were still waiting for Tanner to arrive. He was driving from Frankfort, so it should have been a 30-35-minute ride, but Tanner was probably snug in bed, so add another 10 minutes for him to get up and get dressed.

Kowalski asked in a low voice. "Why ask Johnson who he was seeing at the hospital? We're in and out of there all the time, you know."

"I know, but don't you think it strange that when we were leaving he was just coming in? Obviously, if he were going to see Lawrence and Luke, he didn't know they were gone, either. Was he sent to get rid of them? And why weren't you notified about there being no officer outside Lawrence's room?"

"Not sure. Not sure of anything. It's all spinning before me."

"Kowalski, I want you to think of something. Put your mind to it. Why would the police be involved in an illegal event? Not drugs, not alcohol. Not gambling, I think. Human trafficking? Gun smuggling? What crosses at least two continents and ends up in your backyard? Can you think what that might be?

"No nuclear plants here. No nuclear sites here, save the Bluegrass Army Depot, but that's 60 miles east of Shelbyville. No way those four were involved in something that deep. And Russia makes its own nuclear fuel. No need to get four farmers involved."

"How about something environmental? Have you thought about that?"

"Everyone in this state's a real conservative, environmentally speaking. I mean, coal companies dump raw materials in the rivers and lakes, but the state goes after them really hard."

"Is there anything bigger than that, environmentally speaking?"

"You mean solar system stuff?"

"Think smaller. Global stuff."

"I'm clueless, unless you're going to open my eyes about something."

Jake shook his head. "I just can't figure it out. It's not drugs, alcohol, nuclear, environmental, so I'm not sure why this is happening. These guys weren't being sought out by ISIS, right? So it's not terrorism."

"Let's run this by Tanner when he gets here."

The two sat back and stirred their coffees with spoons, even though both drank their coffee black.

Barker arrived at the hospital. The medical crew had patched his ear, started an IV, and put him on the heart monitor, more for effect than anything else. Barker insisted he walk in instead of being carted in on a stretcher. The paramedics agreed. The four walked into the ER and the crew was immediately assigned a bed.

Barker stood beside the bed as the RN staff helped him take his clothes off. They took his backup off his right ankle and locked it in the ER safe. They gave him a gown to wear. A resident unwrapped his ear and took a look. He asked one of the nurses to get him a suture kit. The resident asked the nurse to give the officer a sedative to help with the pain. Barker sat back and waited.

Tanner pulled up into the diner lot, got out and locked his vehicle. He talked to a couple of the officers on scene. He then entered the diner.

Jake and Kowalski were sitting at the rear of the diner, the back wall against their backs. Tanner sat down opposite them.

"What gives… Ski?" asked Tanner. "You two are running all over central Kentucky, like whirling dervishes. Any idea who took a shot at you?"

"No idea at all," said Kowalski. "Jake here has some ideas he'd like to run by you." Jake looked at Kowalski.

"I don't have any hypotheses, just random thoughts." He shrugged his shoulders. "I think Luke and Lawrence are involved in more than gambling."

"What makes you think that?"

"Just some ideas. Gambling is a chance, both by the house and the players. Most times the house wins, but every now and then, the players win. And everyone is okay with that. The players realize it, the house knows it, and they have fun. So, I think both Luke and Lawrence deceived us. Misdirection is more likely."

"Hmmm," said Tanner. "Not sure I buy that. But here's another question. Why are you still here? I mean, I sent… Ski here to take you to your car, and you keep turning up."

"You know, a lot of cops keep asking me why I'm still here. I kinda don't like it so much. Instead of asking me why I'm still here, ask yourself why no one has caught this big guy, and anyone associated with him." Jake folded his arms across his chest.

"You think this is some kind of conspiracy? We just want this big guy to terrorize the community, kill the police, two citizens, a security guard, seven people in an elevator? I really think those few days in lockup ruined your perspective. I…"

Jake cut him off. "You didn't spend time in jail for something you didn't do. But if you and some others are involved in this, you'll spend a hell of a lot of time in jail, if I have anything to do about it." He looked at Tanner intently. "By the way, how did you know Fry had been killed at Kowalski's house? He never called it in. Just wondering. You got any answers to that?"

Kowalski jumped in. "Wait, Jake, boss. We're here to find out what is happening, why someone shot at us, and what, if any, different theories we can come up with. I called you because someone took some potshots at us, whether to scare us off or take us out, I'm not sure. But this bantering is going nowhere. Let's focus on what is the real issue. Where's Luke and Lawrence?"

Kowalski sat back in the booth. The diner door opened, and Johnson came in.

"Hi, Tanner. We can't find anything. No shells, the trajectory looks like it came from a passing vehicle."

Jake raised his hand. "Not a passing vehicle. Stationary. Three shots. One, pause, two-three. No way a passing vehicle could have done that. Had to be stationary. Window rolled down, shooter on the grassy knoll, whatever. You guys are not taking this seriously. And it makes me wonder what Kowalski and I have walked into."

Johnson put his hands on the table and bent his head close to Jake. "You don't have any authority here. You have no reason to question us or how we carry out our investigation. You need to be on the road to California, right now." Johnson turned and looked at Kowalski and

Tanner. "Since you two can't figure out how to get rid of this guy, I'll have one of my officers take him to wherever his vehicle is, or to the bus station, or down to the river to catch a pleasure cruise at first light. I don't want him here anymore. He's done with trying to help us and the state police. And I mean done now!" Johnson slammed both his palms down on the table for emphasis. "Get him outta here."

Officer Johnson turned and walked over to another officer. He spoke with him, turning his head towards the table as he spoke. He then pulled his cell phone out of his pocket and made a call. The officer with whom he was speaking nodded his head, turned and walked over to the table.

"Jake, is it?" said the officer. "My sarge says it's time for you to go. Either with those two or with me, makes me no difference. But you go now." The officer, whose shirt had the name Lang on it, stepped back. "Ready?"

Jake looked at Kowalski and Tanner. Kowalski started to say something, but Tanner shook his head. Jake shrugged his shoulders, slid out of the booth, and stood up. He and Officer Lang were the same height, but the officer outweighed Jake by about 50 pounds, and by the look of it, all muscle.

Jake started to leave but turned and bent low to Kowalski. "Luke and Lawrence are key to this, I'm telling you. I'm heading west but you're in way over your head, both you and Tanner. You'd better figure this out and fast. And one more thing. Ask yourself why the officer who got shot, Larson, hasn't said anything. He's probably out of a coma by now. He's got to have some idea of what happened that night. You'll be lucky to put any of this together without my help."

Jake turned and walked out with Lang. Tanner and Kowalski shifted in their seats and looked at each other.

"You think this goes way deeper than gambling, boss?"

Tanner shrugged his shoulders. "No idea. But like Jake says, the big guy is still out there."

Barker had his head down one the pillow as the resident finished sewing up his ear. It hurt like a son-of-a-gun. The resident finished and told Barker a nurse would come in with discharge orders and a couple of prescriptions, but he had to take a drug test first. Barker nodded that he understood. The resident left the room. Barker laid his head down on the pillow.

Jake and Officer Lang walked out to Lang's police car. Lang opened the rear passenger door for Jake. Jake sat down in the vehicle, again from left to right as he was so long. His head was behind the driver's seat, his feet under the passenger seat. Jake reclined on his elbow and waited. Jake looked into the diner one last time and saw Johnson sit down with Tanner and Kowalski. Tanner and Johnson were laughing. Kowalski looked perplexed. Jake sat up. Alarm bells started ringing in his head.

"Hey, Lang, you gotta let me go back in. I forgot my wallet."

Lang sat down in the driver's seat. "No, I saw your wallet in your back pocket. Best we just move along, got it?"

Jake looked one more time into the diner. He knew he'd been had.

Barker heard a noise. It sounded like a scuffle. A fight. Then a war. He heard shots. A nurse came into the room and slammed the door shut. "Active shooter!" she yelled. Barker reached down automatically for his back-up weapon on his leg. He had to look down twice to realize the weapon was not on his leg, above his ankle, but locked in a safe, somewhere in the ER.

More shots rang out. Barker stood up and opened the door just an inch. What he saw made his blood run cold. It was the big guy who had shot at him earlier, and he was coming down the hallway, right toward his room.

Lang pulled the vehicle on to the Interstate, heading east. Jake's car lay 33.9 miles ahead of him, still in the parking lot. The vehicle accelerated to 40, then 50, then 60 miles an hour. No chance to open the car door and leap out. That only works in old serial westerns and movies anyway. Plus, this vehicle was a police car, so it probably had security doors, to keep arrested people from jumping out of the back. So, Jake slumped back into the seat, thinking, planning, pondering just how to get out and get back to Kowalski.

Barker moved a surgery cart in front of the door. It did little to keep the door from opening, so he also grabbed the bed. By releasing the brake on the bed, he and the nurse moved the bed so it touched the cart and the back wall, creating an impenetrable barrier. It would stop the big guy from coming in but wouldn't stop his bullets. The shots kept ringing out, closer still.

Kowalski sat in the booth next to Tanner. He kept quiet. All the things Jake had said to him over the last three days kept coming to the surface. Deeper than a gambling conspiracy. Deeper than drugs or alcohol or sex trafficking.

"What do you think… Ski?" asked Tanner.

Kowalski jumped as he heard his name. "Guess I'm tired. Not paying attention. Lost too much sleep with this jack wagon for the past week. I'm kinda drifting, ya know?"

Tanner nodded. "I'll run you back to Frankfort. You can get your stuff together tomorrow and be fishing by next weekend. Sound okay? I'll get the car towed to the garage, so the windows can be replaced." He grabbed his cell phone and made a call.

Kowalski nodded dumbly. Something was rotten, and it wasn't in Denmark. It was right here in central Kentucky.

The door to Barker's room moved ½ inch, but no more. Barker and the nurse were behind the bed, on the hinge side of the door. The shooter couldn't get the gun into the room to turn it almost 180 degrees to affect a kill, so for the moment they seemed safe. But if the shooter shot through the door, both he and the nurse could be hit.

"Get behind me. I'll take the bullet." The nurse cowered behind Barker. He held the rail of the bed with both hands, pushing it to keep the shooter from coming through. His grip was as tight as it had ever been.

Jake rode in silence. About ten miles outside Louisville, off the south side of the eastbound Interstate, lay a rest area. Lang pulled the vehicle onto the exit and slowed down. Jake sat up.

"Gotta hit the head. Best if you used the restroom yourself. We'll get back on the road directly." Lang pulled the vehicle into one of the slots and put it in park. As was the ritual, he kept the engine running.

"Time to get out. Let's go." Lang unbuckled his seatbelt and slid out, then opened the driver's rear door, taking Jake's advantage away. Had he opened the passenger door, Jake might have been able to kick him, slide out of the door, jump him, and take his car. But Lang was apparently too smart for that.

Jake pulled himself to a seated position, which was really uncomfortable because his head was above the doorsill. Jake had to turn his head almost sideways to get out of the rear. It took him a full 30 seconds to extricate himself from the back seat.

When Jake was standing up, he noticed Lang had stepped back and had his right hand on the hilt of his service weapon. Space and time were the advantages Lang held at the moment. And Lang's hand didn't move off his weapon. A trained police officer can clear leather in less than one second. Jake was almost two seconds from Lang.

Barker's grip on the bedrail stayed the same. The nurse behind him was calling to him. Officer! Officer! Mr. Barker?

"Sir, Mr. Barker. Are you alright?"

Barker jerked up. He was in his bed. The bed was in the same position as before. The door was open.

"Did you hear shots?" he asked. The nurse shook her head. "I heard shots. A big guy with a gun was walking down the hallway, shooting." He looked at the nurse. "You didn't hear anything?"

"Probably the medicine I gave you. It makes some people dream hard, crazy dreams. We take weapons away from people because of this." She turned and walked out of the room. Barker realized he was sweating again.

Lang motioned for Jake to walk in front of him towards the building that housed the toilets with a jerk of his head. Jake started walking but noticed Lang still had his hand on his weapon as they walked.

Barker wiped the sweat off his brow. He surveyed the room, then reached up and touched his ear. It was still attached, but he couldn't feel it, because of the Lidocaine the resident had used before he sutured Barker's ear. Barker could feel the strands of the sutures, but there was no pain.

The nurse came back in, this time with Barker's captain. Captain Gibson was grinning.

"Heard you had a little nightmare, Barker," she said smiling. "The nurse said you were ready to fight someone."

"This still has me rattled. That big guy really got to me, I guess."

The nurse said, "This medicine I gave you to relax you while the doctor sewed you up has an almost hypnotic effect. It sedates you but also lets you dream. You go down quick and come back quick, but the dream is unforgettable!"

Jake walked up to the men's door. He had surveyed the parking lot and saw no other cars either parked or pulling into the rest area. It was strange that no one was stopping. Many cars drove by, west to east, but no one was pulling in.

Jake opened the door and motioned for Lang to enter. Lang let out a laugh and kept his distance.

"You first," said Jake.

"Not on your life," said Lang.

Jake shrugged his shoulders and pushed the door open. It was a hefty steel door, with a hydraulic closer at the top. It was hinged on the right side, so the door swung inward from left to right. This was a small advantage for Jake, as Lang was right-handed. For only one second, Jake held a slight advantage. The hinge and Lang's right hip lined up perfectly. If Lang pulled his pistol, Jake would already be in the restroom, turning right. Lang would not have a shot. It was the perfect moment, and Jake took it. Nothing ventured, nothing gained, as they say.

Kowalski walked out of the diner and climbed into Tanner's vehicle. Johnson headed to his patrol car and pulled out.

"That was strange, boss. I can't figure it out."

"What's strange… Ski?"

"That Johnson didn't let us take Jake back to Shelbyville, instead of using one of their officers to do that. Seems like a real waste of talent and fuel, don't you think?"

"I think Johnson wants Jake out of here just like I do. I think he felt if we drove Jake back to Shelbyville to get his vehicle, somehow he'd talk us into turning the car around and he'd be right back in the thick of things. Come on… Ski, Jake's got no dog in this fight. He needs to get going west, and we're keeping him from traveling. That's not very neighborly of us."

Kowalski nodded and sat back in his seat. It had been a long, tiring few days, and he was ready to get some rest and figure out his next move.

Jake weighed almost 230 pounds on a good day, and it was all muscle. A hydraulic door closer is designed to pull a door closed, but it doesn't have a fail-safe override on it to keep the door from closing too fast. It moves at a steady pace, but a strong person can push the door closed faster than the door tracks normally. That's what Jake was counting on.

Jake walked into the restroom and turned right, hesitating for just a touch, then put himself behind the door and pushed with all his might. Lang had just started to walk into the restroom and the door hit him full force. Most people enter a room with their head slightly forward, as if looking left and right. Good tactics if you are in combat. Bad tactics if Jake Thompson is standing on the other side of the door, pushing it at you.

A 36 inch door, also known as a 3.0 door, which means it is designed to fit in a 36-inch opening, has a square footage of 21 feet, approximately. That translates to 252 square inches, with a force of 230 pounds pushing the 252 inches at nearly 10 miles per hour. Lang didn't stand a chance.

The door hit him at the crown of his head and he dropped to one knee. Jake opened the door and kneed Lang in the face, which took him all the way to the floor. Jake reached down and put his thumbs on Lang's carotid arteries, and in 15 seconds, Lang slept like a baby.

Tanner pulled the vehicle on to Interstate 64, heading east. Just under 34 miles to Shelbyville, then another 23 or so miles to the Frankfort exit. Then six miles to his house. Kowalski closed his eyes and sighed from tiredness more than anything. He didn't realize he'd never walk into his house again.

Jake picked up Lang and put him over his back, in a fireman's carry. Jake had never been a firefighter, but he had carried his share of people off the battlefield. Still no cars in the rest area parking lot. This was really strange.

Jake got to the car and loosened Lang's gun belt, then felt for his spare weapon, which he found on his right ankle. He quickly frisked Lang and didn't find anything else that could hurt him, so he pushed Lang into the back seat, shut the door, then walked around the police car and opened the driver's door. Still no cars.

Jake put the car in reverse and backed out. He looked in the rear-view mirror to see if Lang was waking up, but what he saw chilled him even more.

Tanner and Kowalski drove in silence. Tanner's radio buzzed from time to time, but nothing of real importance.

Tanner glanced over at Kowalski and saw he was asleep. He wheeled the vehicle into the rest area just east of Louisville, past the barrels that had been set up just a few minutes before. He saw Lang's police car in front of him, getting ready to pull out.

Tanner flashed his lights twice, and Lang's car didn't move. Tanner pulled up beside Lang's car. Tanner rolled down the passenger window. What he saw made him look again. Lang wasn't sitting in the driver's seat. It was Jake. Tanner hit the gas and pulled his vehicle in front of the Louisville police car. He jumped out of the car, weapon drawn, and pointed it at Jake.

All this unfolded at lightning speed in front of Jake, but it was a position Jake had been in before. Many years before.

While serving in Afghanistan, Jake had been driving a HumVee with his lieutenant and two other soldiers in it, when a car driven by a member of the Taliban had tried to cut off the HumVee. Jake had been instructed in the tactic of bigger is badder, so he hit the pedal and literally drove over the top of the small car, crushing it and the would-be Taliban assassin. It happened in a split-second.

Just as it was happening now. But Jake wasn't in a HumVee; he wasn't armed with an MP-5, and he knew he didn't have three others in the vehicle to think about, but what the vehicle he was in did have, was a deer bumper that could also be used for PIT maneuvers.

What he knew was the axis of vehicles making them the perfect device for traveling also gives them a poor center of gravity. Watch any car careening down the road on wet or icy surfaces, sluicing back and forth. As the arc becomes greater and greater, the driver loses control.

Jake put the car in gear and punched the accelerator. He aimed for the back of the car, the rear quarter panel, and pushed that into Tanner, who still hadn't pulled his trigger. The tires screamed but the car moved quickly. Tanner was knocked down, as the back of his SUV moved over him.

Jake stopped and put his vehicle in park. He climbed out, carrying Lang's service revolver, now off safe, as he approached Tanner's car. Tanner's body lay under the left rear wheel. He wasn't breathing. As Jake stood up, Kowalski came out of the driver's side, holding a bloody head.

"What the hell, Jake? What have you done?"

"Just saved your bacon and mine. Tanner was intent on killing me, and by the looks of it, you, too. I wondered why there was no traffic coming into the rest area. They have barrels set up across the entrance. Any idea who would do that?"

"None, but where's the cop that was going to take you back to Shelbyville?"

"He's in the back of my vehicle. I knocked him out. He was going to take me into the rest area and shoot me, then leave me here for someone else to find."

"There's supposed to be a state worker here, day and night. Where's he off to?"

"My guess is we'll find him in his office, dead. This is way bigger than any gambling ring or drug conspiracy. This has state police involved. And Louisville P.D. as well. This goes against everything I know as sanity."

"Mine, too. Sanity, I mean. I never thought Tanner would turn out to be dirty. What's he got to hide? And Lang here? Is he involved, too?"

"Let's ask him," said Jake.

They opened the backdoor and found Lang on the floor of the car, not breathing.

"Geez, Jake, did you have to kill him, too?"

"He was alive when I put him in. He even moaned a couple of times. I hit him in the head with the bathroom door."

Kowalski leaned in and checked for a pulse. A smell of almonds emitted from the back.

"Cyanide. He just poisoned himself. This is so deep I don't know where it's going to end up."

The two pulled Lang out of his police car and put him into Tanner's vehicle. They then pulled Tanner's car forward and moved Tanner's body into the front seat.

"Best leave the barrels right where they are. The less questions we have now, the better off we both will be."

Jake nodded. "He was going to kill both of us and keep doing whatever it is he and Lang, and I'm sure Johnson were all doing. By the way, remember telling me about a big guy, from the looks of the track marks by the interstate? I think this might be the guy who took a shot at Larson. He was apparently a poor shot and even poorer at situational awareness."

The big Russian and the other two rode slowly to Interstate 64. They turned left and pulled on to the interstate.

"We need to find the two from Shelbyville. I need to make them pay for what they have done," said the big Russian. The other two nodded their heads.

The truck got up to speed and headed west, towards Shelbyville.

Jake and Kowalski pulled out of the rest stop and headed east on I-64. Jake looked at Kowalski.

"We need to find Luke and Lawrence and figure out what they know. They are in way over their heads… unless they're the ones who started this."

Kowalski turned his head.

"We've thought about everything we could possibly think, right? Not gambling, not sex trade, not nuclear, not ISIS. What else is there?"

"When I was in the military, I ran across some bad guys in Europe. They were tied up in a scheme that was taking down banks all over two or three countries. It was happening about the time of the recession back in 2008-2009. The banks had to close because of their losses. Their closings were blamed on the economy, but the State Department figured out it was also due to some bad guys stealing from different accounts. Not much, but if you steal one Euro from a million accounts…"

"You got a million dollars, or more. But that is so time-consuming, isn't it?"

"Not if you're a computer whiz. You can run a program that takes such a little amount most people won't know it's missing. These banks saw it happening, but we thought they were complicit because it was such a small amount. Kinda like a fee for services."

"And if you're doing this in three countries, you might be making a million a month, maybe more. Hmmm, any chance Luke and Lawrence were doing this in the United States?"

"I think we'll find out when we get the FBI to look at their financials. There's something called the dark web, and it's used for more than just sex. I believe those two were using Russian or European assets to fund their unscrupulous dealings."

"But I don't think Luke and Lawrence are around here anymore."

"And we can't go back to Louisville. We're not sure who's involved in this. We know Johnson is, but how many others? And does it go beyond the police department? I mean, we know it goes all the way to the jail in Frankfort. Does it go up the ladder past Tanner?"

"No one knows we're not dead, at least beyond Johnson. And we're in a Louisville Police vehicle. No one is going to question us. Let's go find Luke's daughter. I bet the two of them are there."

Kowalski spun the wheel to the right lane, then took the first crossover, after turning on the lights in the cruiser. He drove west back towards Louisville. This just might end tonight.

The truck pulled into a convenient store on the first westbound exit. The three needed another vehicle, so they could drive into the neighborhoods of Luke and Lawrence. Death would be swift and sure tonight.

They found one—a large sedan, with the motor running. Instead of stealing it and having the driver notify the police about the missing car, they waited. In a minute, a smallish man walked out of the truck stop with a 24 pack of beer.

The man approached his still-running sedan and the big Russian grabbed him from behind. It was over in two seconds. A snap of the neck, breaking C-2 and C-3 meant a cessation of breathing. The other two opened the passenger doors. The one who climbed in the front opened the glove box and hit the trunk opener. It popped, and the Russian carried the man to the rear and dropped him in over the tire.

He slammed the trunk and then went to the driver's side. He opened the door and climbed inside. He had to run the seat back in order to fit. The Russian put the car in reverse, then pulled out onto Highway 35. Luke was first.

Kowalski turned off the lights on the cruiser. He drove fast in the left lane. As he drove, he turned and looked at Jake.

"Hey, Tanner said something funny when you first got here. He told me the big Russian guy came to his office, looking to get you out of jail. Tanner said the Russian tried throwing his weight around. Tanner said he was wearing an Army uniform. Said he had one of those Army looking vehicles. Can you shed any light on that?"

"I've never met this Russian guy. I know how he works, but I've not ever more than laid eyes on him since this past week. My bet is he's not military at all."

Kowalski shook his head. "I don't know how and why I get involved in stuff like this. You know, forensics is going to put this together and figure out it was this car that took out Tanner."

"Not if this car is never found, they won't," said Jake. "I've hidden cars before. Taken them out of plain sight by leaving them in plain sight. Like I said before—it's a magic show. We get taught in the military to make people believe that there's more to the story. Like in World War

Two, the Army Air Corp dropped several bags of cigars over the enemy. The cigars were about two inches in diameter. Big enough so you could hardly get one in your mouth, but in the bag, they labeled them small cigars in huge letters. Trying to make the Germans think the American soldiers were seven feet tall. That kind of stuff."

Kowalski nodded, and they drove on in silence.

The big Russian pulled his vehicle over in front of Luke's house. The three climbed out and walked to Luke's backdoor. The big Russian pressed his shoulder against the door and it popped open easily. They walked in, guns drawn.

Kowalski took the Louisville downtown exit and headed to the hospital. He stopped in the circle in front and walked inside. Jake waited in the car. He was back in a few minutes. He had the Dinkins' addresses on a small piece of paper. He took out a pen and scratched through Luke's Shelbyville address. The next address was Luke's daughter. Kowalski started to pull out his phone, then decided against it.

"Better to not turn on the phone so if anyone is looking, they see us driving around," said Kowalski.

He pulled out an old map of Louisville and turned on the inside light. He used the map locator to find the daughter's address. It was less than a mile from the hospital.

"Funny thing," said Jake. "In all the time Luke and Lawrence were in the hospital, I never saw the daughter or any family member of either one there, did you?"

"No, and it did hit me kinda funny. Maybe they've left town? Gone to see family because it got too hot here?"

Jake shrugged his shoulders. "No way to know till we get over to Luke's daughter's house."

Kowalski put the car in drive and pulled out of the hospital circle.

"*Nyet*," said the big Russian. "No one is here." They had searched the whole house, even the basement. No one was anywhere in Luke's home.

"Maybe at the other man, Lawrence's, no?" said the Russian. They walked out the backdoor and pulled it shut. They got into the stolen car and drove towards Lawrence's house.

Kowalski glided the car to a stop two houses past Luke's daughter's home. Both men climbed out of the car and walked down the sidewalk to the house.

When they reached the backdoor, Kowalski motioned Jake to step away from the door. He reached down and pulled out his .32 from a leg holster.

"Nice," said Jake. "But I thought you were unarmed?"

Kowalski nodded. "I picked this up in Tanner's office when I was taken back there by the SWAT team. I always try to carry, at least something, if you want to call a .32 something." He knocked on the backdoor, once, twice, three times. A light blinked on and a young woman pulled back the backdoor window shade.

"Who are you?" she asked.

"State Police, ma'am. We need to talk." He showed the young girl his badge.

Reluctantly, she opened the door. Kowalski and Jake waited a second, then slowly walked into the room. Kowalski had his weapon by his side.

"Where's your dad?" said Kowalski.

The young lady turned her head slightly. "He's in bed, asleep."

"I need to talk to him, right away. And his buddy, Lawrence, too."

The young lady nodded. "Wait here, I'll get him," she said.

The girl turned and walked out of the room. Jake looked around the room. Everything said it was a young, up-and-coming person's house. Big screen TV, stereo, video game console, all the works. A couple of cell phones lay on a coffee-table. Jake touched Kowalski's arm.

"Two phones. Luke and Lawrence?" Kowalski nodded.

The girl came back to the room. Following her was her dad, Luke. Behind him came Lawrence. Both men were rubbing their eyes.

The Russian pulled the stolen car up to Lawrence's house. Again, all three stepped out of the vehicle. They made their way to the back-door. Again, the big man pushed on the door and it popped open freely. Again, no one was home. The Russian shook his head. "Where can they be?" he asked. The other two men looked at each other, then back at the big Russian.

"Sit down," ordered Kowalski. "We need to talk."

Both men took positions on the sofa.

Jake said, "Lawrence, you look pretty good for a guy who's just had a heart attack."

Lawrence looked up at him sheepishly. "I faked it," he said. "We thought you were the Russian guy. I have pills that mimic the signs and symptoms of a heart attack. I saw you coming up to my house and I popped that pill. Takes about 20 to 30 seconds to take effect. Fools everyone."

Jake and Kowalski looked at each other, then down at Lawrence.

"We know the games you two were playing," said Jake. "We've been following the trail for about six months now."

Luke started to say something, but Jake silenced him with a raised palm.

"We first thought it was a betting gambit gone wrong, but now we know more. What were you doing with all that money?"

"We were planning for our retirement," said Lawrence. "We all worked at good jobs and we take social security, but we thought that might not be enough."

"So, you started importing girls from Russia? Like that's going to make you rich?"

Kowalski looked at Jake. Both Luke and Lawrence flinched back in surprise, as did Luke's daughter.

"Now see here, we did no such thing. Importing girls? No way!" said Luke.

"Alright, what were you doing all this time? Why are the Russians trying to kill you and why did they kill your two friends?"

The young girl gasped and grabbed her stomach as if she'd been hit. "Dad?" she asked.

"No, honey, nothing like that at all. I'd do no such thing." He looked at Jake and a darkness spread across his face.

"How dare you come to my daughter's house and make an accusation like that! We were just gambling and it got out of hand."

"No, it's much more than that," said Jake. "I've been in the military for 20 years, and the Russians do not sanction Americans on American soil without a really good reason. So, if not girls, then drugs?"

"None of that," said Lawrence. "We don't run drugs or alcohol or anything. It was only gambling." He sat back on the sofa.

"Well, you two played the heart attack thing like big screen actors," said Jake. "I think a couple of Oscars are up for the taking."

Luke's daughter looked at her dad. "What did you do, daddy?"

"Honey, it's like Lawrence said, we were gambling, that's all. You need to go back to bed. Let me handle this."

"Go back to bed, in my house? With these two here, accusing you of something really bad? No, that's not going to happen." She crossed her arms in defiance.

"Okay," said Jake. "Tell me the real reason why the Russian guys are looking to kill you."

Luke and Lawrence looked at each other, then at Luke's daughter. Both men dropped their heads at the same time.

"We were working on a line another person told me about. It was bringing in a lot of money for the four of us. I think I knew all along it was wrong, but the money was just too good." He looked at his daughter. "You have to believe me, my little one, we didn't think it was illegal. It all seemed on the up-and-up."

"Well, dad, tell me and these men what you did. Why are people here to hurt you and Lawrence?"

"Not just these four. The Russians have killed maybe ten other people and he's responsible for the deaths of at least three more." Kowalski turned and looked at Jake.

"He and the police are up to their keisters in something. It's all interconnected."

"Dad, please," said Luke's daughter. "What is so bad that people are being killed?"

"We're running nuclear material from South Africa to Iran," said Luke.

"What?" said Luke's daughter. "How is that even possible?"

"We formed a dummy company. I guess I knew that it was wrong, but being in the retail business, I just found a way to make a little more money. The Iranians needed fuel, and they said it was only for social reform, like nuclear reactors. The nuclear material was low-grade, and that means it can't be turned into bomb-making material. The United

States has put so much pressure on Iran, and the people are hurting there so bad, that the Russians offered us big money to form a dummy company. I don't know why I did it, but I did. We did. And we got a lot of other people involved. The State Police were in on it, the local PD, and even the guys at the jail here and in Frankfort. Not all of them, but they put up money so they could get part of the action."

Jake said, "And then the Russians wanted to close you down, right?"

"Yeah, and they made hints that it would just go away, but we were afraid it wouldn't work that way, and we were right. I put out a warning to everyone involved, and when this big guy showed up, we thought he was the one who was going to take us down."

Luke turned to Jake. "Mister, in that restaurant, where you were eating, we thought you were the guy who had come to hurt us. So, we came up with a plan to have you arrested. I walked over to the gas station and shot the clerk in the leg. Then I called in a robbery. When Kowalski took you in, we notified the jail you were coming. We also called Tanner to make it seem like you were involved, and then we had some of the staff at the jail make sure you weren't ever going to get out. The guys in there were supposed to put you in the hospital. We didn't think it through past that."

Jake nodded. "But you never expected what else would happen in the jail, did you?"

"No, and when we heard there was a killing there, we thought someone had killed you along with some others in the jail. It wasn't our intent to have you killed—just scared away. We never thought there'd be another guy out there as well."

"I am just a guy, passing through," said Jake. "I don't have a dog in this fight, at least I didn't." He looked at Kowalski. "How about you? Did you know this was going down?"

"No, Jake, I didn't. Tanner and Luke here are buddies from way back. I know these guys through Tanner, but not enough to run with."

Jake turned back to Luke. "So, tell me more about your company."

"It was called Nary Sales and Service. We took Iran and spelled it backwards and changed the 'I' to 'y'. We even had business cards made up. It all seemed so legit. And, we were told it was humanitarian. We should've checked better, I guess."

"You guess? You put millions of lives at risk by doing this stupid thing. I can't believe you feel you are innocent in this."

"No, we know we're not innocent. I mean, we knew it might be illegal, but it seemed to be just paperwork, not anything more."

Jake shook his head. "There's gonna be hell to pay for this, because the government already knows what you were doing." Jake looked at Kowalski. "Put these men under arrest and take them out to the car." The two men stood and walked outside with Kowalski.

Jake turned to the daughter. "Did you know about this?" Jake asked.

"No, I did not," she said defiantly. "I knew dad and the others were making a lot of money, but they told me they were doing online gambling. You see commercials for it all the time. I thought they had hit it big."

Jake nodded. "I'm going to take care of your dad and Lawrence. No harm will come to them, at least not from the Russians. I'll make sure of that. Pack two bags, and you and your mom get out of here this morning. It's in your best interests." He turned and walked out the door.

The Russians got back into the car. "Let's head to the hospital. I think that's where we can find out where the two others are staying. I'll make someone talk," said the big Russian. The other two knew truer words were never spoken.

Outside, Kowalski stood with Luke and Lawrence. Jake walked up to them.

"Alright, you two. Now the real story. What are you really involved in?"

Both men shook their heads.

"We told you the truth in there," said Luke. "Nuclear material was sent from South Africa to Iran, just like I said."

"No, that doesn't happen. Every ounce of material is accounted for. The IAEA, that's the International Atomic Energy Agency, keeps tabs all around the world. If you had moved so much as a tenth of a kilo-gram of material, you'd be not only in jail, you'd be under it right now."

Jake reached over and pulled the .32 from Kowalski's hand. "I don't mind using this and taking you two out. Kowalski will vouch for me that you two tried to escape custody. And then I'll go back into the house and shoot your daughter and your wife so no one can tell who was here. Talk!" Jake pulled the hammer back on the pistol.

"Okay, okay! We're involved in a Securities scheme. We were moving money around from Russia to here. It went through my company and we scraped 10% off the top. Apparently, the Russians don't like that they were paying us and that we also were taking money from them as well as being paid."

Jake looked at the two men. Lawrence nodded.

"So, SEC involvement, huh? How much?"

"Millions, over about three years. I mean, that's how much we took off the top. So, we moved billions. But it was legit, as far as we could tell. I mean, I even checked with my accountant. He said it was sketchy, but not something that would ring bells, so to speak."

Jake turned to Kowalski and handed him the pistol.

"These two are the biggest buffoons I've ever seen," said Jake. "Anyone with a lick of sense knows moving that much money without SEC approval is monetary fraud." Jake turned and looked at the two men. "And that's why I'm here." He looked over to Kowalski. "My name IS Jake Thompson, and I AM retired from the military, and I AM on my way to see my brother in California, but I am also a Securities and Exchange Commission fraud officer. We've had reports of money being moved around here illegally, and that's why I came to town." He looked at the two men. "I wasn't just passing through. I've been here, studying your bank accounts, your business, and your holdings for three weeks. I knew you four were up to your necks in something, but I had to find out what. And I didn't know if Kowalski here was in on it as well."

Kowalski looked dumbfounded. Jake grinned at him.

"You two are coming with us. We're taking you to jail in Cincinnati. That's the closest place I could find that you didn't have others in on the securities scheme with you.

"But now we have some Russians that are trying to get their millions back, and they're not going to stop until you two are dead. So, you're in my protective custody. Get in the car. Lawrence, you ride up front; Kowalski, you drive; Luke, you're in the back with me. And if either of you two try anything, I'll break your necks. Understand?" The men nodded dumbly.

"We tried to stop," said Lawrence. "But Tanner and Frye told us a lot of people depended on doing what we were doing." He looked at Jake. "Do you think they killed our two friends?"

Jake nodded. "I sure do. And they just beat the Russians to it. One way or another, when you try to quit dirty dealings, you're going to pay, most likely with your lives."

The men climbed into the police car and Kowalski started it up. They pulled out and headed for Interstate 71 North, which led to Cincinnati.

As they pulled away from the curb, Jake turned and noticed Luke's daughter and her mother pulling her car out of the driveway. She turned and went the other way down the street.

The three Russians got into the stolen car and started driving back down the interstate, towards Louisville. It was cool outside, but the Russian rolled down the driver's window. The cool air helped him think.

Kowalski pulled his car onto Interstate 71 North and hit the gas. The traffic was still light, but with the sun coming up in an hour, it would be heavy as they headed north.

Jake turned to Luke. "So, you've been moving money for the Russians, and you think it's all fun and games, but now the Piper has come calling."

Luke nodded his head. "We really didn't mean for anyone to get hurt," Luke said again. "I wish I could pull everything back, just stop what was going on. I've lost my two best friends, and I'm going to lose whatever I have left." He began to cry.

Jake sat up, which was hard for him to do in Kowalski's vehicle. He stared hard at Luke.

"You've put a lot of people in danger, Luke. And now you think you can make a weak apology and then it'll be over." He stared hard at Luke. "As long as the Russians are involved, it'll never be over."

The Russian's vehicle turned left at the exit off Interstate 64. He pulled the vehicle into a slot in the garage and turned to one of his men.

"Find another license plate. Make it from another state, okay?"

The Russian stepped out of the vehicle and walked towards the hospital.

In a few minutes, Kowalski merged onto Interstate 75. He slowed to fifty miles per hour as traffic started building up on I-75 North. Traffic slowed to a crawl, then stopped completely. Luke had fallen asleep in the back seat. Lawrence sat still in the front seat.

"Uh-oh," said Kowalski. "Look up ahead."

Jake sat up and peered around Lawrence's head. The road see-sawed down and then up. About a mile ahead, he saw five Kentucky State Trooper cars parked in a vee, three cars on the left, two on the right, forcing all the cars to filter between them. Most of the traffic went from five lanes to one.

"That's a roadblock. And I bet we're number one on their list. They must have found Tanner and Lang."

Luke woke up, hearing Jake talking. "What happened to Tanner and Lang?" he asked.

"You should know," said Jake. "You as much as killed them both."

The Russian walked into the hospital. It was just becoming light outside. He walked up to the registration desk.

"Help you?" said the lady behind the desk.

"I am from Slovenia. Looking for brother. He had heart attack. I need to see him."

"Name?"

"My name is—"

"Not your name, your brother's name."

"Ah, yes. Brother is Lawrence. This is first name." He hesitated a second. "Last name is Up."

"Lawrence Up? U-P?"

"Ya, Up. Middle name Yers."

"So, Lawrence Yers Up?" She looked at her computer. "No one here by that name. Sure you got the names in the right order? Let me change it. Lawrence Up Yers?"

"Ya, Up Yers." The Russian walked past the desk. The lady shook her head and called out, "Next?"

"We gotta get outta this, Kowalski. Any way you can." The cars were all but stopped.

Lawrence sat up. He began to see light at the end of the tunnel. This would be the way out of his and Luke's incarceration. He began to smile. It was a faint smile, but it was a smile, nonetheless.

The Russian headed to a bank of elevators. He hit the 'Up' button.

Kowalski turned his head and looked to his left and his right, but there was no place to go. Tractor trailers were being directed around the roadblock to the right of the vee. Obviously, the state troopers thought whoever they were looking for would not be in an eighteen-wheeler. Kowalski continued to creep forward. They were now about three-quarters of a mile from the roadblock.

"How about turning on your lights, Kowalski?" said Jake.

Kowalski shook his head. "No reason for a Louisville P.D. vehicle to be running lights this far north, northbound on the interstate."

The elevator doors opened. A couple of doctors and a nurse stepped off. The big Russian stepped in and hit the number 6. The doors closed.

Kowalski moved to the center lane, then to the right lane. The vehicles were moving at less than a mile an hour. Sometimes they sat still for almost a minute. This gave Jake time to come up with a plan. It was a poor plan, but it beat having no plan at all.

The doors opened on the 6th floor. The big Russian stepped off the elevator. He walked forward to the nurse's station. A demure ward clerk sat behind the counter.

"May I help you?" she asked.

"Ya, I look for brother. He had heart attack." The big Russian looked down as if sad. "Can you tell me where is?"

"Name, please?" she said.

"Yes, Lawrence is first name. He changed name when came to America."

The lady looked up from her list. "A man named Lawrence died two days ago. He was the only Lawrence we had here. Maybe you could check other hospitals?"

"*Nyet*, he was here," said the Russian. He leaned forward and stared at the desk clerk for a long minute. She stared back, not flinching. He turned and walked back to the elevator. The clerk behind the desk acted as if she were continuing work, but deftly moved her arm down and hit a silent alarm.

The big Russian pressed the button. The elevator had not been summoned to another floor, so the doors opened again, and he stepped inside. He turned and looked at the nurse's station. The slight lady stood, looked straight at the Russian, then picked up the phone. The doors closed.

"How about moving to the right of those trucks? Use them to cover for us as we drive past the road block."

Kowalski shook his head. "They'll have a car on the right side, just to pick up anyone who tries that maneuver. Best for me to stay to the left and try to talk our way out of this."

"I don't think that'll work. But, maybe if you could jump the grass here and get on to the feeder road?"

"If I were them, I'd have someone watching that as well."

"But there's at least three cars up ahead, then two cars on the right side where the trucks are going. You think they'll have five cars here?"

"If it were me, I'd have ten cars here. There's no going back. Not sure but this may be the end of the line."

Jake sat up in his seat. "Not if you listen to me, it won't be. You'll be fishing inside of a week."

The big Russian hit the 4th floor button as the doors finished closing. The car dropped two levels and opened. The big man walked out onto a med-surg floor. He stopped and looked around. The Russian turned and headed for the stairs.

"Okay, Luke and Lawrence. You may feel this is your Get Out of Jail Free card, but it's not. The two of you are still going down for what you've done, got it?" The car inched forward. Now about a half mile to the road block. Cars around them were honking. Mass confusion trying to be controlled by five State Troopers.

"Kowalski. Put the car in park and let Lawrence get behind the wheel. Luke, move up front in the passenger seat." Both men stared at Jake. "NOW!" he said. "Change those seats fast!"

The three men moved as one. Lawrence moved over the console to the driver's seat as Kowalski slid between the two front seats. He had to crowd Jake as Luke moved up, over, beside, and finally into the passenger's seat. Kowalski slid over behind the Lawrence, who was now driving.

"Put the vehicle back in drive," said Jake. "Keep moving slow. You two are still going to go to jail. No question about it. And don't touch the lights or the siren, got it?"

The car kept inching forward. Still just less than one-half mile to go.

Kowalski leaned over and whispered to Jake. "Now what?"

"No idea, but I know they're looking for you and me in a car, not four, and they're looking for either you or me to be driving," Jake whispered back. "As long as these two lunkheads don't do anything stupid, we should blow through this and be on our way." Jake still held a firm grip on the pistol. This was actually more advantageous, because he didn't have to turn 90 degrees to keep both men in his direct vision.

"But they'll recognize the Louisville police car. Then we're really had lads."

The Russian opened the door to the stairway. He stepped in, stopped and listened. No sound coming from below. That meant both good and bad. Either the police were not there yet, or they were set up and waiting to ambush him. He pulled out his SPS. No time like the present, thought the big Russian. With his good left arm, he reached into his pocket and pulled out his cell phone. He punched a code. The phone started ringing.

The vehicle inched forward. Still about one-third of a mile away. The car was a dead giveaway. The State Troopers would know Jake and Kowalski were in some kind of vehicle, but if the Louisville police car stood out to them, they'd have their guns drawn, no questions asked. If these were northern Kentucky police, it might turn out differently, thought Kowalski. But in just over 10 minutes, they'd all be under arrest, or, even worse, dead.

The big Russian stood stock-still in the stairwell, not moving, barely breathing, to see if he could hear some imperceptible, creeping sound made by police. He heard nothing.

The phone connected. The big Russian heard one of his men say 'hello', as if he didn't know who was calling. Shmuck, thought the big Russian.

"Where are you two, right now?"

"We're waiting for you."

"Yes, but where?"

"We are beside the vehicle, smoking."

"I need a diversion. I need you two to come to the side entrance I used earlier to come out. That is where I am coming down. Do you know which one I mean?"

"Yes, we know," said the man who answered the phone. "We'll be right there."

The big Russian hung up the phone and dropped it back into his pocket.

The car continued moving slowly forward. It was now less than one-quarter mile. But pickup trucks ahead of the Louisville police car had kept it hidden from view.

The two Russians made their way to the bottom of one building.

"Is this the entrance?" one asked.

"*Da*, that is it," said the other.

They opened the door and looked inside. Five Heckler and Koch MP-5 semi-automatic rifles turned towards them.

"Sorry, wrong door," said the other Russian, in perfect English.

They slowly closed the door and turned to walk away.

The door burst open and five SWAT members poured out after them.

"Hands in the air, hands in the air! Down on the ground, get on the ground!" came shouts from the five officers.

The two raised their left hands, looked at each other, then turned and faced the officers. At the same time, they reached down and drew their GSh-18 pistols and got off one shot each before they died in a hail of bullets.

The big Russian heard the shooting in the stairwell. Just the diversion he needed. He stepped out of the stairwell on the ground level and walked away from five officers putting handcuffs on two dead guys.

"We're almost there," said Jake. "Neither of you make a sound when we get up there. I have this .32 in my right hand. If I'm going down, you two will die first. Got it?" They both nodded but said nothing. The slight grin on Lawrence's face was gone.

The police car Jake and Kowalski were in pulled up to the roadblock. The officer on the inside breakdown lane looked at the vehicle. He shone a light in on Lawrence's face, then Luke's.

"Hey, guys, what are y'all doin' all the way up here," asked the officer. Lawrence and Luke shrugged their shoulders.

"We're heading up to Cincinnati for a weapons course," said Jake, from the back.

The officer squatted down and shined the light in on Jake's face. He then tried to take a look at Kowalski's face, but the B post, the one between the front door and the rear door, hid most of his view.

"Really, hadn't heard of a weapons course up this way. Usually they put that out a couple of months early."

"Airport, just south of Cincy," said Jake. "For those of us who couldn't make the original one at the airport in Louisville."

The officer nodded his head. "Yeah, the head of weapons at the airport was my roommate in the academy. You do know his name, right?"

Jake shifted in his seat. "Yeah, his name is, uh…"

"Wrong answer, pull the car over." Lawrence did as he was told. The smile came back to his face. Slightly, but it was back.

The big Russian walked back to the vehicle. He checked to see if the plate had been changed. It had. He opened the door. No keys were in the ignition. Stupid Russians. Their families are better off without them, he thought.

Suddenly the headlights popped on the vehicle. Then the horn honked. Then the lights popped on again. The police were looking for the vehicle that matched the keys. The big Russian turned and walked away from the stolen car. The police would find it sooner rather than later, and with that, the body in the trunk. Time to find another ride.

Lawrence pulled the car to the left and stopped, putting it in park. Jake looked at Kowalski. Their game was up.

The backdoor opened and the officer looked in with his flashlight to get a better view of the rear passengers. He shined the light on Kowalski's face.

"...Ski, is that you? Are you OK?" the officer asked.

"Yeah, it's me," he answered.

"We've been looking everywhere for you. We have roadblocks all over the state. We thought you'd been kidnapped!"

"We were. I mean I was, and my buddy here was as well. But we thought this traffic stop was going to go bad."

"Naw, we're just glad you're alright." The officer reached up to his mic on his shoulder. "Found 'em. Northbound I-75. He's good. Tell everyone else to end their roadblocks."

The officer leaned in. "Man, have I got a story to tell you!" he said.

Jake leaned forward. "These two men are being taken to jail in northern Kentucky. It's the nearest jail I could think of that might not be involved in what they were doing."

The officer nodded. "Securities stuff, I think, right? Your boss called from Washington. He's the one who alerted us to what was going on." The officer shone the light in Jake's eyes. "You Jake Thompson?" Jake nodded. "Washington had us worried stiff about you. You need to call your boss."

Kowalski looked at Jake. "You mean you really do work for the SEC?"

Jake nodded. "Yep. Sure do. I've been on to these guys for months, even before I left the military. Several men working in the Frankfort jail were in cahoots with them. You remember that story I told you about talking to a man who had wronged my father? Nope. I needed to get inside the jail to see if I could get any information on who was in with these two clowns. And, thanks to you, I found out who one of the main players was. Also, several officers from the Louisville department. I've been following their tracks. And they laid a lot of them. Remember when I made a phone call from the jail in Frankfort? No? I guess it was Tanner who was in there getting coffee. I pretended to call an attorney, but I really called my brother in California and asked him to notify my boss. We have a way of talking, in case either of us gets in trouble. Kind of a code, if you will.

"And I think one of the officers from Louisville shot your Officer Larson. I say it was a city officer rather than one of your guys, like Tanner. You wanna know why? Because they missed. State troopers would most likely never miss. I bet if you asked Larson, he'd have no knowledge of what Tanner and the others were up to. Anyway, I called my brother out in California, as I said.

"Tanner was never the wiser. He made up a story about a big Russian or Eastern European guy that fit my profile, but he never realized there really was a big Russian guy, one who was going to kill these four. He also never realized the big Russian guy would come looking for him and the others involved. I think Tanner or maybe Johnson killed their two friends. We were thinking the Russians all the time. Maybe because Luke here was going to end the gravy train. We figure there were about five to six billion dollars they moved though Kentucky over the past three years. That's five hundred to six hundred million dollars split about 12 ways, from what I could add up. Fry, Tanner, Lang, Johnson, these buffoons here, plus the two dead ones. And then there's two others we have yet to identify. That's about thirty-five to thirty-eight million dollars each. A good retirement fund, huh Lawrence? Luke?"

The officer pulled the men out of the police car and handcuffed them. The other officers opened the road and allowed traffic to flow north again.

He turned to Jake and Kowalski. "Anything I can do for you fellows?" he asked.

Kowalski shook his head. "No, I think I want to go fishing. Maybe go up to northern New York. I hear they are biting really good about now. I'll catch up on that story with you later, okay?"

The officer nodded his head. He turned to Jake. "You need to call your boss. He's on my chief's rear, as well as every other department in this state, trying to find out what happened to you."

"I guess he can read it in my report. I've got to head west to see my brother in California. You get these men to Cincinnati and tell the staff to sit on them, hard. I don't want them to get out before I can turn in my paperwork."

The officer nodded and shook Jake and Kowalski's hands. "Good luck," he said. Both men nodded.

"Hey, Jake. Get back in. I'll give you a ride to your car. Shelbyville-bound. You've got a lot to tell me while we drive. Guess we got about an hour. Care to fill me in?"

Jake nodded his head in a yes. Kowalski started the car. Just as he was about to pull forward, the officer came running towards him.

"Stop, Kowalski. Stop!" he said.

"Now what," said Kowalski softly.

"You live on Sunset Drive in Frankfort? Someone just blew up your house. Maybe you better not go back there. I guess there's more than 12, huh."

Jake looked at Kowalski. "Want to come west and visit my brother? He's got a big house. And he could sure use some help from someone experienced in police matters. I mean, when will you receive your DD-214?"

"My what?"

"Your retirement papers. The military calls it a DD-214."

"Oh, yea. Not sure. I left them on the secretary's desk before I took you out of jail. Should be any day now. They contact you by E-mail."

"Well, then. Travel companions?"

"Sounds good, but only if you change your attitude."

"My attitude? What's wrong with my attitude?"

"How you address me. To my friends, my name is… Ski."

"Alright… Ski. So let's go and I'll fill you in."

They pulled away from the breakdown lane with the help of the State Troopers.

Two days later, a big Russian boarded an Atlanta jet bound for Amsterdam, then St. Petersburg. He sat in 2A. It was a single seat with no companion on a Delta 767-200 and it fit him comfortably. He shoved his passport into his top pocket. Plenty of time to recoup their money. *Da*, plenty of time.

* * *